The Baby Tree

For Christina
    Hoping that you keep
liking Kate. So good to
meet you at Denison.

                    Fondly —

                        6/02

The Baby Tree

Erin McGraw

Story Line Press
Ashland, Oregon

Published by Story Line Press, Three Oaks Farm,
P.O. Box 1240, Ashland, OR 97520-0055,
www.storylinepress.com.

This publication was made possible thanks in part to
the generous support of the Nicholas Roerich Museum,
the Andrew W. Mellon Foundation, and our individual
contributors.

Author photo by Jon Hughes
Cover design by Lysa McDowell
Interior design by Valerie Brewster, Scribe Typography

LIBRARY OF CONGRESS
CATALOGING-IN-PUBLICATION DATA

Pending

McGraw, Erin

p.   cm.

ISBN 1-58654-011-4

To my mother & father
for their laughter

and to Andrew
for his.

Someone shouts to me from Seir,
"Watchman, what time of night?
Watchman, what time of night?"

The watchman answers,
"Morning is coming, then night again.
If you want to, why not ask,
Turn around, come back?"

ISAIAH 21:11-12

ACKNOWLEDGMENTS

I owe many thanks to many people. For practical information about women in ministry, I am grateful to the Reverends Julie Carmean and Deborah Steed. For her exhaustive knowledge about abortion services and availability, my thanks to Dr. Pat Hudgins. For their close reading and advice, I am indebted to Leslie Jennings Cooksy, Samuel R. Delany, Anna McGrail, Richard Powers, and James Schiff, and for her careful oversight of production, I am grateful to Lysa McDowell.

I am also grateful for support provided by the Mac-Dowell Colony and the Taft Foundation at the University of Cincinnati. To my editor, Robert McDowell, and my agent, the indefatigable Gail Hochman, my thanks are boundless.

Above all, ever, thanks to my husband, Andrew.

The Baby Tree

One

At seven o'clock on a September morning, the cool air still half dark, Pastor Kate Gussey stepped out of the parsonage. She hadn't bothered yet with breakfast, or a shower. She had half-combed her hair, in case one of her parishioners drove past, but her feet were sockless inside beat-up outdoor shoes, and the cotton shirt she'd thrown on was too light for the gray morning.

The dewy grass—a little long, as one of her flock was likely to tell her—sawed at her ankles, and chilly moisture seeped into her shoes. Stubbornly, she dragged her feet where the grass was longest. After her sleepless night the rough textures of the outside world felt good; she pressed her cold fingers against her cheek and gazed at the autumn wreck of her garden. Maybe she should have tried sleeping out on the grass. She wouldn't have had a worse time.

Around midnight she and Ned had exchanged a stiff kiss, he turned off the light, and she had forced herself to take slow breaths, waiting for sleep to come. Instead, the fidgets came, twitching her feet, then her knees. Eventually she was flipping from side to side like a dolphin in a net. She twisted her pillow into a stick, kicked the covers off, then pulled them back on, then off. Ned lay beside her without stirring. He always dropped into slumber as if he were shutting himself in a drawer, a habit she had used to admire.

At two o'clock she crept into the living room to watch middle-of-the-night movies. By four she was nibbling on saltines and watching "Ag Report"—late rains could be trouble for soybeans. If she strained, she could hear Ned's breaths lapping serenely from the bedroom, a sound that made her own nerves chatter like telegraph wires. At the first sign of light she bolted outside, but anxiety still roared through her. Gazing at her garden, she felt a new and urgent desire to weed it.

The task had been overlooked all summer; dandelions rioted under the lilacs and right over the phlox. Work would ease the outrage clamoring in her veins, and sweat might steady her fingers, which had started trembling sometime around dawn, when Ned snored once, enjoying the pure rest of a man certain of his clear conscience. Kate strode toward the shed for a weeder and a trowel.

Beside the lilies, quackgrass fanned like a skirt, dotted with broadleaf and clover; she knelt down in the middle of the rampaging vegetation and started wedging her trowel into the hard dirt. But the sound of Ned's reasonable, confident voice needled through her thoughts, and she crawled further into the lilies, where the grass stuck up in tufts and some weed whose name she didn't know had spread an impudent mat of leaves. Unsystematically, she ripped at all of it, reminding herself that the weedy takeover of her perennial beds was no special symbol or surprise—the garden was always hell in a handbasket by September. Every year some parishioner chided her, a parishioner who wouldn't have dreamed of criticizing a male minister for the state of his garden.

Normally Kate cultivated a sense of humor about her old-school parishioners. Some of them got so rattled on Sundays, when she wore her robe and collar, that they asked how her wife was. Let them get used to a woman in the pulpit, that was the trick. But she had been in the pulpit for five years, and this morning she was sick of extending extra charity to people who extended little to her.

Wrapped up in her thoughts, chipping at the cement-like soil, she was startled when a voice called her name. She yanked out a rope of ground ivy, then turned around to see Barb, who volunteered at the church and told the only funny jokes that came Kate's way.

"Wow. Up and at 'em. Guess I didn't need to worry that I might catch you in your nightgown." Barb gestured at Kate's handful of leafy weeds. "You know, most people wait till the sun is actually in the sky before they start gardening."

"Take a look at this flower bed, and tell me it can wait one more minute. The dandelions are about to achieve a voting majority." She peered at Barb, who usually rolled into the office after ten o'clock. Something brittle in her voice and expression put Kate on alert. "I was up," Kate said, watching Barb's fingers pleat and smooth her shirt cuff.

"I wanted to find some little, manageable task. That was before I discovered that weeding the garden is going to take a backhoe."

"Typical. Just when you think everything is all right, something goes haywire."

"If life was easy, we'd all get lazy," Kate said, reaching for an amiable, pastoral tone. She'd never seen Barb so ragged, raising and lowering her red eyes like a wretched beacon. For an unworthy moment Kate wondered just how much she was going to have to cope with this morning.

"Nothing goes right. We know this. Why do we ever get our hopes up?"

"Are you going to tell me what happened?"

Barb shrugged helplessly, and Kate was already standing, brushing her dirty hands against her pants, and leading the way to the church. The middle of a chilly garden was no place to talk. In the office Barb sank into the plaid armchair, and Kate pulled another chair beside her, close to her friend's tense, averted face. "Somebody threatened you?" Kate asked. "You've been hurt?"

Rigid cords running down her throat, Barb shook her head. "Mindy —my niece—came to church with us on Sunday," she said.

"I saw her." Kate scrambled to remember anything that could have brought hurt or offense—what joke gone sour, what mangled prayer. Usually she could count on one of the camp of chronically dissatisfied parishioners to tell her how she had not measured up. All she could remember was the girl flipping her hair, bright as cornsilk, from one shoulder to the other.

"She came to church as a favor to her parents, which was a good thing, because she's been doing them precious few favors lately. Even then, she twitched like a six-year-old. When her mother wanted her to go up and greet you after the service, she started crying, ran out of the parking lot, and walked every step home. Two miles, in high heels."

"What set her off?" Kate asked.

"She's preggers." Barb let her head tilt back. Her face, in its exhaustion, was stiff as a mask. "Assuming that her walk didn't jog anything loose, such as whatever's left of her brain."

"Oh," Kate said, helpless and relieved. "Oh, Barb. This must be killing you."

"Nineteen years old. Halfway through a dental tech degree, a year and a half of school in the trash. When people used to ask her what she wanted to do in life, she'd say, 'I want to see every place in the world.' She'll be lucky to see Bedford now."

"Does she have a boyfriend?"

"Not one she's admitting to. She sits there and cries. And then she stops crying and says she hasn't done anything wrong."

"She's young," Kate said.

"She doesn't have the first idea about what she's done. You should see the look in Cathy and Dick's eyes. She's their only baby; Dick used to say she'd be president of the world." The corners of Barb's mouth quivered; Kate plucked a tissue from the box and put it in Barb's right hand, picking up the left one and hanging on.

"How far along is she?"

"Six, seven, maybe eight weeks. Plenty of time to go to the clinic. I'd take her there myself, but she freezes if you even mention it. She looks up from the dinner table and says, 'I am in harmony.' I got mad enough to ask her what she was in harmony with, and she said, 'I am fulfilling my destiny.' Two years of college, and she thinks her destiny is to be an unwed mother."

"I could talk to her. If you think it would help," Kate said carefully. She had a good idea that the girl would turn away any counseling, but Barb's choked voice filled her with the helpless ache to offer something. Barb so rarely asked for help. Even on the rare occasions when she talked about her husband, who had driven off one morning and never come back, who sometimes sent Barb post cards that left her silent and shaking, Kate had never seen her cry. Now she watched the tears wash over her friend's rough skin, and was ready to offer money, food, bone marrow.

"Of course it would help." Barb paused to blow her nose without opening her eyes, or letting go of Kate's hand. "I've been telling her so for two days, solid."

"I'll call."

"Don't bother. She sits there and looks moony, and don't you just know she thinks she's a romantic heroine. Aw Jesus, she's a fool." Barb sat up then and covered her face with her hands, her shoulders shuddering away from Kate's touch.

"There's still time," Kate murmured. "She can reconsider. It can't feel real to her yet."

"It feels real, all right. It's her destiny."

"The romance will wear off. Wait until she can't button her favorite pair of jeans. She'll need to talk to somebody."

Barb wadded up three tissues and tossed them short of Kate's wastepaper basket. "Look, if you run into Mindy anytime soon, don't say anything; she's as jumpy as a flea. But I'll keep working on her. If she had any idea what she's opening the door to—"

"—she'd be forty, not twenty," Kate said. "She'd have learned the hard way."

"Like us," Barb agreed.

Kate's glance skated across her cluttered desk, and she felt the familiar, sorrowful frustration swell; so much of her life seemed to be half gestures, statements of intent, actions taken that were rarely sufficient. Did every minister feel inadequate? Yes, she immediately knew. She'd heard enough of them say so at conferences. "I'll talk to her," she said again, more forcefully.

"Don't do anything yet. I just wanted to tell you," Barb said. "A minister should know these things. Now you can tell me how come you were out in your garden at seven-thirty."

"It's complicated. I don't think you want to sit through the explanation right now," Kate said. Before Barb could press her, the phone rang; Kate caught it on the second ring. Barb got up and left the room, pausing to squeeze Kate's hand on the way.

After the phone call—an easy one, Arnet Wilson checking on the time for the next Committee on Outreach meeting—Kate got up and made a pot of coffee. A stack of unanswered letters waited on her desk, and she could answer them while she was still wearing her gardening clothes. Sharp energy rattled her hands, and she knew she'd better use it while she could; by the afternoon, no matter how much coffee she drank, she would be muddy with exhaustion.

Back at the desk, she re-stacked some of the letters and sat them in front of the photo of Ned. Not that Ned was her real problem. Her real problem was Bill-o, her first husband, had appeared yesterday on her welcome mat, where she had hoped never to see him. But Ned, her second husband, had asked him to stay.

She made a muttering noise, the closest she permitted herself to swearing, and snapped a rubber band against her wrist. This time Ned had really done it. In a move that was stunning even for Open-Door-Policy, Have-A-Heart Ned, the doctor who treated half his patients for free and made generous time for every blowhard and malingerer in town, who was beloved by everyone he treated, who had started the soup kitchen and volunteered at the animal shelter, Ned, her Ned, had invited Bill-o to stay in the parsonage with them. The mere concept made her lungs squeeze. On the scratch pad by the phone she drew box after box, coloring each one in until she wore holes through the paper.

For fifteen years Kate had been training herself not to check for Bill-o before she entered a room, not to listen, rigidly, for his sly voice on the telephone or scan every parking lot for his dark hair and fleshy face. Day after day, she'd practiced believing that the world might contain uncomplicated pleasures, that lives could be honorable and people trustworthy. She had spent all these years recuperating, edging an inch at a time into daylight. The notion that the husband of her youth might re-enter her life now felt like the recurrence of an old disease — a sucker punch delivered by a snickering fate.

The blow felt all the more sneaky because Bill-o had returned in the middle of an ordinary afternoon, sunlight resting on his hair — still dark — like a gentle hand. Never, in all her nightmares, had she imagined that he might simply appear on her front porch, ringing the doorbell as if he had a right. Operating out of pure pastoral habit, she'd invited him into the house, where he accepted a cup of coffee and told her that he was going to manage the new NaturWise garden center at the edge of town.

"You?" she'd blurted. "You don't know a lilac from a tulip."

"I've learned a few things," he told her. "I trained. And once I got my hands in the dirt, I found out what you already knew; dirt's the right place to have them."

She'd smacked a cupboard door closed. "These days I keep mine clean."

But he kept talking as if he didn't see every molecule in her yearning to push him out, *out*. And then Ned had come home in time to hear Bill-o's modest, sad tale — the corporation that was supposed to be building him a house, the crews that didn't show up, the delays. For the time being, he was sleeping on an air mattress at the new store, a building also unfinished, half of the walls unpainted, the telephones sitting on the dusty concrete floor. She could see that Ned was moved by Bill-o's speech, saw the impulsive offer filling his mouth before she could cry out to stop it. And then saw Bill-o produce a toothy, hayseed smile. "You're real kind," he said. She blinked, and barely kept herself from saying *You've got to be kidding.*

She would have known how to deal with Bill-o's anger, or with his pure, idle viciousness. But this sunshiny Bill-o glad-handed Ned like a Rotarian, chuckled, and offered clichés about small-town life in a voice from which all the old, mean fury had been rinsed. Talking about his job, his hopes for life here in Elite—which he pronounced Ee-light, as residents did—his voice was boyish, guileless, drenched with happy optimism. She would never have imagined him capable of such a tone; he sounded like a beginning actor trying to communicate Sincerity or Eagerness or Charm. She wondered what he was trying to put over, and answered his many questions in monosyllables, not seeing him to the door when he finally left. Why bother? Ned was right there with him, every step of the way.

"What do you want from the man?" Ned asked after dinner while he washed the dishes, his sleeves folded four precise inches above his wrists. "He came offering friendship. Are you holding out for blood sacrifice?"

"Only if it's his blood. What I want is for him to go away. What I don't want is him anywhere near my house."

She picked up the kitchen sponge and went at the countertop, working on a smudge in front of the toaster.

"Look, Kate, I don't think this is an ideal arrangement. But nobody should have to sleep like a refugee on the floor of a half-finished warehouse. You know that."

She rubbed harder, then tossed aside the sponge. "Would you stop for a minute and listen to me? I used to be married to the man. I have some authority on this issue. Having him stay here is a terrible idea."

"It's pretty strange," he said. "But it's still the right thing to do."

"There are all kinds of right. It's too bad that he's sleeping on a concrete floor, but why do we have to be the ones to take him in? Has it occurred to you that there's a reason divorced people don't generally seek out each other's company?"

Ned turned off the water and sat down at the kitchen table, flattening his hands, his tactic to gain patience. "Honey. You haven't seen him in all these years, but you still have bad dreams about him. Now here's a chance to get past that old stuff. It could make things better for you. And whether we like it or not, he needs our help."

"Look—when you brought home a wino you found half in the bushes by the courthouse, I agreed that he should stay. When you called and said you'd met a man who'd lost his job and needed a breath of hope, I put fresh sheets on the guest room bed."

"Stanley," Ned said. "He had a name."

"He stayed six weeks. And then Lucille, whose food stamps got screwed up."

"You never told me you objected. I thought you wanted to help."

"I'm just pointing out that I've earned a little credit here. Nobody can say we haven't been kind to the sick and the needy. But Bill-o isn't another lost soul who's stumbled onto our doorstep. He has a place to stay."

"Come on, Kate. You wouldn't let a dog stay out there."

"That's different. I like dogs."

"Pretend he's a collie," Ned said. "Put a leash and collar on him. It's what you want to do anyway."

True enough. She'd like to put a collar on Ned, too, which he probably knew. "Tell me how I'm going to explain to my church that I'm living with both my past and present husbands. The District Superintendent isn't as high-minded as you."

"The District Superintendent understands homelessness."

"Any other husband on earth would be territorial if his wife's ex showed up," Kate said, her voice rising. "Any other husband would be suspicious. But Ned—Ned claps him on the shoulder! Invites him in! Gives him a shelf in the bathroom!"

Ned pulled off his glasses and polished them—first one lens, then the other, then the first again. "I don't think that makes me the bad guy," he said at last. "Bill-o came here, hat in hand. How often are we supposed to forgive?"

"Oh, knock it off." He had been doing more of this sort of thing lately, quoting Scripture at her and wearing an expression of inquisitive sanctity that scraped on her nerves. She took a shaky breath. "I wouldn't ask this much of you."

"You could. I wish you would."

"Now what are you talking about?"

"We get up, we go to bed, and in between, our major challenge is whether we should go out for dinner two nights in the same week. Believe me, I'd like it if you asked me to take on a challenge. I'd love it."

"Okay. I'm asking."

Ned surveyed her, his mouth curled with disappointment. "You would call him in that half-finished building where there isn't even a bathroom and tell him he's no longer welcome here? It isn't a phone call I could make."

Kate started to nod, but as soon as she tried to envision the scene, her imagination jammed. Not even to Bill-o could she say, Sorry, you can't come anymore. We changed our minds. Tough luck. "You win. But only a day or two. Enough time for a room to open up at the Travelinn."

"I'm sure he'll be grateful," Ned said with heavy sarcasm.

"His gratitude isn't what I'm looking for." The phone rang then— Bill-o, of course, saying that he had business calls to return and clothes to pack; why didn't he plan on arriving the next day? Ignoring the slam of Kate's coffee cup against the counter, Ned encouraged him to come as soon as he could. Kate waited until the conversation was over before she turned on the TV, where she found a celebrity biography filled with despair hidden behind a glamorous façade.

Ned watched her watch the show; she watched him arrive at judgment. He was likely finding her to be unforgiving and irrational, in need of correction. It was a bad judgment, made in ignorance. If Ned had truly understood about Bill O'Grady, even he, whose heart was open to the whole world, would have closed the door. But Ned had never allowed Kate to tell him about Bill-o. When she'd tried, early in their dating days, he'd soothed her, pressing his hand on her wrist, and told her that none of the past mattered anymore. "It's important," Kate had said. "I want you to know. I want you to understand."

"I want *you* to understand," he'd interrupted her. "The past is the past. There's no point in dwelling there." Hearing the tightness in his voice, Kate had stopped. She had, of all things, agreed with him. Stroking his hand, she'd convinced herself that Ned was right; they would be wise to put away those destroyed years, bury them and start afresh. But now the memories were arrayed around her, shining, branched, fragrant, detailed down to burl and bud, apparently more vigorous for their time underground.

The office phone rang again, and Kate reached for it, but Barb, at her desk, got to it first. "Dove Methodist," she said, and then, more flatly, "It's me."

Barb rarely took personal calls at the church, and Kate strained to hear as much out of surprise as curiosity.

"Situation normal," Barb said. Kate heard the quaver in Barb's voice, the sour laugh. "You can buy baby clothes or point her to the door. Myself, I'd get down on my knees and pray for a miracle."

"Huh," Kate said softly; she'd never heard such words out of Barb's mouth before. And although she tried, Kate couldn't suppress the instant memory of Bill-o, stone sober, smiling at her and saying that he always liked her best on her knees.

Two

The day Bill-o first entered Kate's life, a day she would later call ruinous, she was seventeen years old and working in her parents' nursery in Indianapolis. It was May, and the auto race had taken over the city; every basket of flowers that Kate sent out featured a little black-and-white checkered flag tucked in among the daisies. A quarter of Speedway Flowers' budget was made in May, when Indianapolis society held giddy black-and-white parties and businesses ordered thick banks of bedding flowers, competing for the brightest, the newest, the most surprising. For a month Indianapolis—India-No Place, Nap Town—came alive, its inhabitants happily screaming over the howl of car engines.

Kate's parents enjoyed the excitement, but Kate herself was sick of the race, its heat and rowdy crowds and numbing noise. She set up camp in the nursery, watering, pinching, thinning, and rotating, and she put in extra hours once the time trials started, making the concrete floor vibrate under her feet. Her friends all knew which drivers had sponsorships and who had qualified on the pole, while Kate could distinguish varieties of lilac at a glance and would talk about them to anyone who would let her.

Hardly anyone would. The customers who didn't want to discuss the Unsers or Andrettis usually asked what she planned to do with all her knowledge—landscape design? Travel? Keeping her eyes on whatever tally sheet she was working from, Kate would shake her head. "I guess I'll just keep doing this."

She could hear how spiritless she sounded from the way strangers pressed her; her whole life was ahead of her! She needed to raise her sights, look around; when was she going to dream, if she didn't dream now? "I hate when they do that," she told her mother after a woman followed and prodded her for ten minutes. "How do I know what I'll want in twenty years?"

"She meant well," Kate's mother said. "Maybe she's just rich. Maybe she can map out every minute of the rest of her life and it'll work out just like she says. The rest of us don't get to call the shots. Things happen. People get sick. Somebody's car gets hit. You can dream as much as you want; you've still got to take what comes."

So Kate took Bill-o, who wandered into the nursery to pick up 1,500 bedding plants that Kate's father had been holding and checking every day. They took up a third of the greenhouse. While he went to wheel them to the front, Bill-o explained to Kate that he was an assistant at the track—seasonal work. He'd been pushing the lawn mower for the last two weeks, and as a reward the groundskeeper had sent him out to pick up marigolds and dusty millers, the worst combination of bedding plants Kate could imagine, to arrange on the embankment next to the ticket booth. Kate's father pulled flat after flat from the back of the greenhouse while Bill-o lounged against the tray of begonias and talked.

"They do this every year, make a huge deal about getting the flowers in just right. The morning after the race the flowers are dead; people stomp on them going in and rip them up coming out. I don't see why we don't just cement the whole thing over."

"It wouldn't look worse," said Kate.

"Last year the crew was up past midnight, making sure the lines between the colors were straight."

"We need stupid chores to keep us out of trouble," Kate said, echoing her mother.

Bill-o leaned toward her until she looked up, and then he grinned, slowly. "Somebody else can do all the planting this year. I'd rather get in trouble."

"Smooth," Kate said scornfully.

He really smiled then. "I am, aren't I? Smooth as glass. My name's Bill O'Grady; the whole world calls me Bill-o."

She laughed out loud and said, "My name's Kate. The world doesn't have a name for me."

"It's coming. Sooner than you think," he said, and she felt her breath hitch. He seemed graceful to her, even though he was heavy around the arms and padded at the waist. His clothes fell softly over his thick legs and shoulders, not so much sloppy as loose; they gave the impression that they would drop from his body with a touch.

"What else do you do?" Kate asked. "When you're not buying flowers." She was expecting him to tell her that he liked to drink beer; she was hoping he would suggest that she meet him later, after he had gotten a six-pack. In Speedway, that was a date.

"I like to get people to talk," he said. "People give themselves away as soon as they open their mouths, and they don't even know it. I listen for what they don't even know they're telling me."

"Well," Kate said, pinching off a begonia shoot. "Guess I'd better keep my mouth closed." She wanted to ask about some of the things he'd discovered, and how anybody had a chance to say anything when he was talking all the time, but just then her father called from the cash register to ask Bill-o whether he could transport these flowers himself. Bill-o winked, pinched Kate on the back of her hand, and wandered to the front of the store. In her confusion, Kate put a daisy down on the watering tray, where nobody found it for a week and its roots had already started to rot.

Bill-o had come back to the nursery twice by then. He liked to stand behind Kate so she was never sure just how close he was; once she tilted her head to ease a cramp, and his hand closed around the back of her neck. He rubbed his thumb under her collar in slow circles, but he never stopped talking. His money was on Unser this year —literally. Thirty bucks. Employees weren't supposed to bet, but it didn't take much to figure out where to slide an envelope. All you had to do was watch, pay attention. Some of the other guys, who'd been at the track since the '50s, couldn't believe Bill-o was only twenty.

"You seem older," Kate said. Her eyes were closed, her hands motionless in a bucket of potting soil while Bill-o slipped his fingers up into her hair.

"I've gone around the track a few times."

Kate believed him. He didn't scramble like other boys. He strolled, he drawled, his smile worked across his mouth like a long wave. He didn't even drive fast, which Kate thought was funny for somebody who worked at a racetrack. Herself, she was hurtling, reckless under his slow fingers. By the time he finally drove her up to a practice track north of town two weeks after the race, when nobody had any reason to be there, she practically flung her clothes off while he sat without moving, laughing softly and listening to the car engine's tick.

And he didn't drink. This fact by itself set Bill-o apart from the other boys Kate knew, and made her uneasy. She didn't want liquor for herself—she was a terrible drinker, weepy and then sick—but she was embarrassed that he could watch her so coolly in the car's dimness, night after hot, desperate night. Her body began to feel strange, rubbery, and when she came home, she scrubbed herself in the shower with her eyes closed.

She started urging Bill-o to relax and have a cold one, and made jokes about working up a thirst; when they drove around town she read all the liquor billboards. The night in early July that he finally reached into the back seat and fished up a bottle of Jim Beam, she was relieved. "You first," she said when he held it out to her.

"Oh, no. I got this with you in mind." He untwisted the cap and held the bottle in front of her lips, so Kate sipped a little, wincing at the burn. "More," Bill-o said when she pushed the bottle back to him.

"I don't like it."

"So?" He pressed the bottle against her mouth and with his other hand pushed her forehead back; whiskey spilled across her face and down her collar. Kate choked, trying to force his hand away while he kept dribbling alcohol into her mouth. She swallowed despite herself, her throat feeling sanded by the drink and her rough tears. Fighting to breathe, she struggled under Bill-o's arm, heavy as an iron bar. Only when the bottle was empty did he let her sit up, sobbing now, her blouse and the seat underneath her soaked. The whiskey had run into her eyes and nose; her whole face stung. "Why did you do that?" she cried, her breath ragged.

"You wouldn't quit," he said. "You wouldn't stop nagging."

"Jesus, Bill-o. I was just playing. I was only trying to get you to relax."

"Will you stop trying now?"

Kate huddled against the door and cried, pushing his hand away when he tried to snake it around her shoulders. After a moment, he settled back into his own seat and started the car. "What are you doing?" she said. "It isn't even ten o'clock. You can't send me home like this."

"Don't you think I know that?" He steered toward the track without bothering to turn on his headlights. Watchmen were posted, she knew, to keep vandals out—every year a story went around the high school about somebody stupid enough to try to break in. He stopped in front of an unmarked gray metal door, and came around to Kate's side of the car.

"What's this?" she said without moving. "The secret entrance?"

"You got it."

"I should have guessed you'd know anything secret."

"That's right. You should have." He pulled her out and gave her his arm to lean on. She needed the help; whether from the drink or her weeping, her ankles and knees had gone loose. He had to balance her against his hip as they stumbled to the door, where he slid away a small piece of cardboard that had kept the deadbolt from catching. "Come on, drunky."

Kate opened her mouth to protest, but Bill-o was leading her down an unlighted hall that smelled like cool cement. He was careful with her, warning when they approached a step she might stumble over. Silent and woozy, she trailed beside him, half enraptured by the echo of their footsteps. Her head throbbed with sound, and she rested her forehead on Bill-o's shoulder, where he stroked her wet hair.

They turned twice. She heard the sound of a door swinging open and smelled dampness, and she must have been drunk already because she thought Bill-o was taking her to some underground greenhouse. Only after a few shapeless moments, when she heard water rush on, did she realize that she was standing in a shower room.

"This is the drivers' shower room," he said. "It's kept really clean."

"I can't see."

"Take my word for it. We'll get away with this if we don't turn on the lights." Tugging on her elbows, he pulled her into the water, which was lukewarm for the first moment, then cold. She tried to jerk away, but Bill-o pinned her arms and turned her around so that the water shot into her face, and she could feel her blouse and shorts mold themselves to her skin. He kept her arms pinned at her waist, his own arms crossed over her chest as if he were doing an old-time dance step, and when she realized that at least he was getting soaked too, she relaxed.

He held her under the hard jet of water until she was shivering, any smell of liquor long gone. Then he led her back into the long corridor, their shoes squelching with every step, and out into the soft night. At the car he made Kate wait until he pulled towels from the back seat, a pair of his old jeans for her to slip over her shorts, and then a department store bag that held a new blouse, crisp white, nicer than what she'd been wearing; she turned her back to put it on. Her trembling fingers slipped over the pearl-shaped buttons, and she swore she'd burn it when she got home, but Bill-o let his slow smile unspool when she turned back to show him, and her arms fell uselessly to her sides. "It looks good," he said. "I went to three stores. I'll get you a skirt to wear with it."

Later, Kate would hate the fact that she could remember the sunburst pattern of the clock on Bill-o's dashboard, the striped white and blue blouse they had spoiled, the green check of Bill-o's fresh shirt, which had felt warm when she'd leaned against it. In particular, she would hate remembering that she had felt, as she turned her face toward his sweet breath, cared for.

She had learned her lesson, though, and no longer risked challenging him. The summer bled away, and she woke up several times a night, her teeth clamped and her jaw aching. She was sure that she was losing ground with him, slipping backwards, that she was knowing him, somehow, less. He rarely talked about himself anymore. While they drove back and forth across Indianapolis, he made her tell him about her days and dodged any reference to his own; she didn't even know whether he had worked since the racetrack job had ended. In his car, watching his eyes move over her, she imagined what he was seeing: her square, flat face and sturdy shoulders, the thick brown hair that resisted curling and flew into its own stubborn shapes, tiny eyes that almost disappeared behind their heavy lashes. Not charms enough to give her confidence. So she answered his questions and asked none of her own, maintaining such a high mix of hope and fear that she felt as if she were breathing high-altitude air.

In August, the night before her eighteenth birthday, he drove her north, up past Noblesville, and parked where they could look out over the reservoir. To Kate's surprise, the water, faintly scummy by day, looked milky in the moonlight, as romantic as a tiny, private sea. "I thought we should celebrate your last night as jailbait," he said.

"Aren't you Mr. Funny."

"Things change now, Kate. Better face it."

"What," she said, trying to control the wobble in her voice. "Are you going out tomorrow to find a younger woman?"

"I might. Get me a twelve-year-old and help her with her homework. When we're done I'll swing by and pick you up."

"I'm not interested in meeting your twelve-year-old."

"She can be flower girl. I thought we'd get married."

"What?" Kate said, her head jerking back.

"Married. I do, you do, then we go home and do some more."

"What?" she kept saying. "What?"

Bill-o reached over and pulled Kate across the seat until her hip was wedged down beside the gearshift. "'Get a smart one,' everybody told me. 'Sex doesn't last. Get one you can talk to.' So who do I pick? The village idiot." He mimicked her then, squeaking, "'What? What?'" over her whimpering giggles.

"This will be a story to tell our grandkids," she said, her voice rippling.

"The night Grandpa took Grandma out by the reservoir? I don't think so."

"Not that." She squirmed in the tight space. "How Grandma kept saying What? because she didn't think she was hearing right."

"What did you think you were hearing?" His voice suddenly tightened.

"I don't know, Bill-o. You surprised me, all right?"

"You don't think we should get married?"

Kate tried to shift to a more comfortable position, but Bill-o wouldn't let her move. "Yes, okay? Yes. I do."

He said, "Because I could take you home, you know. I could leave right now, believe me."

"I believe you," she said. "Please don't go. Please marry me."

"You better want what I'm offering."

"I do. Like a bride, right? I do."

"Maybe," he said, gazing out the driver's side window. "If that's the best you can offer."

When this scene came back to Kate at odd moments—as she

washed dishes, or watched a movie—she wished she could hurt that mean boy, pinch a tender piece of skin and twist. But her dazzled, un-done, seventeen-year-old self had looked at his profile, turned sullenly away from her, and felt joy. Understanding had burst upon her with the force of a waterfall. What he had been trying to hide all this time was his own plain need for her. Love had broken out despite his best efforts to hold it back. His moods, his hard, angry words and selfish ways—he wouldn't have acted so careless if he hadn't cared so much. Happiness pulsed through her, and in a moment of wild assurance, she took Bill-o's head and turned his face toward hers. "I do," she said again, and waited for his slow smile.

She was happy on her birthday, happy the next day when she and Bill-o went to the justice of the peace, happy for the week following, while they were still living in her bedroom in her parents' house be-cause the lease on his apartment had run out. Then he told her about Linton, a town she'd never heard of, where he'd read about an opening for a mechanic and called to tell the garage owner that they were on their way.

"You didn't ask me," Kate protested, trying to keep her voice low, so her parents wouldn't hear them disagreeing. "I don't know anybody in Linton."

"How many people do you need?"

"A few." He looked at her with an appraising expression, and she said, "More than one, anyway."

"We can't stay here, with your parents listening to every breath."

"I can't just go to Linton. I don't even know where it is. What would I do?"

"People have gardens everywhere. You can always sell flowers. But I've got to go where there's something for me. I'm ready to have a life."

"We have a life. What do you call this?" she said, gesturing vaguely at her soft bed, the yellow curtains she'd awakened to since she was a baby.

"Your life," he said. "Your bedroom. I've still got my razor in a box on the floor. You can keep your life, or come with me and make a new one. I have to go." He waited for her to say something, but all her brain could fix on, stupidly, was how long his hair had grown, long enough to show a hint of curl. Bill-o pulled her into his lap and stroked her shoulder. "I hope you dream about me after I leave."

Kate leaned into his hand. After a few minutes, she stood up and started folding clothes. She was embarrassed to have him, of all people, point out that she had dreams.

Once they arrived in Linton there was no nursery, of course. Had the job for Bill-o actually been waiting when they arrived? Here the story became hard to remember. Jobs diminished and dissolved the minute Bill-o wrapped his hands around them; he and Kate would drive seventy miles on a rumor he'd half heard, for a job he meant to talk his way into. Even when the jobs existed, even when the gas station managers or assistant machinists took Bill-o on, nothing ever lasted; after a month of following orders he would take a four-hour lunch break or give free gas to customers, just to see what would happen. Kate got so she could tell by the sound of Bill-o's step at the door that it was time to pack again.

After the first three years, she let the toaster and pots stay in their boxes. She worked when she could, bagging groceries or sweeping up hair in beauty salons, although often enough the towns were too small to need even that meager help, and Kate spent her days sitting in front of grimy, dented trailers, waiting for Bill-o to get fired.

"We'll find something better," he always said when they were back on the road. "That was no place to live. We'll land pretty soon, and we'll land on our feet."

"Let's land in a town that has a Laundromat," Kate would say—or a shoe repair shop, or a grocery store. Before she left her parents' house she'd had no idea how small a town could be. Not so much communities as postal conveniences, they offered drafty trailers that she learned to dread in the winter, a single gas station, and churches with names so dire they made her laugh: The One True Holiness Church, The Church of the Single Truth, The Church of Christ's Cross Daily.

Members of these churches would come to visit in the first week after she and Bill-o moved in, asking her opinions on faith and redemption. At first she went ahead and admitted that she didn't have any opinions, that she wasn't what they might want to call religious. But after the third town where a church member leaned forward, her eyes glowing and acquisitive, Kate abandoned her frankness and began indicating that her faith was tiptop, robust, in need of no help. Then, for a while, she took to telling visitors that she was a Buddhist, just to watch them scuttle off the porch. In the end she took Bill-o's advice, kept the shades drawn, and didn't answer the door.

Not that she didn't pray, although haltingly, to a force she couldn't name and was afraid of. She prayed when she came home from discount stores or parks, and she used the same hurtful, defeated words: "A baby. Please. My own baby." After a while, a child was her only clear desire, and she carried it from town to town, trailer to trailer, the steady ache lodged in her lungs so she felt it with every breath.

In the aisles of grocery stores, she stared at mothers, some of them younger than she, women who snarled at their rabbity toddlers and kept hiking up the infants slung across their hips. Kate gripped the shopping cart to keep herself from reaching for the children's grubby hands; she knew that her yearning bordered on the violent, and she scared herself. In front of baby food displays and pyramids of disposable diapers she read every word on the packaging. Once she even bought a jar of strained carrots to keep in the cupboard as lure or promise, although Bill-o laughed at her when he found it. "What do you think, that babies show up in houses where there's baby food? Gee, Katy, why don't you check the produce section? I hear they're right next to the spinach."

As if in spiteful validation, Kate was pregnant only two weeks later, waking Bill-o up three mornings in a row when she scrambled from the bed. "Of course I'm happy," he said sleepily, pulling her into his lap after she had rinsed her mouth. "But this isn't the time. You can see that, can't you?"

"I want a baby," she said.

"I know. I know you do. But things haven't come together for us yet. How can we have a baby now? Where would we even put it? Ah, don't cry, Katy. We'll land on our feet soon, and then we'll have six babies. Ten." He pulled her head to his shoulder and Kate cried away all of her hope. She knew that mere desire couldn't provide clothes for a baby, or a crib, or pay for one visit to the doctor. After Bill-o left she spent half a day on the phone, finding a clinic in the next county that performed abortions but stopping shy of making an appointment. For a week she crept out of the trailer at dawn, vomiting outside so that she wouldn't wake Bill-o. Then, without warning, she awakened one afternoon to a sharp cramp and hot liquid streaming between her legs, and the baby was gone.

"Now you know we can do it," Bill-o said when he came home that night, after they cleaned, as best they could, the sheets and the mattress. "That's some kind of good news, right?"

Kate shrugged. For several days she scarcely left the stained bed, and then for months more her only moment of genuine wakefulness came at the end of the day, when Bill-o lifted her hair from the back of her neck and told her that he loved her, or that she was a slut, or that she wasn't much, but she'd do for now.

Ten years. Kate felt dull surprise when she and Bill-o actually made it to their tenth anniversary, even though she couldn't imagine an alternative life. As they drove into a new town, Bill-o liked to say, "This is home. Things will last here. This is where we've been meaning to get, all along." He had so many tones of voice; he could sound encouraging when he wanted to.

But then he turned thirty, and suddenly he wasn't hearing about new jobs; once, in Vincennes, Kate had to stand in line in a church basement for groceries. "Not from around here, are you?" asked the woman packing dry milk in a sack.

"No, ma'am," Kate said humbly.

Bill-o swore he was working his networks, calling in old chits, and for once he was truthful, more so than Kate could have wished— it was one of his old girlfriends who found a job for him, in the same auto-parts plant where she worked inventory. The day before he was set to start, she invited them over to her duplex for a drink. Kate sat wretchedly on a kitchen chair, humiliation crawling up her throat, while Bill-o and the woman laughed together. When she couldn't suppress a whimper, the woman flicked a glance at her and said, "For Christ's sake, get a grip. If you can't take it, then take off. He'll get along." Bill-o gazed inquiringly at Kate, and the woman nodded at the door, which hung half open.

And leave her with nothing? No child, no happiness? Nothing doing, Kate thought, shaking her head. She had pinned up her life to his promises and dangled from them; she wouldn't drop now.

So finally Bill-o had to be the one to leave Kate, not the other way around, and for years she derived stringy pleasure from the thought that there had been one thing, in ten years, that he hadn't been able to make her do. Three weeks after they moved to the old girlfriend's town, Kate came home to find his clothes and the good lamp gone, along with some frozen pork chops — the girlfriend's touch, she guessed.

She spent a week without leaving the trailer, getting by on boiled potatoes dressed with salt and salad oil. On the eighth day she walked to the community center and asked about a class to get her GED, then spent a month in a basement with refugees and flat-haired girls who looked, she thought viciously, as if they'd whelped every year since they were ten years old. "I know I'm a snob. I don't care!" she railed at the break, drinking murky vending-machine coffee with Helen, the high-school teacher who was in charge of their class. "I know how to make change. I can read a newspaper. It's stupid for me to be sitting in this room."

"Yup," said Helen, putting her cup in Kate's hand. "I'm going to make a phone call. Finish this for me." By the end of the week she had arranged for Kate to take the exam early and presented her with a typewriter and application forms to Indiana University, Ball State, and Indiana State.

"What are my long-term goals and aspirations?" Kate read from the application form and glared at Helen.

"You hope to acquire a broad-based education that will allow you to be a vital participant in today's society," Helen said, and Kate started typing. Later, when Helen asked if Kate would like to accompany her to church, Kate agreed with a sense of leaden obligation, and seven years after that, at her ordination into the ministry of the Methodist Church, she named Helen first among those agents that had raised her life from the pit.

The memories, fragmented and out of order, teased at Kate all morning. After a quick shower at the parsonage, she returned phone calls, kept an uneasy eye on Barb, took up every small task she could find. But nothing distracted her from the dread lining her lungs. How easily the slippery fear had found her again. And what a clown she'd been to believe that a new husband, a new faith, a whole new life would somehow obliterate the whole old life.

At the side of her desk sat a sheaf of papers for an upcoming statewide conference on abortion; she was supposed to write a statement, a chore she'd been dodging for weeks. She needed Ned's medical perspective, but that conversation would have to wait until they quit stalking around the parsonage like angry cats. Right now he would probably suggest that she turn the parsonage into an orphanage and a home for unwed mothers. Assuming that it stopped being a refuge for former husbands.

"Crap," she muttered. The man hadn't been back in her life twenty-four hours, and already her thoughts skidded toward him as if he were magnetized. She was on her way to pour another cup of coffee when the back doorbell rang. On the step sat a three-foot-high arrangement of roses and ferns, lavish and not quite Methodist. Dove received flowers every other day, deliveries for weddings and funerals, and sometimes even flowers meant for other congregations—Kate and Barb joked that all churches looked alike to a florist. When she checked the envelope, though, expecting to see the name of Episcopal St. Mark's on the square, the card was addressed directly to her: Kate, Here's a down payment on all that I owe you. —B. Automatically, she shielded the card from Barb, who poked her head out of the office to see what had arrived.

"Who are they for?"

"They're not for us." Kate propped up a rose that had slipped out of its Styrofoam prop. "I'll go ahead and redeliver them."

"For heaven's sake, Kate, let me call the florist. You shouldn't have to do their job."

"I don't mind. I have to make hospital visits. I'll just drop them off on my way." As she spoke, Kate read the card again, then ripped it in pieces, regretting the action almost immediately. It would have been smarter to have the card as evidence. Still, she could tell Ned about it—the insinuating words, the inappropriate, blowsy flowers. Once she had his attention, she would finally be able to tell him about her past, that grim story he was so sure he didn't need to know. Shaken out of his world of happy accidents and good intentions, he would start to understand the danger Kate felt licking at the sides of her heart. "I'm not saying this to punish you," she rehearsed. He needed to feel what she did. That would be the start.

Three

Because Kate had loaned her car to her student associate Gabe so he could go to his AA meeting, she walked the mile and a half to the El-erette County hospital, peering through the red and green fan of Bill-o's roses. At corners she rested, gazing over yards lined with played-out zinnias and petunias, and practiced words that would help Ned understand Bill-o. "Untrustworthy" was a good one. "Sly" was bet-ter. She brushed her cheek against one of the softly bristling ferns. Ned had never met anyone like Bill-o; he didn't know how goodness could be turned on itself. "Sometimes trust needs to be earned," she said, smoothing the words in her mouth.

She took the quick back route, cutting up an alley behind the Sunoco and through the grade school parking lot. If she hustled, she could catch Ned before he finished his morning rounds, when the staff still knew where he was. In the afternoons he often adroitly left his of-fice, slipping out to perform good deeds—helping someone fill out tax forms, or someone else repaint a barn. Other afternoons he paid house calls, actual house calls, on aging patients who'd been feeling puny. Kate didn't hear about these visits from Ned, but parishioners often stopped her and praised her generous husband. "Why don't you tell me?" she would ask Ned later, her mock frustration bleeding into real frustration.

"It didn't seem important," he would say, a statement she knew to be a kind of lie. It was important, all right, but he was practicing his good deeds in private, not letting the left hand know what the right hand was doing. She only wished he would pause to think that his wife, the minister, might want to work in conjunction with him. Secretive, she thought. Tight. At the back of her skull a new thought flared like a match: Selfish.

She slipped inside the hospital's back door and trudged up the service stairs, pausing at the top long enough to stretch her throbbing arms. Then she strode onto the floor, scanning corridors and checking with nurses, none of whom had seen Ned recently. All of them smiled at Kate's towering flowers. "Misdelivered," she kept saying. "Thought I'd donate them to somebody with a taste for bordello décor."

She carried the flowers from room to room, showing them off for her parishioners: on the third floor, Sally Plummer, age seven, who'd seared the full length of her arm on her parents' sizzling barbecue grill; on the second, Lynn Ann Lennox, scheduled for gall bladder surgery, and ancient Ed Worley, whose blood pressure jetted up every time he was released from the hospital—this was his fourth return in three months. In each room she rested the flowers on the sink, then stood at the bedside long enough to squeeze a hand and murmur a prayer, while she kept one eye on the corridor in case Ned strode past. She didn't sit down until she came to the bedside of Janelle Speckler, and only stopped there because Janelle was her favorite, and loved roses, and was dying.

Diagnosed with pancreatic cancer two years before, she had undergone the months of chemotherapy and radiation treatments with a sweet courage that touched everyone who talked to her; even doctors who weren't on her case stopped by to visit. She had emerged from the disease sweeter than ever, and Kate thought that she'd never understood, before looking at Janelle, what it meant for a person's face to shine.

But Janelle's last routine checkup had revealed a fresh explosion of cancer cells, spread now into the liver, and Kate had lived with a doctor long enough to know that liver patients didn't come back. Janelle seemed to know that, too—her face looked shriveled, and what hair she had left clung to her skull in damp, exhausted patches. Still, even through her pain she could produce a gentle smile, and when Kate entered her room, Janelle opened her eyes and said, "Now things are looking up."

"You're going to give me a big head." Kate squeezed Janelle's hand and set the roses next to some maroon chrysanthemums on her windowsill. Pushing the pot aside, she dislodged a two-inch New Testament with a green vinyl cover, the sort given out at grocery stores and high school graduations. "This isn't doing you any good on the windowsill," she said, handing the tiny volume to Janelle. "Although if you'd like, I'll bring you one myself. One with bigger print."

Janelle blinked at her. "I thought this one *was* from you. Your husband brought it around yesterday morning, when he came in and prayed."

"You must have gotten us mixed up. I'm the one who prays. He's the one who reads charts."

Janelle looked at her knees—knobs under the white hospital blanket. "He put his hands on my head and called on the power of the Holy Spirit. It isn't good of me, but I was embarrassed. I'm not used to that kind of thing."

Kate opened her mouth, then closed it again and bent to pick up some get-well cards that had slipped to the floor. Ned taught the adult Sunday School class at church and occasionally volunteered to talk to the youth fellowship, but this on-the-spot witnessing was nothing she'd heard about. "I would have been embarrassed, too. I'm embarrassed just hearing about it."

"I'm sure he meant it as a kindness."

"Kindness can be tricky," Kate said. "Not everybody wants what we have to offer."

Janelle closed her eyes, so Kate moved over to the sink and sorted through a basket of little gifts there—sachets, buttons, slender books of meditations. Wedged at the bottom was a figurine of a simpering girl in a yellow dress holding a sign: When God hands you lemons, make lemonade! What kind of idiot gave such a thing to a woman with liver cancer? The other arm of the statuette was missing, and Kate hoped that Janelle had been the one to snap it off.

She slipped the figure into her pocket and turned back to face Janelle, who had opened her eyes again. "I'm a little better today," Janelle said. "Not so weak. I think I can make it nine more weeks."

"What's in nine weeks?"

"I started watching a new Masterpiece Theatre. I'd hate to think I won't find out what happens." She turned her sunken eyes on Kate. "Don't you think that's a good goal?"

Wordless, Kate rubbed Janelle's bony shoulder until the woman closed her eyes. Kate swiftly prayed, then hurried down the corridor.

She was shaken by how quickly Janelle was failing, and angry with Ned, who hadn't told her that his daily rounds now included the laying-on of hands. Did he figure he could just step in for Kate, do her job with his embarrassing prayers and twenty-five-cent Bible? Was this one more secret good deed?

She checked the rest of the rooms on the second floor, while her anger ballooned. "Presumptive," she muttered. "Arrogant. Half-assed." She slowed down to ask one of the nurses whether Dr. Gussey was still in the hospital, and saw the merest bloom of surprise widen the woman's eyes. Did she believe that wives always knew where their husbands were? She must never have been married.

No one in the hospital had seen Ned, so Kate trotted down the block to the medical arts building where he saw patients. His waiting room was empty—even Donna, the receptionist, was gone—and Kate went ahead and opened the door to his office. She visited him here two or three times a week. Even so, Ned's head jerked up as if he'd heard a gunshot.

"It's just me."

"Looking like thunder. What's wrong now?"

Kate groped in her pocket and set the lemonade figurine on his desk. "Janelle wants to know if she'll make it nine more weeks."

"Maybe. She may not want to, though." Then, nodding at the figurine, "Are you going to glue the arm back on?"

"I'm going to drop it in the trash. I can't believe how insensitive people can be."

"It's just a joke."

"Not funny. Janelle won't be making any lemonade, ever again."

"Take it easy. I gave her that statue. She's on restricted fluids, and she told me that she stayed awake at night fantasizing about lemonade. She said, 'It isn't much of a fantasy, is it?' So I brought her up six ounces of lemonade and this. She laughed."

"Sorry."

"Forget it. You didn't know." He tapped a pencil on his blotter, although there was no hurry that Kate could see—no waiting patients, a clean desk. She leaned over and tapped his desk herself, to get his attention.

"Okay, I'll tell you something else I didn't know. I didn't know you've added Bible-dispensing to your rounds. Janelle told me about how you went in and prayed over her. She didn't sound grateful."

"She's dying, Kate." Ned frowned, and his mouth flattened to a thin line. Looking at his expression, Kate made an attempt to loosen up her own. He said, "She's already on morphine. She's either gorked or in pain. You tell me what kind of comfort to give."

"What you did for her wasn't comforting. How do you think she felt, having her doctor resort to praying over her bed? You might as well have just announced that you were throwing in the towel."

"She knows what the odds are. If there's ever been a time to pray, this is it. Although it never occurred to me that you would object. Frankly, I thought you'd back me up on this."

"I might have, if you'd told me what you had in mind. I would come to Janelle at three in the morning if I thought I could help her. But you just scooped up this responsibility yourself, stood next to her bed like a Roller and got Jesus on the main line, and didn't bother to tell me what you were planning to do."

"So you're mad at me for poaching on your preserve? Is that what this is about?"

Kate picked up the figurine, rubbing her finger against the rough stub. A less restrained, less responsible woman would throw the little statue at him, Kate thought. For the moment she liked feeling the broken porcelain's edge. "I feel like I'm behind the curve all the time. When I go to visit Grace Heinkel's laid-up uncle, I find out you were already there. When I sit down to balance the checkbook, I see that you sent off two hundred dollars to World Vision. I go to visit Janelle and discover that you left her a Bible. It's getting so that more and more of the time I feel like I'm married to a stranger."

"Well, you're not the only one. Guess I'm the chump; I didn't realize I was supposed to get permission. When Janelle wakes up at night afraid and hurting, at least she has something to bring her comfort. I thought you'd like that."

"I love it. Bring Bibles in by the truckload. But why am I always finding out afterward?"

Ned leaned forward, his mouth so flat his lips were nearly invisible. "Maybe I'm tired of defending everything I do. 'Don't think about taking Bill-o in; it will give me trouble with my church.' 'Don't bring

Bibles to the patients unless I tell you it's okay.' 'Don't give money to charities; I might want to give it away myself.' When was the last time you said, 'Gee, Ned, good idea. I'm glad you thought of that'?"

"The last time you had a good idea."

He snorted softly. "You're a gem, Kate. You really are."

"In a good marriage, husbands and wives tell each other things. They don't sneak off to secretly save the world."

"In a good marriage, husbands and wives share goals. They don't have to check in every morning. They work together. One unit."

"And so you're saying that we're two units? The wonderful Doctor Ned and his unfortunate harridan of a wife?"

He pulled off his glasses and started polishing them, although Kate could have told him that the lenses were so clean they were spotless. "You don't make things easy, you know that? I've never seen anybody like you for finding problems with anybody else's ideas. You want the whole world cut according to your measure. So when somebody comes in with a different piece of cloth, you just snip, snip, snip at it. The right way, the wrong way, and Kate's way."

"Oh, honey," Kate said, so furious her arms trembled. "There's a word for what you're doing. We call it 'projection.'"

Ned shrugged. "I'm not the one who wants to refuse a man a decent bed to sleep in."

"I'm trying to keep my life decent, but you won't listen to that," Kate said, looking at his pale, almost lashless eyes, his complexion the color of Cream of Wheat. Everything about him looked bled, ethereal, scarcely mortal at all. "You just love being *right*, don't you? I wonder if anyone has ever been quite so right as you are."

"I might agree, if I knew what you were talking about."

"You want to take Bill-o in because you're in love with how good it looks. You're the cowboy wearing the world's biggest white hat. You want the whole world to look at you and say, 'My, that Ned Gussey. Isn't he *right?*'"

Ned opened his mouth, then closed it. "What?" she said.

"Choices can be easy. But you won't let them be."

"I see what I see," she said.

A long pause followed, and Ned looked out his window onto Central Avenue and Bender Hardware across the street. His hair needed combing and his tie hung crooked, but he still managed to look tidy, a man with no thought beyond his next golf game, though he didn't play golf. A rectitudinous man, who could be depended upon to act with justice, mercy, humility. What, she wondered, would happen if just once he acted out of plain desire? What would he find if he explored the sealed-up crevice in his brain where his human wants were stored? Kate would give him leather-upholstered sports cars, ruby rings, a movie-star mistress, just for the satisfaction of seeing his outstretched, hungry hands. Then her thoughts plummeted: What desires was she secretly nursing, and would Ned be as eager to provide them?

"Is this why you came?" he finally said. "To tell me that everything I do is wrong?"

"I—look, let's just go to lunch."

Ned's eyes actually darted from side to side as if he were looking for an escape, and Kate began to tell him that she wasn't that hard up for a date when a knock came at the door—probably Donna, announcing that she was back from her break. Kate propped her mouth into a bland smile and opened the door, then felt the smile freeze when she found Bill-o there, the look on his own face as pure as an illustration entitled Bashfulness.

"I guess this isn't a good time," he said.

"It's fine." She stepped back to give him room. "No time like the present."

"Have you packed up your things?" Ned said. "Kate can move you in now, if you're ready."

"I'm still tying up a few loose ends," Bill-o said. "I just dropped by to say hello, maybe get some lunch."

"I have appointments," Ned said. "Kate?"

"I have appointments of my own."

"Just dropping by," Bill-o said. "Nothing important. I can see you later."

"Too bad," Ned said, standing and slipping his lab coat on. The extra pairs of glasses in the pocket made a fussy click. "You caught us on a bad day. Come around next week and we'll go downtown. I can introduce you to some people." Kate stared at him. Ned didn't spend two afternoons a year lunching downtown, and here he was coming off like the Chamber of Commerce. Was this another gesture that he expected her to congratulate him for?

"That's good of you," Bill-o said. "I can't get over how friendly people are here."

"Just wait," Kate said, sorry for her sour tone as soon as the words were out of her mouth.

Bill-o only laughed. "Can I at least offer you a ride back to church? I saw you out walking over here, carrying flowers. You looked like the world's fastest-moving camouflage unit."

"I was in a hurry," Kate muttered. She felt Ned's gaze pressing on her and rashly lifted her chin. "Sure. I'll take a ride."

"Good. I can return your big favor with a little one," Bill-o said. Ned showed them to the exit and stood in the doorway as Bill-o led Kate to a stodgy silver sedan. A company car, she guessed. Nothing he would have chosen for himself—if he still liked British cars, if he still preferred bucket seats, if he still favored red. She knew all his old tastes. She was sick with what she knew.

She relaxed a little when he quietly pulled onto the street and headed right back toward the church, no funny business, but he hadn't gone two blocks before he pulled into a parking place on the square and looked at Kate, his posture and face now denoting eagerness. "So—did you ever get that piano for the fellowship hall?"

"Last year. How did you hear about our piano?"

"Your mother sends Christmas cards. She's proud of you. Of Ned, too."

"I know." Although she didn't really know so much as assume. Kate's talks with her parents usually focused on old neighbors and new plants. On the one occasion she had tried to tell her mother about her call to ministry, her mother said, "Isn't that a little dramatic?" Now Kate said to Bill-o, "They're thinking about closing the shop. I told them they'll be getting rid of the last unpaved patch in Speedway."

"I'll have to go see them before they leave," Bill-o said. "Make a farewell to the greenhouse. Lots of memories there."

"Yes," Kate said. "How's your new house coming along?"

"I'm always surprised at how long things take. I tell myself that waiting is useful instruction in patience, which I could use. I guess you feel the same way."

"Yes. Has the company given you even a tentative date?"

"Several," Bill-o said. "I'm learning not to put too much stock in what they say. In the meantime, the contractor gives me lists. What kind of drawer pulls do I want? What kind of hinges on the kitchen cabinets? Houses are more complicated than you realize."

"Yes," Kate said. She let silence gather between them until the happy expectancy drained from Bill-o's face.

"I'm not going to bite you," he said.

"If you say so. But you can't expect me be a clean slate. When I look at you I remember things, and those memories aren't pleasant."

"Give me a chance," he said. "Let me give you new things to remember."

On the windshield in front on her a thin streak curved exactly at eye level, blurring the storefront ten feet away. "I thought I'd never see you again, and that was fine with me. Now you show up and seem surprised that I'm not hurrying to kill the fatted calf."

"It's going to take a while to get used to hearing you sound like a minister."

She smiled grimly. "Several of my congregants think I lay it on thin."

"I wasn't criticizing. I like hearing it. If anybody ever needed a minister—"

"I'll be happy to give you the addresses of other churches in town," Kate said. "They will welcome you."

"Isn't it in your job description to welcome me?"

"Yes, it is. I'm falling down on the job."

"Kate, it doesn't have to be this hard. Strange, yes, but not impossible." His voice was steady. A person overhearing the conversation would imagine Bill-o to be the reasonable one. "It's been a long time since you've seen me. My life hasn't held still. You of all people should be able to see how much a person can change."

"The old things don't just go away."

"No. But they get modified. The old things don't just stay."

Kate shook her head, and, still looking at the streaky windshield, flexed her mouth softly around several different words. "You're asking a lot. Don't expect anything to happen overnight. Don't expect anything," she said.

"I've got all the time you want."

Again she listened for some slick threat, but heard only a kind of matter-of-fact hope that she would have admired in anyone else. She was starting to feel churlish, Ned's precise opinion.

"So," she said. "Did you just happen to wind up in Elite? Is it grace that steered you here?"

"My supervisor told me I was the ideal man for the site. I used to come through Elite all the time when I was working as a rep, and I liked how the place looked. Families, grandkids, a street where everybody says hello. I'm ready for that. Am I making sense?"

"Of course. Forty doesn't want what twenty did." She almost added, Twenty didn't want what twenty got, but that was just more churlishness. "You wake up one day, look around and think, 'This isn't what I'd meant my life to be.' And then you go out and make changes."

"That's it," Bill-o said. He turned off the ignition. "I thought you would understand."

"After you left, I spent a year crying," she said. Bill-o let his glance drop; he looked abashed, which she appreciated. "I was already pretty low before you went, but I had to get all the way down. It's like being in a swimming pool; you need to push off the bottom if you're going to shoot back up to the top."

"Good example."

"I've used it in about twenty homilies," Kate said. "So I went to college because I couldn't think of any other option. I wasn't even thinking of the future. I was just trying to survive the present."

"I know how that feels. Every day tightens around you."

"Is that what you thought? Loose was how it felt to me. I couldn't get my feet underneath me. If anybody suggested anything, I did it," Kate said. Bill-o chuckled. "No joke. I took drugs, even though I didn't like how unstrung they made me. I tried yoga. Then one day when I was in a mall, I walked past a guy who was hectoring people about how their new blue jeans would lead them to the fires of hell. Everybody was looping way around to avoid him, but any kind of distraction was okay by me. I stood still, and as soon as he saw me he dropped the hell business. He said, 'There is still time to change your life.' He came at me, his hands stretched out. 'Is it you? Are you ready to change your life?'"

"And you were."

"Isn't it something? He was exactly what I'd been waiting for." Kate was surprising herself. She almost never told this story, filled as it was with the kind of emotional arm-twisting she wouldn't permit in her own ministry. She couldn't look at Bill-o as she talked. "He made me kneel down, right there, with the shoppers veering around us, and he told me to pray to be changed. As if I knew how to pray. When he put his hands on my head I imagined my brain cracking open like an egg."

"Did it?" Bill-o asked.

Kate looked out the side window. Handbills in shop windows advertised the monthly Boys Club catfish fry. "You have to remember—everything seemed the same to me. God or yogic breathing or learning to be a legal secretary. I'd already been to church a couple times with a woman I knew. After the run-in at the mall, I dared myself to go back, just to see if this guy in his blue suit had changed me. I couldn't tell, so I dared myself to keep going. Half the time I didn't know what the pastor in the church was talking about, but I felt clean when I was there. I liked feeling clean."

"Oh, yeah," Bill-o murmured.

"Maybe it was grace, maybe pure chance." Kate was talking fast now. She'd never told anyone the whole story all at once, not even Ned. It was a good story. Why didn't she tell it? "But I started to see a new world, a system that I hadn't seen before. People were all connected, lifting one another up or tearing down. Everybody doing one or the other. The whole universe was being created and destroyed at the same time, every minute. Once I started to see that, I wanted to be one who lifted." She hadn't thought in these terms for a long time—years. But they were still good terms.

"You were converted," Bill-o said.

"—And I was the most obnoxious kind of convert. After all those years of feeling no responsibility to anyone, I was ready to take on responsibility to everyone. I had a new notion of myself as part of a huge picture, cosmic, bigger than anything I'd seriously thought about. I started to pray just so I could say Thank you."

"Did anybody say, You're welcome?"

Kate shot a look at Bill-o, but the question seemed genuine. "Nobody hears an actual voice talking back. Or at least we should worry about the ones who do. But everything seemed possible then. You should have seen me; happiness was pouring off."

"It still is," Bill-o said.

"Not like then." Kate shook her head; this was the good part of the story. "I changed my major from accounting to religious studies, and I started seminary two days after I finished my B.A. I was in a hurry to get out in the world and start doing good."

"You're a whole new woman."

"I am become incorruptible," she said, and laughed. "It helps a lot to believe your life is following a path."

"I know."

Kate peered at him. He leaned toward her, his hands cupped as if to catch something. "Do you? Then you really have changed."

"I've been trying to tell you."

"Okay. Tell me."

He held up one of his cupped hands. "You finish first. I want to hear the end of the story."

"Well, you see the end of the story: It's right here." Kate gestured at the shop window across the sidewalk from them with its back-to-school plaids and bright construction paper leaves, wholesome and steadfast. "I felt as if my life had been saved, and I wanted to save lives for other people. The years I was in seminary—I was blazing all the time. I'd wake up in the morning already overjoyed. I met Ned then and thought he was a part of that happiness."

"Wasn't he?"

She paused. "Nobody's life blazes forever. But I looked at Ned and figured he could show me how to live the life I wanted, and I was right about that."

"I can see that. I'll bet he keeps you on the straight and narrow."

"He has high standards."

"I'm surprised you haven't had kids."

Kate cleared her throat. "Maybe I'll be like Sarah, get pregnant at ninety. She laughed when God told Abraham that she would have a baby, and when she did have a son, she named him Isaac, which means,

'He laughs.' I love that story."

"It's not as good as your story, Kate. You've come a long way. You're lucky."

"Don't I know it. When I think about where I could be now—well, I don't need to tell you."

"I envy you. I admit it. You've already got a whole new life, and here I am just starting. I feel like a baby next to you."

"Babies are unscarred. They're fresh slates."

"I'm a stale slate."

"Your turn. Tell me."

He started up the car again, reversed into the street and turned toward the church, his expression hardening.

"This may be tough for you to believe, but things got even worse for me after we split up. I started knocking on people's doors, offering to do odd jobs for money. And tomcatting—" he glanced back at Kate and blushed, something she hadn't known him capable of. "I lived off the girls who would let me."

"I'm not surprised," Kate said.

"You shouldn't be. It was the same old story, getting worse all the time, but never quite bad enough to make me stop. I managed to clean myself up enough to get a rep job with AgPro, and that was the worst thing that could have happened. I had two suits and a company car. I didn't have to get scared looking at the other guys in line for a free meal at some community center. I got engaged twice. God help those poor girls."

"You never had trouble getting girls."

"Too bad for all of us. I don't think there's a motel in three states that doesn't know my face. I didn't have a house; I didn't have a family. There was a cat for a while, but I got rid of it. I had a job that kept me on the road. I didn't have one thing in my life built to endure, but I thought I was the last word."

"And then what?" Kate asked. She knew it must be past one o'clock, and she was expected back at church, but appointments would have to be patient. Bill-o bumped the car into the church parking lot and Kate was leaning toward him, practically lunging across the seat to hear how he suffered after walking out on her.

He left the engine running and ran his fingertip across the top of the steering wheel. "What can I tell you? I went to Damascus. I can show it to you, if you want. It's a Knights Inn just outside of Indy, a room with purple crushed velvet bedspreads. I met a woman there. This dark room with horrible lighting made her look like a hag, so I wanted to turn the lights off, but she wouldn't let me. 'Don't you want to see?' she kept saying and giggling as if she'd said something really raunchy." He stopped, sucking at the inside of his cheek.

"So the lights stayed on," Kate prompted.

"So the lights stayed on. And the whole time she's undressing all I can think is that she's a wreck. Her skin was covered with these awful little puckers; and the light was gray in this motel room I wouldn't have wished on a dog; and her breasts, jeez, they must have been beautiful once, just laid down flat over her chest. I thought, 'This is the most pathetic sight I've ever seen.' I mean, I couldn't even make myself touch her, and she's standing there tossing around hair that's so bleached it doesn't look like hair anymore and waiting for me to ravish her."

"And you didn't?" Kate said. Her breath had grown hoarse as a cough.

"I looked away from her and caught sight of myself in the mirror. In that crappy light it was like looking at myself underwater. But there I was, with pimples all over my chest and love handles hanging out over my boxers, and my mouth dangling open like some old pervert's who shows himself to little boys. I looked twisted, Kate; Christ, I looked like some kind of gargoyle. I couldn't stand to even imagine that this reflection could be me, so I shut my eyes."

"Just that?"

"For a long time. I stood there with my eyes shut and listened to the gal—Linda, I couldn't forget her name if I wanted to—get dressed again and leave, offering a few opinions on the state of my manliness. And I stood there for a long time after she left, holding my arms out from my sides so I didn't have to touch myself. It disgusted me to put my clothes back on, but I finally did it because it disgusted me more to be standing there with all this flesh hanging off me."

"You hated yourself," Kate said.

"I bought an electric razor so I could shave without a mirror, and I still get dressed in the dark."

"Still? Bill-o—listen, there's such a thing as too much remorse." Kate unbuckled her seat belt and turned fully to face him, but he sat with his face turned away from her. "Remember—" she began, but he cut her off.

"Remember. I've got more miles racked up on me than your common guy. I'm dirtier, and it will take more than one bath to scrub all this off. But that's the thing, Kate; I'm ready now. That's why it was so important for me to see you. The girls are gone. I'm living clean. All I want to do is get things solid under my feet. I need to wake up in the morning and know I'm not hiding anything. Do you understand what I'm saying? I'm counting on you, Katy."

"I do," Kate said. "You're starting a new life. You're just like me." She swallowed and blinked. Of all the healing she had hoped for in her life, this was a greater gift than she had imagined: to meet Bill-o in the territory of grace. "It's good to see you," she murmured and reached out with her damp fingers to touch his wrist. Awash as she was in her astonishing new joy, she stiffened slightly but didn't draw back when he took her hand and turned it up, then lowered his head and pressed it against her palm, like a penitent.

Four

"I'm sorry," Bill-o said. He raised his head from her hand, but she meant to keep this new door between them open, no matter how awkwardly it was held.

She said, "I should apologize, not you. It's good to have you here."

He laughed softly, clasping her fingers and quickly releasing them. "Who would've thought?"

"Anyone who believed in solid-gold miracles."

"That's what you are, Kate."

"In your eyes, maybe. I feel more like a lead miracle." She was finding it hard to talk; her mouth had gotten clumsy. "I've got to go. I have work to do."

"Good. You'll make me get to my own work. All heck's probably breaking loose down at the garden center."

"You can say 'hell' around me. I'm familiar with the concept."

He shook his head. "I was just telling you; I want to play by the rules."

"The rules aren't as strict as you think. They allow for a little hell now and then." He rolled his eyes, reminding her of the afternoons she'd spent happily trying to decide whether his eyes were green or gray or brown. "So Ned and I should plan on seeing you in the parsonage tonight?"

"You may come to regret your generosity—I'm in and out a lot, and I keep late hours."

"When people ask what you're doing here, I'll tell them that business is being conducted," Kate said, and touched him lightly above his elbow before she opened the car door and headed back out, toward the church, hearing how the very tap of her footsteps sounded delighted.

At her desk, Barb was on the phone. She motioned Kate to wait while she finished giving the times for the youth group pizza supper, then hung up and hit the answering machine's replay button before Kate could even say hello.

"Here's a little something to brighten your day," she said, as the pinched voice of Lucinda Akins came on. Lucinda was a lifelong church member, a mercilessly upright woman married to a genial, laid-off stonecutter whom Kate had never seen, at any hour, fully sober.

"Your new fellow just called on us," Lucinda began. Jolted, Kate raised her hand to her face until Barb mouthed "Gabe," and Kate remembered that he'd been assigned to visit church members after his AA meeting. "I would like you to speak to him. I'm sure it's a fine thing that he has managed to stop drinking, but we are not interested in the details of his debauches. We do not expect a minister of the church to tell us where people he's known have hidden bottles. We are not interested in his opinions of our habits. I would like a call back from you as soon as possible." Not until she hung up with a controlled, ladylike click did Kate exhale.

"Another satisfied customer," Barb said.

"I thought Gabe knew what he was supposed to do," Kate said, shaking her head. "'Just visit with people,' I told him. 'Be friendly. Let them talk. Sometimes they'll tell you things at home that they wouldn't want to say at church.'"

"Lucinda wouldn't tell anyone where Hank hides his bottles if she was in front of a firing squad."

"I'll talk with Gabe when he's done with Youth Fellowship. Any other calls?"

Barb elaborately sorted through the notes on her desk. "Do you mean the message from the paper supply company? Or the window washers, to remind us that it's that time of year again? Or do you mean the five different parishioners who want to know whether it's true that your ex-husband has moved into the parsonage?"

"Tell them no. He hasn't, yet." Lifting her hand to her hair, avoiding Barb's gaze, Kate smoothed a curl into place beside her ear. "There just aren't any secrets in this town, are there?"

"Marie Moeller's been working the deli counter at the IGA, and your ex has been coming in for sandwiches. When he told her that she wouldn't be seeing so much of him, she naturally asked where he was going to be eating, and he told her that he was being taken in by the world's kindest-hearted minister ex-wife. Marie thought this was news worth sharing."

"I can tell you already that it isn't as thrilling as she thinks."

"Kate, I don't want to sound like your mother here, but have you thought this thing through?"

"It wasn't my idea. Ned's the one."

Barb capped her pen. "Go slow. I'm interested."

"I was all in favor of putting him out in the street, preferably in Montana. Then Ned came in, and when Bill-o said that he's sleeping on the floor at the garden center until his house is done, Ned wouldn't rest until he promised to stay with us."

A moment passed, then Barb shook her head as if recollecting herself. "This is going to be a whopper of a hard sell. Bob Peters has already called twice—the second time he said, 'Oh, she's still not in?' as if he knew just what *that* meant."

"I tried to tell Ned how it would look, and he kept talking about bad backs and air mattresses and reminding me that it's my responsibility to take in the homeless, which didn't really leave much ground under my feet."

"Are you going to be able to keep standing?" Barb said softly.

Kate shrugged. She felt uncomfortable not saying more; Barb was her best friend, and they didn't keep secrets from each other. But Kate had a whole new Bill-o to get used to—a penitent Bill-o, a new creation. Her breath snagged at the thought. "Things are complicated. We can talk about it when there's more time."

"You just let me know when that will be. Have you got this week's homily written yet? We have to post the title."

"I'll get to it today. I swear."

"Before or after you call Lucinda back?"

Kate groaned. "I'm going into my office to spend five minutes getting some clear space into my head. Then I will deal with Gabe, write the homily, and end world hunger."

"I'll hold your calls," Barb said, already turning back to the typewriter, leaving Kate feeling dismissed, so she closed the door that separated their offices with a hurt click.

Sitting at her desk, where Barb had left phone messages scattered over the drifts of paperwork, she put her head down, resting her cheek on a week's accumulated memos, questionnaires, articles, and notes. In seminary she had been warned about days like this, when there were too many balls to keep in the air, too many bullets to dodge—somewhere in the office was an article on the subject she'd half-finished reading. The author had offered a checklist of common stress inducers, including low salary, unrealistic expectations from parishioners, and lack of intimacy—that was a good one—with spouse. Nowhere had the list mentioned a resurrected ex-husband, the biggest bullet of all, a cannonball that had hit her squarely in the chest. And no article ever explained how to make phone calls and write prayers as if there were no cannonball lodged between her lungs. Congregants don't want to know their minister's problems, the article had said. Congregants look to their ministers for stability.

Sighing, she lifted her head. On top of the pile were the few notes she'd made toward a homily—three cites and a vague half-paragraph about rights and respect. As she looked at the measly start, suspicion, borne on Ned's voice, murmured that she hadn't been able to write anything because she couldn't ever let anything be easy—the right way, the wrong way, and Kate's way. "I see what I see," she muttered, picking up the phone to dial Lucinda's number. When she heard the busy signal she gave quick thanks, then looked up as Barb came into the office with a handful of letters for Kate to sign. "You're just in time," Kate said. "Lucinda, one. Homily, one. Kate, zip."

"Bill-o, one?" Barb said.

"Bill-o, ten. He brought the element of surprise."

"He must have been counting on that." She set the letters at the edge of Kate's blotter. "So how did he look? Has he grown a beard or anything?"

In fact, Kate had been surprised at how dark and thick his hair had stayed and had felt a quick pinch of regret that she'd let her own hair become so drab. "I would have recognized him anywhere," she said, picking her words.

"That's what I would have guessed."

"Look—it wasn't a wonderful reunion. If I had it to do again, I'd push him off the porch."

"But you didn't. Isn't that the point? We make our first blunders early, and then we just keep remaking them." With a rough motion, Barb pulled her hair back from her face, then let it drop. "You shouldn't listen to me this morning. I hate every man on the face of the earth, except Dr. Ned."

"I wouldn't make an exception for him," Kate said.

"I thought about having Mindy go see him. I thought maybe he could get her to see that having a baby now means closing every door of her life."

"He's kind of a loose cannon right now. I don't think you want to get him involved."

"And then I just think about force marching her down to the clinic myself and getting it over with. Kate, I'm driving myself crazy. I start out thinking about what to have for dinner, and fifteen seconds later all I can think of is Mindy with her belly out to here, acting like she invented pregnancy. I go from rage to misery, then back to rage. I'm wearing a groove in my brain."

"This is still new. Things will get better."

Barb produced a watery half-smile. "Promise?"

"They'd better. I'm telling myself the same thing." Kate paused. "Isn't this where I say that we must have faith? We must have faith." The phone rang then, and she and Barb both grabbed for it, Barb beating her by half a second. She answered, then handed the phone over to Kate. "It's Bill-o," she said and turned to the door.

Kate sat with her hand over the mouthpiece, nodding and smiling encouragingly, but she could see from Barb's locked-shut face that she, the minister, was hiding none of the excitement that had splashed up at the mention of his name, or the impatient guilt; as Barb closed the door, Kate held back the urge to make a hurry-up motion with her hands.

Bill-o said, "Am I getting you in trouble, calling like this?"

"I'm here to serve."

"Well, I guess I'm counting on that." She heard the nervous quiver in his voice, a quiver that made her nervous, too; reaching for a note that had fallen off her desk, she brushed two pens to the floor. He said, "I need a favor, and I didn't know who else to call."

"Good. I'll do whatever I can."

"It's not anything you might think. What I need is a gardener."

She felt the smile slide off her mouth. "Haven't you heard? I'm out of that line of work."

"Look, I hate to even ask. But I've got three hundred chrysanthemum plants that have to be watered and pinched over here, and two lugs from the high school who don't want to do anything except carry around bags of mulch. I know this is an imposition, but if you could just come in and take care of the flats, I could start putting displays out front. I wouldn't ask if I knew anybody else."

"You've seen my garden. Do you think somebody with more weeds than flowers should be let anywhere near garden flats?"

"I'm sorry," Bill-o said. "I shouldn't have called. You were the only one I knew."

Kate stared at her desk, at the papers that seemed to be breeding there, and felt her guilt rise higher. "I'm not saying I won't come." She squeezed her eyes shut. "But it's been years since I've messed with new plants. I don't want you to think you'll be getting expert help."

"I'll be getting your help. Ah Katy, you're too good to me," he said, relief purling through his voice.

"Not too good. Maybe good enough."

"You're helping me. I didn't mean to come to town and have you keep doing me favors. I'll pay you back."

"Don't worry about payback," she said. "Compared to what's going on around here, pinching mums will be a pleasure." She hung up quickly, before he could tell her again how splendid she was, and lingered at the desk only long enough to dial Lucinda Akins's number—which, happily, was still busy. Then she tiptoed down the corridor toward the Fellowship Hall to eavesdrop on Gabe and the youth group, another one of the aspects of his ministry that she was supposed to evaluate.

"You're making it too hard for yourselves," he was saying. He had a country voice, high and reedy, that Kate liked to listen to. "Prayer is just talking. You don't need special words or a separate place. Just pray where you are. Hang out. Know that God is all around you."

"How about at work? I'm pretty sure God's not there. I mean, I wouldn't be," one of the boys said, and a few of the kids laughed.

"How about in the locker room at school?" another boy asked.

"How about the whizzer?" The kids really laughed then.

"Why not?" Gabe said, and Kate nodded. He sounded flexible, open, and she wished he could have been this willing to listen to Lucinda. "You don't need to draw any lines. Every place you are, God is."

"Every place? I'm in trouble," one of the girls said. Kate smiled and walked back to the office to gather her jacket and purse. Barb lifted her hands from the keyboard. "I thought you were going to stay here this afternoon."

"Bill-o needs help at his garden center. Lucinda's line is busy, and all the rest of the work can wait. I can't tell you how good it sounds right now to get my fingers into some potting soil."

"Beats talking to Lucinda, that's for sure."

"We're done, aren't we?" Kate said. "What we were talking about? I can stay if you want to talk some more."

"Go." Barb pushed at the air. "Get out while you still can."

"I'll bring you back an African violet for your desk."

"Goody—a present. I guess his coming was a blessing after all." She and Kate exchanged sharp smiles, and the first thing Kate did when she arrived at the new NaturWise was look over a tray of African violets that had been left outside, on top of stacked bags of manure. She set aside a vigorous plant with double flowers in a full crown, then let herself in through the propped-open door.

The structure, built like a warehouse, still smelled of plaster dust and paint, and Kate could see why Bill-o wanted help. Two long, empty, white metal shelves ran across the back wall—otherwise, nothing had been unpacked. Aisles were formed by four-foot-high warehouse boxes holding bags of grass seed and sevin powder. Bright signs advertising specials on slow-release fertilizer lay under an armload of rakes, and from another box with a stain across the bottom rose the thick smell of fish emulsion.

Listening to her steps echo and crunch on the concrete floor, she wandered to the far end of the store. A forklift squealed out back. "Bill-o?" she called. She had to call three times, the last with real annoyance, before he hurried out from a set of swinging doors.

"Here you are! The angel of mercy." He opened his arms to her, looking so purely happy that her irritation fell from her like a drape.

"Just a friend. Helping a friend."

"The best friend a fellow ever had."

"You won't say that after I've forgotten to pinch a few stems."

"You? You're a pincher from way back. Nothing's safe around you."

Kate laughed, partly amused, mostly startled. Years had passed since a man had dared try the kind of flirty teasing other women heard every day. Bill-o didn't even know, she thought, a fresh chuckle rising into her mouth. He couldn't imagine. He was taking her back into the land of the living.

"Gosh," he said. "I'm funnier than I thought."

"You're a stitch," she said. "Show me what you've got here."

He took Kate's arm as he steered her through the swinging doors. The add-on, with its bright light and shelves of watering trays, wasn't a greenhouse so much as a holding zone for plants that were shipped from all over the country. This arrangement meant he could offer exotics, plants that could never be propagated in Indiana—big, orange-snouted clivea, baskets of twining mandevilla, even orchids. "We've got plants you won't find anywhere else," Bill-o said, nodding at a sweet pepper. "I'm going to get people in this town thinking beyond marigolds and daylilies."

"Good luck," Kate said.

"Don't be negative. We'll start a show garden out in front of the store with new varieties, some ornamental grasses. Let people see what's possible." He grinned. "Foster a little healthy competitiveness in the garden club set."

"I don't know that I've heard of a garden club in Elite. Look, I'm just trying to warn you; people here like growing the plants their grandmothers grew. They'll come in to see the orchids, but you'd better keep your stock of marigolds up."

"Let them see, that's all," Bill-o said stubbornly. "Give them a choice. Those are Martha Washington's Plumes across the back wall." He dropped her arm in order to point. "You can't get more old-fashioned than that."

She could see he was disappointed in her, and so she murmured appreciatively at the giant pink feathers, although she couldn't imagine anyone in Elite thinking a nine-foot plant was a good choice for the garden. As he kept talking about hardiness and all-season color, Kate was tempted to tell him about her enchantment, when she had been twelve years old, with apricot tea roses. The hybrids were new then. She'd plastered pictures around the shop, invited customers to heft the bushes, kept chattering about vigor and floriferousness while her father loaded white "Peace" and pink "Helen Trauble" roses, available anywhere, into car trunks. By September, the shop had sold three apricot rosebushes. "People like what they know," her father said, trying to console her. "If you remember that, you won't get disappointed." But Bill-o was beaming at the tiny, purplish-blue fans of a scaevola, his face soft with appreciation. "Lovely," she murmured.

He toured with her for a full half-hour, lingering over the white peppers and finger-long Japanese eggplants, before he brought her to the long trays of maroon and gold chrysanthemums. Kate smiled, touching one of the bobbing, firm flowers. "I love these," she said.

"Everybody does. Chrysanthemums pay a lot of bills." He handed her the watering wand. "Just pinch off any minor buds or dead leaves, and give them a decent soak. These guys are shallow rooted, so they're thirsty."

"Thank you, Professor Botany."

"Sorry. I'm not used to dealing with people who actually know something about plants."

He loitered at the table next to her for a few minutes, pretending to read the faint, computer-printed labels on the begonias; but Kate could tell he was keeping an eye on her, and she passed the wand so quickly over the first tray that she missed some of the plants completely.

Bill-o drifted behind her, watched for a moment, then said, "Don't worry—the knack will come back before you know it."

"It's you," she said, trying to slow down. "You're making me nervous."

"Guess we still have to get used to each other."

"You've always made me nervous."

"Guess we need to start again, then," he said, taking the wand away from her. His hand steady, he moved the rod evenly over the plants. The stubby leaves, lobes like little fingers, glistened. When he handed the wand back she imitated his motion, watering in long arcs, watching the flowers shine as she passed over. "Still nervous?" Bill-o murmured.

"Yes."

He laughed, squeezed her shoulder, and slipped back through the swinging doors to the main store. Kate was relieved—now that he was gone she could lean over the tables, pinching off dead leaves with one hand while she watered with the other, settling into the old, pleasant rhythm.

Bred to it, her father had used to say proudly. There were pictures of her as a toddler embracing a long amaryllis stem, and of onions she'd planted in the front border because she'd mixed them up with the daffodil bulbs. When she was six she had plunged her face into a blooming lilac to inhale the fragrance and a bee stung her square in the fold of her eyelid. She had to stay in bed for the rest of the day. The next morning, she ran out to the lilacs and buried her face in them again. Her father, two steps behind her, said, "You're a slow learner."

Without taking her face from the blossoms, Kate said, "Mostly they don't have bees."

She'd used that story from the pulpit when she needed an illustration of faith, but she thought now that the story had another, truer moral: People who knew where happiness was shouldn't let a little sting scare them away. She turned off the wand and held up a particularly good plant, its yellow flowers like sculpted butter at the top of strong stems. There was no telling the last time she had studied a flower's silky petals, a beauty almost opulent, and she wondered whether she'd been missing her own moral. At least, for years now, she'd missed looking at plants.

During her courting days with Ned, afternoons of long walks, he had gotten annoyed with her habit of interrupting his conversation in order to point out a well-established Japanese maple, a fine use of pyracantha. "Do you have to name every plant we pass?" he would say. "Am I going to be tested tomorrow?" She kept a miffed silence for a while, trying to listen to him while still nodding at the pretty candytuft verbena they passed, vowing that she'd find a man who liked to look at plants when he walked.

Kate replaced the damp, heavy pot. She hadn't found that man, of course. She'd kept walking with Ned until the urge to point at a plant, name it, sniff it, and rub its leaves between her fingertips had almost died away.

Carefully, she set the chrysanthemum on the rack to drain and reached for another one, running her fingers over the densely packed petals, the faintly fuzzy leaves. When she put her face down, she smelled its sharp, vegetable scent while the flower heads bobbed against her cheeks. Glancing around to make sure Bill-o wasn't sneaking back up behind her, she ripped off a corner of a petal and tasted it. The flavor was coarse and grassy, earthier than she'd expected, and she wasn't sure whether she liked it or not. She swallowed the bit of petal, glanced around again, and then, feeling reckless, ate the rest of it.

Five

Bill-o had been living in the parsonage for a week before Sharon Werth, head of the Pastor-Parish Relations Committee, called a special meeting. "I don't know about you all," Sharon said while committee members were still pulling out chairs and hanging up purses, "but I've been swamped with phone calls about Kate's situation." Looking at her earnest face, Kate felt dismay prickle through her. Sharon was one of the parishioners who always defended her. This meeting would be almost as hard for Sharon as it would for Kate.

Around the table people were nodding, and Terri Knorr flashed an embarrassed smile. "Bill heard at work. He came home and asked me just what kind of church this is."

"The Church of Whoopee," Bob Peters remarked, a line he'd obviously looked forward to delivering. His son had a church up in Chicago, and Bob thought he knew everything there was to know about ministry. Every time he was unhappy about Dove, and he was often unhappy about Dove, he threatened to write a letter to the District Superintendent. Now he flashed his teeth. "The Church of Let the Good Times Roll."

"People are calling," Sharon said again, shooting him an irritated look. "And I want to know what to say."

"Bring on the dancing girls! The Church of Let It All Hang Out."

"Thank you, Bob; we get your point," Kate said. "I understand that this is a troubling issue, but my ex-husband hasn't moved in to stay. He was sleeping on the floor of the new garden center while his house is being finished, and none of us, I think, would expect him to live like that. He'll move into the Travelinn as soon as space opens up." Although she was beginning to wonder if a room would ever become available;

Bill-o called the motel every day. She swallowed and quoted Ned, much as it rankled to do so. "He came to our door and he was homeless. It was right to let him in."

"You couldn't have put a twenty in his hand and let him find a room down the road?" said Bob.

"The Bible is pretty clear on this, Bob," she said, but he was already talking over her.

"Pardon me for saying, but with two husbands in residence you look more like the woman at the well than a pastor. What do you want me to say when people ask what the three of you do at night?"

"We talk," Kate said. "That's all."

He snorted and sat back in his chair, his arms folded. He knew what he knew. Kate sat back in her own chair and folded her own arms.

"For pity's sake," she said. "What do you think is going on? Do you imagine that we're holding orgies? You're welcome to come and see. But it seems to me that you're spending a little too much time worrying about something that really isn't yours to worry about."

Bob jerked so hard he actually moved his chair back a few inches and perfect silence held in the room. Sharon examined her pink fingernails.

"Talk," Kate repeated into the silence. "This is what you can tell people. Tell them to come by. Drop by and hear for yourselves. We sit up and talk."

Which was true, as half-baked as it sounded. With Bill-o in residence, Ned and Kate weren't retreating into the grim silence and elaborate politeness that characterized most of their fights. Instead, they were talking. Every evening, every morning. To Bill-o.

Ned pulled out tales from medical school, new to Kate: the plastic surgeon who, fancying himself an artist, required that the operating table be shifted so that he could work with north light; new mothers groggy with anesthesia who named their babies after viruses or antibiotics. Kate countered with stories from pastoral counseling, anecdotes she'd never told before because there had never been reason before — the one, for instance, that all seminarians heard about the holy pastor who hung a curtain around one corner of his living room and disappeared behind it for a half-hour every day. "What do you do there?" his parishioners asked, imagining visions, raptures, transports. The pastor only smiled, making them ask with greater urgency, "Do you meet with God himself?" The pastor's smile broadened, which they took as his modest acknowledgment. So one day, when they heard slapping sounds from behind the curtain, they imagined the pastor engaged in furious battle with the devil and whipped back the curtain to come to the pastor's defense. The man was kneeling, slapping down playing cards as he laid out a hand of solitaire. He arose in wrath and drove them out, crying, "You have every other inch of my church and home and life. You won't allow me even one corner in which to be alone?"

"Good story," Bill-o had said. "Where's your corner?"

"I'm still looking. Let me know if you see one."

"I wouldn't say she needs a corner just yet," Ned said, but Kate, already on her feet, didn't bother to answer. She was acting out the marriage she'd performed between two Cameroonians who had only been in America a week. Neither the bride, the groom, nor most of the guests spoke any English beyond hello and thank you. Kate had smiled and congratulated them in the Fellowship Hall reception and prepared to leave, when the entire group—bride, groom, and congregation—had headed back to the parsonage with her. "They brought the food and stayed for hours. I wound up driving everybody home."

"I would have let them stay," Ned said.

"Great big family weddings," Bill-o said. "All that celebration. Nobody wants them to end."

"I did," Kate said. "I was afraid to look onto the porch the next morning, in case they were ready to celebrate some more."

"God forbid they should be happy beyond their appointed time," Ned said.

"Ned doesn't work in the same place he lives," Kate said. "He forgets that other people have different kinds of responsibilities."

"Other lives always look easy, don't they?" said Bill-o.

"We had a house filled with joyful people. Let me tell you, that's a rarity," Ned said.

"It was past midnight. You could hear them a block away," Kate said.

Cocking his head toward Bill-o, Ned said, "You would have let them stay, wouldn't you?"

"Hard to know. I'm not much on weddings—" he looked at Kate and made a face, "—but I always like a good party."

Kate made a face back at him and went to pour more coffee. Fighting this way, using Bill-o as part umpire, part jury, part backboard, was inexcusable, as she well knew. When couples came to her for counseling, her first rule was no arguing in front of audiences. But she hadn't figured on how utterly Bill-o's presence in the house would burst open the dams and sluices that had developed between Ned and her. Now that they'd started, they couldn't stop talking. Kate found herself hurrying through meetings, choosing new choir robes, and rescheduling the ushers' meeting chop-chop—impatient to get back home and pick up the conversation.

Ned had jumped in to describe a patient, a little boy so frightened of his measles vaccination that a waiting room full of patients heard him wailing clear across the parking lot. In the end, the boy would only let Ned give the shot if Ned would let the boy stick him in return.

"What did you give him to stick you with, a pencil?" Bill-o asked.

"The boy wasn't an idiot; he could see how shots worked. I gave him a hypodermic."

"For crying out loud, Ned," Kate said, coming in with the mugs on a tray and setting them on the table, aggravated enough to address him directly. "What's happened to your sense? Where did you let him stick you?"

"In my finger. I'm not an idiot either." Ned paused, then added dryly, "His mother looked a little stunned."

"I'll bet that's one kid who can't wait until his next shot," said Bill-o.

Ned said, "When they left he looked at me and said, 'When I come back I'm giving it to you in the butt.'"

Kate, caught off guard, sprayed a mouthful of coffee, and Bill-o turned his gaze back on her. "You two have great stories."

"Stick around. There's no telling what you'll hear."

"It helps to have an audience," Ned said, wiping off the table.

"Ned thinks I don't listen to him," Kate informed Bill-o.

"She hears what she wants to hear."

"I hear a heck of a homily," Kate said, "about how you can be surprised by the very people you think you know the best. I'll wrap it up with a story about a little boy promising to stick it to his doctor in the butt."

"Pastor Gussey," Ned said. "Minister to the Crude."

"They need saving, too," she said.

"You know," Bill-o said, "I don't mean to be insulting here, but the life of the cloth isn't quite what I'd expected."

"Me, neither," said Ned.

"Me, neither," said Kate.

They stayed up late that night, and when they got up the next morning, words were already spilling out of their mouths. To this cheerful, nonjudgmental Bill-o, Kate and Ned could voice emotions long suppressed—the old resentments, the new uncertainties, the hurt feelings, lost opportunities, slights and fears and suspicions. Words flew from their mouths, and all the while Bill-o intervened like a graceful emcee, chuckling at Kate's jokes, nodding as Ned made a cogent point. Kate's dreams, which came fitfully, were plotless descents into voices that talked, talked, talked. Her brain banged with them.

After two weeks the wear was obvious to anyone who looked. By herself she was drinking two pots of coffee a day, so much caffeine that her hands trembled when she raised a cup to her mouth. The shadows under her eyes were dark as bruises. She kept blinking, trying to draw the world into focus, and the little time she was able to spend without church members or houseguest or spouse felt like moments of cease-fire.

So she was grateful to find herself alone in the dark on a Friday night, watering the new Bradford pear tree set off the east side of the church. Nearly three hundred dollars' worth of tree, it was Bill-o's thank-you gift to her and Ned and the church. He had planted it himself, taking over an hour to chip a hole in the packed dirt. He'd also meant to water it, but he was working late tonight, logging the inventory of new materials that seemed endless: tools, pesticides, herbicides, fertilizers. Kate imagined him standing with a clipboard in a whirlwind of white chemicals, and she hoped he'd remembered to put on a mask, a concern she wouldn't have had for careful Ned who was out too, working through paperwork in his office; he could be hours yet. Velvety quiet settled around her, and in celebration she sprayed S-shapes at the base of the spindly tree trunk, playing with the nozzle and watching the water bubble up before it soaked into the newly amended soil. Bill-o had situated the tree so that she would be able to look up from her office window into its wand-like branches, which still, even freshly transplanted, held a few soft leaves. In the spring those branches would be as frothy and white as petticoats.

Assuming she kept them alive that long. Although October had arrived, heat had come roaring back. Temperatures in the afternoon were over ninety, and farmers bringing in late harvests were passing out in the fields.

"This isn't Indian summer," Barb had panted at her desk, where the fan was pointed straight at her. "This is hell."

Everybody was complaining, Kate included. The church's air conditioning converter was out being serviced, work scheduled almost a year ago, and church attendance on Sunday had been down to thirty-four. Only three out of the usual fifteen attended Ned's Sunday School class. The faces in the congregation had shone with such misery that Kate had felt as if she were punishing them even though she was preaching on forgiveness, on how people give up on themselves, forgetting that they are infinitely forgiven, infinitely forgivable.

Watching Alma Vyrie pluck at her polyester blouse to keep the fabric from adhering to her skinny chest, Kate had found herself saying, "We put ourselves to tests that God would never put us to. We practically smother in hot churches when God would just as soon have us go home, where it's air conditioned. Let us stand and pray." She'd had to motion to make people get up, and while the congregation stirred to its feet and Ellen Phillips hurried back to the organ, Barb caught Kate's eye and mouthed "Good call," making a circle with her thumb and forefinger.

Now Kate closed her eyes, enjoying the mist settling on her hands and wrists like cool gloves, engrossed enough in her task not to pay attention, at first, to the car pulling up, its engine stopping. She listened to quiet footsteps crossing the lawn, and in the languid moment before she turned she felt certain that whoever stood there must be a friend, because the evening was soft as cloth, and she was at peace.

Lights from both the church office and the parsonage cast enough brightness for Kate to see clearly the little delegation clustered on the grass: two men, two women, two little girls. The men wore boxy suits and white shirts, the women flowered dresses with sleeves and high collars. The two girls fingered full-skirted party dresses, the sort Kate hadn't seen in years. Wearing a cotton blouse and skirt, she felt underdressed in her own yard.

"I'm Pastor Gussey." She shut off the hose at the nozzle and extended her wet right hand. One of the men, with the bulky, padded shoulders of an ex-athlete and a thick crest of hair rising from his forehead, reached forward to clasp it.

"We know who you are," he said, his voice rich and musical as a horn. "I'm Robert Efrim, and this is George Mellot, Mrs. Efrim and Mrs. Mellot, Nancy and Veronica." Like him, the other adults lightly dipped their heads. George Mellot produced a smile crammed with long, horselike teeth. The woman whose pale hair rose over her head like a cloud moved self-consciously into the shadow, and the other stared at Kate with huge, bloodshot eyes, the girls pressed to her side.

"You're welcome here," Kate said, the phrase she always used with strangers. Judging from the confident way these folks held themselves, they were already sure of their welcome. To the girls, she added, "Thank you for coming to visit me," and watched them grin and twist.

Robert Efrim said, "We come from The Church of Sanctuary Christians. We're eager to talk to you."

"Would you like to come inside?" she asked, trying to keep the resignation out of her voice. She'd never heard of Sanctuary Christians; they weren't from Elite, or even nearby, but wherever they'd swooped in from, they stood before her glowing with high purpose. She had a good idea of what was coming, and started to line up her defenses: he would be leaving soon; he was in need; it was right to take him in. "I have lemonade."

The woman with the bloodshot eyes—Mrs. Efrim or Mrs. Mellot—said, "It's so pleasant and warm out here; it's like a summer evening. A shame to waste it."

"Well then," Kate said, fingering the heavy hose, as much relieved as insulted at their refusal to enter her house. "How can I help you?"

Robert Efrim said, "Last week I happened to drive past your church and saw the title of your sermon posted: Turning Our Backs On Joy. I found that title striking, I don't mind telling you."

"Thank you," Kate murmured.

"'What could that mean?' I asked myself. 'Who would say no to joy?' And then I understood. Only someone who had turned her own back on joy would be able to talk about it."

"Now, hold on here," Kate said.

"We haven't come to criticize," the long-faced woman said, stroking the older girl's hair. "We just want to tell you a few things. People are curious about you. A member of our church was in town last week and saw you in the hardware store. He came over to our house for coffee and kept saying, 'She was wearing a preacher's collar, right over her dress. Standing there, buying a hammer.' He says that he slunk around the back of the store until you left."

"A wrench, actually," Kate said. "One of our radiators is going."

"The whole idea upset him—he talked for half an hour. And I couldn't help wondering if you don't get tired of this, people looking at you like you're in a zoo. How much good can you do, if people hide at the back of the store when they see you?"

Promptly, Kate's complicitous brain projected an image of Lucinda Akins, her straight spine never touching the back of the pew, her nostrils pinched during Kate's homilies as if she were smelling mice. "All change takes time." Kate wished she could find something less banal to say. "I'm like a missionary."

"It must be hard work," said the woman softly. "People expect so much of you. They feel like they can comment on everything you do."

"That's true," Kate said, surprised that the woman understood so well.

The second woman moved back into the light, where her hair glowed like the moon. "People don't know whether to expect you to be a woman or a man, so they expect both, only better than either. You have problems, all the time, that men don't have. Every single day, you have to re-create the wheel."

"Yes," Kate said uneasily, feeling herself coaxed into the warm, familiar waters of self-pity. Usually she only discussed these issues at the annual district conference, in meetings set aside for women ministers who looked, always, more tired than the men.

"It shouldn't be so hard. Nobody but a soldier should have to fight every day. But this is what happens when you challenge the order of things." The woman's face, as unlined as plaster, wore a serene expression, and Kate thought briefly that the woman's greatest daily task might involve bringing a cup of tea to her lips.

"Listen, there are compensations," Kate said. "I don't have a miserable life. I help people; that's what I'm called to do."

The long-faced woman stooped to pick up the smaller girl, her bright yellow dress matching her ruffled anklets. Trustingly, the girl held out her arms to Kate, who set down the hose and took the child, her heart swelling as it always did at the touch of new, plump skin. "Aren't you a nice girl," Kate murmured. "It's good of you to come visit me." In response, the little girl burrowed her face into Kate's neck, and Kate felt helpless love splash over her like rain.

"We take what is so simple, and we make it so complicated," the woman said. "Just look at yourself. Have you done anything all day that you liked better than holding this child?" She moved forward and rested her cool hand on Kate's elbow. "You were made for this."

Resettling herself, the little girl wrapped a damp arm, smelling lightly of soap, behind Kate's neck. Kate felt a tendril loop around her heart, and for a moment, she couldn't speak. "Plenty of women ministers have families," she eventually said. "I haven't closed any doors. Not a day goes by that my husband and I don't pray for a child of our own." A sentence too late, she closed her mouth. She usually knew better than to confide in strangers about Ned's and her struggles.

Robert Efrim brightened. "I don't need to tell you, Pastor—anything is possible, if you have faith."

"Thank you," she said quickly, but not quickly enough. He was going strong.

"—But sometimes we need to believe more, harder. So the question is, how can we do that? How can we believe more than we believe?" He paused again, encouraging her to nod in agreement. She buried her nose in the child's sweet hair, and he said, "We believe by our actions. We show by what we do that we expect prayers to be answered. And if that means we make new decisions, take new roads—well, that's fine."

"And what if I've already taken a new road?" Kate said. "You don't seem to believe that I've gone where I heard myself called."

"Ah. A call. What did you hear in your call?" Robert Efrim said. "What words did you hear?"

Beside him, the woman with the moon-white hair said, "It's so easy to imagine we hear something. My children are all grown. Still, at night, I hear a baby."

"A path. A direction," Kate said, although the confident intimacy of these people made words shrivel in her mouth.

"You might just try testing that path," Robert Efrim said, and added, "I mean this in the kindest way." On that cue, all four of the adults and the child who was standing bowed their heads and stood in a silent, prayerful half-circle before Kate. Only when they took, in near unison, a step toward her, did she realize they were praying for *her*. She could see the glints of silver in Robert Efrim's hair.

She twitched and stepped back. Although none of the Sanctuary Christians reached out a hand, she felt as if they were squeezing her between them, and the flowery perfume worn by the wife with the bloodshot eyes rose and clung to Kate's face. Kate smoothed the hair of the child she held, reminding herself that she could use some prayers. Besides, so long as they were all quiet, she could keep herself from ordering them to leave, to get off her church's property; a statement they would almost certainly find gratifying.

In the same rough unison all five heads bobbed back up. George Mellot straightened his jacket, looked at Kate, and said mildly, "You might still find happiness. It isn't too late."

Kate stared at him. She saw the long, yellow teeth, the sharp-edged gray suit. She wondered how he would react if a stranger came into his yard and informed him about the state of his heart. "Is there anything else?" she asked, handing the child, who whimpered at being disturbed, back to her mother. "Because as you can see, I have chores to attend to."

"Anything you have done can be undone. You just need to admit you've made a mistake," Robert Efrim said.

"Show me a human life that doesn't have mistakes," Kate said. "I don't want to get personal here, but I have to imagine that you've made a few yourself. My ministry isn't ruining my life. It saves my life."

"And the members of your congregation? Are their lives being saved, too?" he asked.

"Yes," she snapped. If he was going to ask the impossible question, she'd give him the impossible answer. No minister she knew could answer such a question—although if anybody talked chummily with God every night and got the divine thumbs up, this Robert Efrim would be the one. He gazed at her appraisingly, and she gazed back, wondering how long it had been since he'd been forced to stand on the victim's side of four against one. She bent to pick up the hose at her feet to start watering the tree again, but must have jogged the release on the nozzle. The hose jerked in her hand and shot a hard blast of water directly onto Robert Efrim's closely laced, unscuffed shoe. She could see the leather shine in the moment before he yelped and jumped away. She fumbled the water off.

"That was an accident. I know it didn't look like one," Kate said. "Please let me get you a towel. I'm so sorry."

"I accept your apology," he said, quickly unlacing the shoe, managing to look dignified even when he held it up and tipped it as if he expected water to gush forth. A thin stream dribbled off the heel.

"You're nervous," said the bright-haired woman. "Ideas only upset us when they carry some truth."

"I wish you would let me dry you off," Kate said, but Robert Efrim had already smiled, held up his hand as if in blessing, and stepped back into his wet shoe to lead the group back to the car. The shoe squeaked with every step. Kate followed them, her jaw clamped; she would not, *not* offer one more apology.

At the curb in front of the church they climbed into a station wagon, strapped the girls into car seats, and squeezed the two women between them. Before they pulled away Robert Efrim rolled down his window and called to her, "It was charity that brought us to you. We came out of love." Kate smiled without showing her teeth and waved as the car drove off. Once they had rounded the corner she said evenly, "Come back anytime. Don't be strangers." Not that they would need the invitation.

She turned back to the yard, her breath so uneven she felt as if it could, like Absalom's long hair, catch on a tree branch and jerk her to a stop. But the feeling that sheered through her as she hurried across her dark lawn wasn't fear, or wasn't only fear. It was something closer to recognition, the sense that she had battled these coaxing, confident people before. And not in the abstract, either. They sounded, these people, in their perfect confidence, like Ned.

No sooner had she allowed the thought into her brain than she batted it down again—the comparison was unfair and absurd, the malicious result of days of fighting. But after she let herself in the back door, she sank onto the hard beige sofa and sat with her hands clenched. The nubbly curtains behind her were beige, too, and also the flat carpet—the same beige, everlasting parsonage beige, selected with practicality in mind. Kate, who loved bright colors, wouldn't have chosen it herself, but Ned would have, with his eye for what was durable, his preference for what was correct.

One Sunday, hungry and distracted, she'd preached that heaven rejoiced over every lost sheep. From the front row, Ned had called out loudly, "Back up, Kate." The congregation laughed, and Kate tried to laugh, too, but later, over dinner, she was close to tears.

"I just misspoke. Nobody but you noticed," she said. "Everybody knew what I meant to say."

"You got it wrong, Kate, as wrong as it could be. That kind of thing can't go uncorrected."

"So you had to humiliate me in front of my whole church? Correcting me was that important to you?"

"If you're preaching, you'd better get it right," Ned said, his voice unruffled and clear—his doctor voice, which didn't allow for shades of meaning or hurt feelings. If she'd truly heard, if she'd let herself listen to that voice when she first met Ned, would she have married him? Could she have seen other roads, if she had only looked?

Kate groaned and blinked up at the low, textured ceiling over her head. "Crap," she said. "Oh, crap," an utterance from her deepest soul. In seminary she had been taught that God hears all utterances and knows them to be prayer. "There is no such thing as bad prayer," the teacher assured his class. Well, the teacher was wrong, Kate thought now. There was such a thing as bad prayer, and this was it.

Before she could follow her thoughts any further downhill, the front doorbell rang—unusual, so late, but not unheard of. Smoothing her hair on the way to the door, Kate hoped she wouldn't find Robert Efrim in dry shoes, back for round two. Instead, craven and swollen eyed under the porch light, stood Mindy Leaf, Barb's niece. "Well, Mindy. Come in," Kate said. "Welcome."

"I'm sorry it's so late, but I didn't know where else to go," the girl said, her voice rigid. "My parents kicked me out of the house. Where can a person go at ten o'clock in Elite?"

"Here," Kate murmured, opening the door further. When the girl stood unmoving on the porch, Kate took her hand, spongy in the humid night, and pulled her one step inside. "You came to the right place."

"You may not think so for long. I'm going to have a baby."

"I know," Kate said. Mindy's head shot up, and Kate added, "Pastors hear things. You've been in my prayers."

"I guess I need prayers. Here," she said, handing Kate a note. "This was on your door."

"Come on in. Sit down," Kate said, but the girl didn't move. Kate glanced at the note and recognized Bill-o's hurried handwriting. *Good news! The house is almost done! Come on out and I'll take you on a tour.* Kate looked up again at Mindy, who was watching her.

"Nothing important," Kate said. "Relax. Let me get you some lemonade." She had to lead Mindy to the couch and touch her shoulders lightly to get her to sit down; the girl kept jerking like a wary horse, glancing at the door, calculating the distance. Kate rattled from cupboard to stove, chattering about the weather. "Usually at this time of year we're worried about heating bills," she said as she brought a tray with the pitcher and tall glasses into the living room. "Now when I go to see people they're wearing T-shirts."

"You don't need to tell me it's hot."

"Hard weather to be pregnant in," Kate said.

"You don't need to tell me that, either." She took the glass Kate offered her and drained half of it in a swallow, then looked up. "I throw up a lot," she said.

"Slow down," Kate said. "That will help."

Mindy shook her head. "Taking in requires emptying out. That's pretty basic. My body wants to be pure."

Mindy held up her glass and stared at the lemonade. She was dressed for the weather, in a sleeveless top and shorts, and while there was nothing improper about her clothing, her body made it seem improper. Her arms and legs were round and lustrous, her skin the color of moist apricots. She had as many curves as a bowl of fruit, and Kate could well imagine a boy's urgency to reach out, touch, bite. The only surprise about Mindy was that she hadn't been knocked up before. Keeping her voice gentle, Kate said, "Do you know what you're going to do?"

Mindy closed her eyes. "I can't stay here?"

"Of course you can. We'll be cozy. But do you know what you're going to do with this baby?"

The girl's eyes, the pale blue of shallow water, snapped open again. "Try to get a good night's sleep. I need to start remembering my dreams—forgetting your dreams is losing half your life. Is there enough room for me to stay here? I know you've got the man from the new garden store here, too."

Kate listened but didn't hear any edge or accusation in Mindy's voice. But then, how could there be, considering the girl's own situation? On a wave of rueful affection, Kate said, "You can have my bed. You'll sleep best there. When Mr. O'Grady moves, you can have the guest room." Kate and Ned could sleep on the lumpy foldaway, and she would dare him to complain.

She stood to get fresh sheets, but before she was quite out of the room, Mindy picked up Bill-o's note and said, "Are you going to go out to see this house?"

"I imagine so, after I get you bedded down."

"I'm not tired. If I try to sleep when I'm not tired, I never fall asleep at all."

"Well then, we'll sit up and watch TV, and I'll see the house another time."

"You can go," Mindy said. "I can go with you. I don't mind. I haven't gone anywhere new in a while."

"I don't think so."

"It's a good idea," the girl said, sucking down the rest of her lemonade and standing. "We'll go see it, shake ourselves out a little, and by the time we come home, I'll be ready for bed. And you'll have done what you're supposed to do. You don't want to just stay here, do you?"

She extended her hand, gesturing at the room like a model on TV, and Kate saw the room as she supposed Mindy did: couch wedged between wall and bookcase, armchairs brushing the coffee table, a room so small that Mindy's backpack, dropped near the door, made it feel cluttered. "You came here asking to stay," Kate said.

"Not every minute," Mindy said. "I'm pregnant, not in jail." And then, as Kate still hesitated, the girl picked up her backpack. "Come on," she said. "This will be fun."

Six

The Hills of West Elite, the subdivision that held Bill-o's house, was new, new, new. Backhoes and graders still cluttered the stumpy cul-de-sac, and yellowish dirt from the slick, unlandscaped yards had already washed over the fresh curbs. No stop signs, no street lights. While Mindy hummed in the passenger seat, Kate trolled around the curves, inspecting every corner and peering down lanes that so far held only surveyor's stakes and piles of lumber.

Once she found the right street though, Bill-o's house was impossible to miss. Stretching like a boxcar across its treeless, shrubless, lawnless lot with light surging from every one of its unshaded windows, the house was as brilliant as a department store. Even from a distance, she could make out the pristine walls and the glittering doorknobs. "Eureka," she said.

"Somebody lives here? It looks like a warehouse," Mindy said.

"This is a ranch house. It's supposed to look simple. He must have every light in the place on; it looks like he's throwing a party."

"It looks like he's opened a 7-Eleven," Mindy said, opening the car door as soon as Kate pulled into the driveway. The girl sashayed up the walk, her round behind swaying like a sweet invitation, and for a perturbed moment Kate wondered what she'd taken on. Then she hurried after Mindy to the porch and had hardly lifted her hand to knock when Bill-o opened the door. "Hey," he said. "A crowd."

"This is Mindy," Kate said. "She's going to be staying at the parsonage. She wanted to see your new house."

"New houses have new spirits," Mindy said, testing her weight against the flimsy porch railing, which swayed a little. "Have you greeted the spirits of your house yet?" Bill-o caught Kate's eye, and she shrugged. *Boy crazy*, she mouthed, though she doubted he could understand her.

"Come in," he said. "Welcome to my castle. Check your spirits at the door." Closing the door behind them, he had to yank on the handle to get it to latch. "Needs a little adjustment," he muttered, prompting Mindy to put her own hand on the fixture, as if her touch might heal it.

Kate strolled into the hollow living room, its air still sharp with new paint, while Bill-o recited dimensions and pointed out where the couch and entertainment center would go. She nodded, turning as he directed her and hoping he couldn't see her dismay. Close up, the shiny fixtures she had admired from the street were cheap and badly fitted; their finish was already peeling. The paint job was patchy, with roller marks not even reaching the ceiling in two places. "Of course, everything will look better once the carpeting's in," Bill-o was saying. "This is a little raw."

Nodding, Kate murmured, "Houses never feel right without carpets and curtains." Across the room, Mindy was drawing on the dusty windows. "Homey touches are important," Kate added.

"I've never had a house built for me. I'd expected things to go a little smoother." Bill-o pushed his thumb against a spot in the drywall where a screw protruded. "I can't help worrying. But it will be all right, don't you think? All it needs is the fine tuning?"

"It will be fine," Kate said. "You've got a lot to work with here."

"Once you get furniture and some pictures up, no one will notice the paint," Mindy said.

The girl was pressing her hand to the rough molding around the door, and Bill-o's expression turned grim. He went over to one of the spots where grayish drywall showed, took a pen from his pocket, and drew a black line across the wall. "Bill-o," Kate protested.

He drew a second line, perpendicular to the first, bracketing the spot where the paint trailed away. "There's a window in one of the bedrooms that won't shut."

"The heat," she said. "Wood swells."

"Well, that's just fine. By Christmas I should be able to shut every window in the place," he said.

"Unless they're frozen," Mindy said. "You don't have storm windows here, do you?"

In the kitchen the track lights wouldn't come on, and the bathroom cabinets didn't close; Bill-o kept trying to bang them shut, but they popped merrily back open. Mindy counted the three shelves inside and pointed out that three was the number of unity. Bill-o kicked the cabinet.

"Easy, boy," Kate said.

"Every time I turn around, it's something else. Woodwork. Paint! If people can't paint a room, are they going to get the wiring right? Imagine the possibilities once the appliances get here."

"All houses need a few adjustments," Kate said. "The main thing is, you've got room. Just look at this place! You can put every bath towel and washcloth in its own cupboard."

"And have them all on display whenever I come into the bathroom."

"Still," she said stubbornly. Square footage was the house's single aspect she could admire in good conscience, and she meant to make sure he heard her. With its three bedrooms and separate dining room, Bill-o's new house was easily twice the size of the parsonage; and shoddy and faux-genteel as the fittings were, by the time he showed Kate the second bathroom, her dismay was ebbing. "You could have houseguests and never know they were here," she said. "You could take in boarders."

"Boarders might be a good idea," Mindy said. "Fresh spirits. You might could use some young ones."

"Feel free to come visit," Bill-o said, then leaned toward Kate. "The company's supposed to ship out furniture after the carpet gets delivered. A girl called to ask me about my preferred colors, and I told her I like anything that doesn't show dust. She said, 'You can have brown or you can have green.' So I said green. Seems right for a plant man, doesn't it?"

"Plant man," said Mindy. "Planet Man."

"Don't you think green is better?" he said. Before Kate could speak, the girl shrugged. "It's your house."

Kate walked to the window, where she rested her forehead against the gritty glass and tried to see into the back yard. "How big is it out here?"

"These lots are all a hundred by fifty."

"Plenty of room for a garden."

"I never get home before dark. I'd have to weed by flashlight."

"And it's a new neighborhood," Kate went on morosely. "You don't have to worry about trees shading you out. You can put in tomatoes, peppers. You can put in sunflowers."

"Sunflowers bring birds," Mindy said. "Birds bring generosity, and mirth."

Kate squinted into the dark back yard. "The parsonage lot is all shade in the afternoons. I can't grow one tomato plant. When the trustees first showed me the house, I argued that we should take out a couple of the trees to let in some sun. 'It's right for a parsonage to have a vegetable garden,' I told them. 'We can feed people.' But no one would believe I really wanted to cut down that moth-eaten sycamore."

"Vegetables take work," Bill-o said, standing close behind her. She could see his loose white shirt reflected in the window and, fluttering in the background, Mindy, humming tunelessly. "You need to be out there every day, no matter what. You can't turn your back on them."

"I'd do the work. That's what I'm telling you," Kate said.

"Except for the days when your committee meeting runs late. Or you have to be off with the youth group. Or there's a funeral. I don't think pastors can be gardeners, Kate."

"Well, I wouldn't be a pastor, would I? I could be Elite's gardening queen, with nothing but time and a garden to fill up."

"Trying out a new life?" Bill-o said.

"Maybe."

Mindy said, "Look. Here's a window that closes."

In an overflow of self-lacerating satisfaction, Kate made Bill-o show them every closet and storage cupboard, where there was room enough to store her entire parsonage, including bricks and shingles, and still have room left over for sheets.

Back in the living room, Mindy rocked back and forth on a loose flagstone, and Kate pulled Bill-o to the room's opposite corner. "The company only builds two models," he was saying. "They build them over and over. I figured they'd know how to build them right."

"People get away with whatever they can," Kate said.

"I feel like a sap. Bill O'Grady: homeowner. I thought I was really going places." He watched Mindy's hips, moving as easily as a pendulum. "I thought that having a house would mean something about me —how far I've come. Maybe it does."

"You've got to knock this off," Kate said. "The company cut corners and bilked you. But there's nothing here that can't be fixed, and nothing that's your fault, and plenty to be grateful for."

"I guess the breeze from all those open windows is just blowing my gratitude away. Unlike you, Pastor Mary Sunshine."

"Everybody in my church can tell you that I'm a world-class complainer. I just wish I had a few of your open cabinets."

"Done. I'll throw in one of the half-painted bedrooms. That will make one fewer room I have to repaint myself. Is it unreligious of me to care about this stuff?"

"Religions are big on paint," Kate said. "Think of the Sistine Chapel."

Mindy had picked up the pace of her rocking. She spread her feet so they were resting on the very edges of the stone, which kept bouncing against the underlayment. Just as Kate was about to warn her, the stone shifted and cracked. A piece pinged across the room. "Sorry," Mindy said.

"Is that something else I can pin on the contractor?" Bill-o said.

"Yes," Kate said. "A girl should be able to walk on your floors." She glared at Mindy, who was looking with interest at the mantel. "We'll have to get home," Kate said before she could announce some new shortcoming. "Can we give you a ride?"

Bill-o kept his eyes on Mindy's flagstone. "I'm not sure I should join you. Quarters are going to be pretty cramped, and now I have this house."

"Don't be silly; there's enough room. You don't even have a mattress here." Kate lowered her voice. "I didn't take her in to kick you out."

"Still," he said. "There's all kinds of work to do at the store. I have to set up a fertilizer display."

"You have to sleep somewhere."

"I'll sleep in my office. It's still set up."

"Bill-o, *please.*"

Mindy swiveled her head and looked at them with feral interest, and Kate shut her mouth.

"Okay," Bill-o said eventually. "Thank you. Don't wait up; I'll come in late."

But he didn't. He didn't come in at all, and neither did Ned, whom she supposed was staying at the hospital, although he usually called to tell her. It was unlike him to be so inconsiderate, a point Kate intended to make when she saw him again. For now, she thrashed through the night, her eyes flying open at every slight noise, her hip digging into the meager, foam-rubber mattress. No matter how she strained to hear, no step sounded on the porch; no key rattled in the lock, and when morning came she was alone in the house with Mindy.

She waited until seven o'clock, then drummed her fingers on the bedroom door. "I've got coffee going. Would you like toast?"

"I like little foods. Berries are good. Blueberries, strawberries. Do you have any of them?"

"I'll go to the store later. For now, I can fix you a little egg." The bedroom door flew open. Mindy ran past, white faced, and slammed the bathroom door behind her. Kate lingered in the hallway until the sound of the girl's heaves made her feel furtive, and she returned to the kitchen.

By the time Kate finished her cereal, Mindy was back in bed, assuring Kate in monosyllables that she didn't want even dry toast, she would wait for her berries, her strength was holding up fine. Kate started to head out the door to the office, but just as she reached the door, the phone rang. Seven-thirty in the morning. She caught it on the second ring.

"I want you to know, I'm behind Ned a hundred percent," Bob Peters said, not bothering with hello.

"He'll appreciate that, Bob. It's pretty early. Are you calling about anything in particular?"

"I expect you to be behind him, too."

"We're a team. You know that. But what are you talking about?"

In the pause that followed, she heard trouble coming at her like a locomotive. "Read today's newspaper," he said and hung up.

Kate quietly put down the phone, went out the front door, and started searching through the shrubbery for the *Bugle,* vowing while she looked to address some words to Bob about his phone manners. The paper, as usual, was wedged between the house and the yew, two front pages snagged on a twig. Filled with airy dread, she worked the pages free, but didn't open the paper until she was back inside the house.

RIOT! ran the headline. Underneath it a triptych of photos showed limp demonstrators lolling hand in hand on the steps outside the women's clinic on the edge of town. Taking up the bottom of the page was one more photo, bigger—a woman, her mouth shapeless and her hair wild, weeping in Ned's arms. The caption read, "'We must decide what we're willing to stand for as a community.' Dr. Gussey takes his stand." Kate sagged onto the couch. Oh, boy, she thought. Oh, Ned.

> Violence and abusive language broke out last night
> at a candlelight demonstration in front of the Elerette
> County Women's Health Services Center. Members of
> the Sanctuary Christian Church, chanting, "All life, always,"
> clashed with supporters of the Center, and threw rocks,
> mud, and cans. Police made fifteen arrests.
>   "We don't mind getting dirty," said Dr. Nedrick Gussey,
> Elite physician and husband of Pastor Kate Gussey of
> Dove United Methodist Church. "We're here to save lives.
> That's our priority."

Kate nodded at the paper. Ned thought priorities were important. But abortion had never been a priority before.

Protests sprang up at the Center regularly, but Kate and Ned had always kept their distance. Though they discussed the issue until words were ragged in their mouths, they had never been able to come to a conclusion. "A right is a right," he or Kate would say, and the other would counter, "A life is at stake." Now, apparently, Ned had made up his mind. He had decided to stand shoulder to shoulder with sanctimonious thugs, and he was content to let the Elite *Bugle* inform Kate of that fact.

The article went on for columns, threading through the whole front section. The paper hadn't had such a good home-grown story since four Elite boys returned from the Persian Gulf, and Kate compulsively read every word. Then she flipped back to the front page and stared at the picture of her husband.

His arms were wrapped around the woman's thin shoulders; his lips were pursed—Kate could see he was gently shushing her, telling her everything would be all right. The expression on his face as tender as a mother's. Anyone seeing the picture would be moved by his compassion. Kate herself was moved.

No one was ever sweeter than Ned, no one more calming. When Janelle's cancer was first detected, he spent half an hour walking with her son Frank, and by the time they finally came back to the hospital the young man's face had lost its white despair. No one but Kate could imagine that Ned would return to his office and write up a summary of Janelle's biopsy results, including her wretched prognosis, and then go on to see other patients without even stopping for a drink of water.

"Your heart bleeds on schedule," Kate had told him later. They hadn't been quarreling; she was just trying to figure him out. "It's amazing. You can walk with Janelle's boy for half an hour, then go in the next room and tell jokes."

"It's the practice of medicine. I give patients whatever they need."

"But do you care?"

He looked puzzled. "How can you look in the face of suffering and not care?"

"I mean once you've stopped looking in that face. Do you care at nine o'clock that night, when you're watching TV?"

"Life isn't just suffering, Kate."

Which was certainly true; she'd be the first to admit it. But she wondered whether the woman from the photo was still crying now, and where Ned was, and whether he was bearing her misery in mind. Then, suddenly making the connection, she looked again at the article: *Police made fifteen arrests.* "Oh, Ned," she said aloud, then hurried to Mindy's room.

"I'm going out," she called through the closed door. "I'll probably be out all day. There's food in the refrigerator. Fruit. Oranges." She waited, but Mindy made no sound. "Is that all right? Should I call your aunt to look in on you?"

"*Go.*"

Kate did, zooming out of the driveway. She'd been to the county jail before, to visit church members caught shoplifting or brawling or driving under the influence. She and Ned had actually laughed about the holding cell's cheerful pink walls and agreed that if they had to be held, they'd want to be held in Elite. She darted through an intersection on a yellow light and wondered how many times through the night Ned had remembered that conversation.

The officer behind the desk—just a dented metal desk, nothing like the imposing wooden barricades on TV shows—was no one Kate knew, a middle-aged man with a soft brown moustache and a hound's haggard eyes. Yes ma'am, he said, Ned had been brought in the night before. Disturbing the peace, unlawfully blocking access. Two hundred dollars.

"I'll post his bail," Kate said.

The officer smiled gently. "He has a lot of friends. You're the third person to come for him."

Kate rubbed her aching eyes. "He's my husband. Can you tell me who he left with?" Some patient he'd called on at home, she supposed, some high-minded hospital colleague or Bob Peters, who would have carried him home on a throne. Not his wife, in any case. The officer flipped through a sheaf of papers.

"William O'Grady," he said.

Kate backed out of the building. Later she would hope that she'd been polite to the officer, who had been kind and discreet. All she could do at the time was keep shaking her head as if she had water in her ears and drive first to NaturWise and then to The Hills of West Elite, while she scrutinized every car she passed to see if Bill-o was driving. But Bill-o was a specialist in the getaway. By now he could have crossed two state lines, Ned sitting beside him in the passenger seat, trustingly telling stories about his practice and his patients and his new anti-abortion activities—stories he would never think to tell Kate.

She imagined them shambling into some truck stop, laughing, affectionate, their eyes full of secrets. Although Ned, of course, didn't believe he had secrets, and Bill-o never admitted to any. Was it the nature of husbands to have secrets, or only of *her* husbands? Kate pressed harder on the accelerator. What she needed was a secret of her own, some shield to cover her stupidly vulnerable life. A secret would provide a light skin of solace between Kate and the humiliating awareness that Ned, in jail, would rather reach out to Bill-o than to his wife.

On a whim, she turned down a gravel road, then saw a sign for a U-pick farm that she'd always meant to visit. She followed the rutted driveway to a barn where two unsmiling women in straw hats and shorts watched Kate pull up. "What have you got?" Kate asked.

"Melons," the taller woman said. "Corn. A few late raspberries. Mostly melons."

"We'll rent you a basket for two dollars," the other woman said, her vowels lazy and long. Her eyes fixed on Kate and evaluated her; Kate could see that they were not impressed with their findings. "Weigh when you come back. Melons thirty cents a pound, berries by the pint. Honor system not to eat in the field."

"No problem," Kate said. "Just show me where to go."

She rented a basket and headed for the raspberries, striding to the furthest edge of the canes. Unexpectedly, she found herself hungry and supposed that all her anxiety had used up the morning's mingy bowl of cereal. Standing and shading her eyes, she gauged her distance from the barn and the two harpies there. Then, at the end of the row, she bent and pulled off every berry from the long, prickly canes, even the berries that were half green, even those already pulpy between her fingers, and dropped them in the basket. Once she had stripped the nearest canes, her hands cross-hatched from the stickers, she sat back on her heels and ate, inserting each berry tidily into her mouth so that stained lips wouldn't give her away. The sharp stems she buried in a shallow hole. Slightly sick to her stomach, she moved down the row, picked more, and ate again. Only when the overripe fruit started to make her choke did she stop eating and pick a third basketful to bring home to Mindy—about three dollars' worth, she calculated.

Queasy as she felt, she rested twice on her walk back to the barn. There the tall woman, her hat pushed back so that the brim framed her face to surprisingly dainty effect, poured the berries onto a scale and said, "You didn't get much, for all your time out there."

Kate shrugged. "I'm slow."

"Berries are high, now that it's the end of the season. If you'd come in July, you'd have been quicker. More people here then. Folks always pick quicker when they're not alone. Funny."

"I like to be alone," Kate said.

"Fifteen dollars," the woman said, and Kate opened her mouth to protest, then shut it again. The woman glared at her. "End of the season. You pay for whatever you get."

"Can you take a check?" Kate asked, digging through her purse with red-stained fingers. While she wrote, the woman looked over her shoulder.

"Well. Reverend. I've heard of you."

"Nothing bad, I hope," Kate said, the answer she always gave. The prick of actual fear she felt this time, though, was new.

"I've heard of you," the woman repeated.

A beat passed before Kate said, "Join us some Sunday." Even to her, the sentence sounded gimpy. She added, "We always like to see new faces."

"And you come on back here sometime," the woman said, taking her check and handing her a sack. "But don't look for any more raspberries. You got the last of them."

On the drive back to Elite she let her mind drift between her chaotic stomach and her unease over Ned, absently changing lanes and making turns. Preoccupied as she was, she almost didn't notice Bill-o's silver sedan parked smack in front of Dorrie's Coffee Shop and looking nothing like a getaway vehicle. She whipped clumsily into a parking place, then hurried out to look inside his car.

Its floor, front seat and back, was a mess of rags, cups and empty doughnut cartons—but no maps, no wadded receipts, no signs of stealthy, nighttime flight. She stared at the doughnut cartons. Ned didn't eat doughnuts, but maybe he'd joined Bill-o in order to be convivial. She should ask him whether he was a chocolate-covered or glazed man. Her raspberry-filled stomach lurched a little, and she turned from the car and pushed open the door to the coffee shop.

Ned and Bill-o had taken a back booth with wide seats, the table furthest from Dorrie's TV. Their elbows wedged between plates and coffee cups, they leaned toward each other, not noticing Kate pick her way down the narrow aisle until she was halfway through the restaurant. "So, Ned. You've been busy," she said, taking pleasure in the way he jerked upright.

"I tried to call you." He looked pretty clear eyed for somebody who'd been up all night, clean enough and tidy around his hair and collar. Bill-o was the one who looked terrible; his eyes sunk into his face like raisins in dull white dough. "I called you at home, but no one answered."

"I was pretty shocked to read about your evening's activities. But you rely on the element of surprise, right?"

He folded his mouth into a line denoting extravagant patience. "I wasn't trying to surprise you. At least no more than I surprised myself. Alma Vyrie came to my office while I was going over billing. She told me about the demonstration and invited me to join her. I tried to call you."

"You know I don't stay out late. If you'd waited fifteen minutes, I'd have been home. At the very least, you could have called me when you got to the jail."

"I didn't want to wake you up."

"Oh, for God's sake, Ned." Catching the expression of a man sitting near them, she tried to lighten her tone. "Shucks, honey—I would have been happy to hear from you. You've got stories. You can tell me what life is like inside the big house."

"You've been there," he said. "It's pink."

Kate stared at one of the empty coffee cups on the table; dark veins raced around the interior. "I think I know why you didn't call. And I'm really sorry you didn't want me to be the one to spring you."

"You're getting it wrong, Kate. You don't have anything to apologize for," Ned said, reaching over to pat her hand, which she held stiff under his touch.

"There's a difference between apology and regret. I truly regret that Bill-o was the one to post your bail. I was worried when you didn't come home."

"I didn't mean to worry you," he said right away, then stood up. "I'll be back."

As he headed for the men's room, Kate and Bill-o looked at each other. She slid into Ned's place.

"He's a good man," Bill-o said.

"I'm told that a lot."

"People in town think the world of him. Even girls who get lectures when they go to him for birth control say he helps them; he treats them seriously."

"The serious treatment is his long suit. Are you talking to many girls about their birth control?"

"I've been interviewing kids to work the registers, remember? You ask them whether they're available for the evening shift, and before you know it, you're finding out about their boyfriends and their mothers and how many times their periods have been late. Believe me, they tell me more than I want to hear."

"I don't believe you. No one's ever told you more than you want to hear." She smiled and he smiled back, and she wondered whether her smile looked as bleak as his. "How long have you and Ned been sitting in here?"

"An hour, maybe. We drove around for a while."

"Did he tell you what happened?"

"Apparently things got out of hand—it was supposed to have been a peaceful protest. Ned was trying to talk to a woman, and the next thing he knew he was being handcuffed. 'I didn't plan to get arrested,' he said. 'Most people don't,' I told him."

Ned probably didn't mind, Kate thought. Like St. Paul, he would have waited for an angel to come and free him. Making Bill-o the angel. She coughed.

"We drove out west of town," Bill-o said, "way out; I kept waiting to cross the Illinois line. He likes to drive around there, he told me. Some afternoons he just leaves the office and drives. It was three, four o'clock, and I had to keep pinching the back of my hand to stay awake. Every once in a while he'd point out a water tower or somebody's big farm, but I couldn't see a thing."

"And then?"

"And then we came back. He didn't want to wake you up, so we came here."

"He was afraid of what I'd say," Kate said slowly. "He knew I wouldn't care if he woke me up. He just didn't want me to light into him."

"Come on, Kate. He didn't think you were waiting at home with a rolling pin," Bill-o mumbled, glancing around. The place was almost full, noisy now with voices and the tootling cash register and the shiver of cutlery on heavy china. Dorrie had turned up her morning show, where someone was noisily grinding cantaloupe in a blender.

Kate dropped her glance back down to the table; all of a sudden she was irritated at the pile-up of used plates. Why hadn't Dorrie cleared some of this away? "It's not a good thing, you know, when a man doesn't tell his wife he's been arrested. That's not being considerate; that's hiding things."

"You're way off the mark here. Ned loves you. He spent half the night rehearsing what he was going to tell you."

"I imagine that he did. But this has nothing to do with love—love's easy. This has to do with opening up your life to the person you see first thing every day, showing all your holes and bumps. Sharing your plans. Letting that person see you right down to the bone. It's a terrifying concept, in case you want to know."

Bill-o ran his finger along the table and pushed the spilled grains of sugar into a thin line. "We never did that, did we?"

"Bill-o—" She swallowed and started again. "We had no idea."

"You want to know what hurts? Coming back and having the idea, but not being able to do anything about it. Wanting to tell you everything, show you everything, and not being able to. Although I would, Katy. I would. I'd reach up, if you'd lean down and pull me to you." His line of sugar began to waver. Appalled, Kate felt her mouth tremble, and she found it hard to reach across the table and tap his cheek, make him look at her.

"When I said that I was talking about your house. We're friends now, you and me," she said. "That's more than I ever hoped for. Standing side by side. But Ned is my husband. I made a commitment."

"Dry word."

"The big word, the important one." She was ready to go on, but the bathroom door clunked and she glanced up to see Ned threading his way back to them. "He's coming," she added, and Bill-o leaned across the table.

"I didn't tell him about Mindy," he said.

"Why not? That's no secret. He'll see soon enough that she's moved in."

"There was so much going on—I just wanted to tell you that he doesn't know."

"Okay," she said. "Fine. This isn't a problem; Ned isn't going to mind that I took in a pregnant girl."

"Who's ready to greet the new day?" Ned said, flattening his hands on the edge of the table. His collar and hairline were wet; he must have washed his face while he was in the men's room, and the action seemed to have rejuvenated him—his hands were steady, his eyes bright. No one would take him for last night's tub-thumper and jailbird. Looking from Bill-o's haggard, sagging face to Ned's fresh one, she wished she could say aloud, to both of them, I have made a choice. Ned, she knew, would echo her, and neither of them would admit where that choice had brought them. How dreadful marriage was.

"Ned, you're a wonder," she said instead.

"You mean I'm wonderful or that you wonder about me?"

"You fill me with wonder," she said, meaning to sound chipper but hearing how her voice slanted and trailed off. She stood and led him out to the car, and though he protested that the walk to the hospital, only a half-mile away, would do him good, when Kate opened the door for him, he slid in, sniffed the sweet air, and closed his eyes.

Seven

Kate started the car's engine to get the air conditioning going while Ned, his eyes still closed, appeared to be practicing deep breathing. Fatigue pinched his features; she was reminded of his residency, when he would come off of thirty-six-hour shifts looking drained but purified, his face chiseled into clean lines like a saint's effigy. She'd laughed and accused him of thriving on deprivation, and he'd laughed too, flexing his stringy biceps and calling himself Superdoc. "What do I smell?" he said now without opening his eyes.

"Raspberries." She looked at his unshaven face, its sunken planes so different from Bill-o's cheek, spongy as he made his forlorn declaration. The big word, the important one. She said to Ned, "They're the last ones of the season. I'll make us a pie."

He nodded, and let the silence inflate between them. "Honey?" she said softly. "Are you sure you want to go in? You could call someone to take your rounds for today."

He shook his head and sat up. "I'll be fine. I don't feel too bad."

"Doc Ned: able to leap tall buildings. Bill-o looks like he staggered out of a bar brawl, and he wasn't even the one who got arrested."

"He might be doing better if he had. Being in jail wakes a fellow up."

"Do inmates still bang their cups on the bars and yell, 'Hey, screw!'?"

"Not that I heard." He nudged the air-conditioning fan to a lower speed. She could see from his stiff posture that he wished she would go ahead and back the car out, although, politely, he was waiting until she was ready. "You took a stand," she said. "Not everyone would be willing to do it. That should make you proud of yourself."

"But you're not proud of me, are you?"

"Of course I am," she said without hesitating, but the lie was a waste—too prompt, too hearty, tinny as a toy horn. "I wish you hadn't had to do it," she added when he didn't say anything.

"Everybody wishes that." He sighed. "I don't think this is such a good time for a heart-to-heart. I'm awake enough to read blood pressure, but I'm not awake enough to talk about how I took a stand."

"I'm trying to be your ally, Ned."

"Will you stand with me next time?"

"I don't know."

"I didn't think so." She had expected him to sound disappointed, but he sounded accepting, which was worse, in its way. "Some of the people there have given their lives to this. They're that sure. I was in awe."

Kate knew some of those people too. Thinking of them made her want to weep. They were passionate, and gave of themselves, and were unforgiving, and perfectly sure of their righteousness. It was amazing that Ned had taken so long to find his people.

Eventually he said, "I'll come home early this afternoon and take a nap."

"There's one more piece of news you need to know." Kate pulled out of the parking place and turned toward Ned's office building. The bag of raspberries scudded across the back seat. "Mindy Leaf asked if she could move in. Barb's niece. She's pregnant, and her parents kicked her out."

"I know," Ned said. "About her being pregnant."

"I must be the last person in Elite to get gossip. How did you find out?"

"Educated guess. I saw her washing her face in the drinking fountain outside the IGA last week; she looked green. Two months?"

"Less, we're hoping. She isn't interested in giving out any hard facts, like pertinent dates or who the father might be."

"How long is she going to stay?"

"Until the baby comes, I guess. It didn't occur to me to set a check-out date. We never have before."

"You're not going to want that girl for seven more months." Ned frowned.

"I don't especially want the girl now," Kate said. "She's not big on the social graces. But she came to me at ten at night, and I didn't have a manger to send her to. Anyway, I thought I was acting the way you would have. I thought you'd be pleased."

"There are easier girls," he said shortly. Kate squinted at him, trying to guess when he could have spoken to Mindy, who wasn't his patient and whose lavish curves didn't make her look like the Candy Striper sort. For a whizzing, unsettling second, Kate imagined Ned leading Mindy by the hand down a motel corridor, but the idea was too ridiculous; when Kate tried to envision their joined hands, all she could conjure was the way Mindy's features had drawn together that morning just before she threw up.

"You know her?" she asked.

"I've seen her in action. She was in the hospital a lot when a friend of hers was working there. Unpleasant little vixen."

"She's a child. A girl in trouble. I told her she could have our room until Bill-o moves out. You and I can make do with the foldaway for a week."

"You're sure rolling out the red carpet."

"I hadn't guessed she would be the one person on earth you'd have shut the door on," Kate said, trying to keep a hold on her temper. "Look, can we stop here, please? I'm sorry I let her in. I truly thought you would have wanted me to."

"I just wouldn't have given her our bed," Ned said. Glancing sideways, Kate watched him frown as they passed the park. "She's hard to like. She used to stand in front of the nursery and look in at the new babies. She'd announce which ones she thought looked ugly or stupid, which baby looked so nasty she wouldn't even want to pick it up. She'd stand out there and yell her opinions. New mothers could hear her in their rooms."

Kate started to laugh. She knew she shouldn't, but the girl's sheer audacity impressed her. "Funny, all right," said Ned. "The baby she wouldn't pick up was Marnie Vyrie's daughter. The one who has Down syndrome."

"Sorry," Kate said.

"If I were you, I'd talk to her parents right away and lean on them to take her back home."

"They're not going to unbend until she tells them who the father is.

And she's not talking." Kate hesitated, remembering the girl's odd, serene pronouncements, and her ruthlessness in uncovering the flaws of Bill-o's house. "She needs a place to go. We've taken in Bill-o. I don't see how we can refuse Mindy."

Ned was silent until Kate pulled into the parking lot beside his office building. "The timing of this could have been better," he said. "Now that she's installed, I don't suppose we can ask for our own bed back."

"She needs some privacy, Ned. And I don't think any of us want to stumble out on her in her sleep."

"We're all going to be stumbling on each other. But it's done now. I'm going to work." When he opened the door he plunged into the hot air as if he were making an escape. Kate understood the impulse; before the back door of the building had closed behind him, she was bumping across the lot to the hospital. A sudden hunger to see her parishioners rippled through her, the yearning to distract herself from a husband whose every word lately baffled and frightened and angered her.

Sally Plummer's room sat only a half a corridor length from the nursery. Kate dawdled at the big picture window, studied the sleeping babies, their scrawny, shocked bodies so tightly bundled, and tried to differentiate one minuscule face from another. A tuft of black hair rode low on the forehead of one frowning boy, giving him a menacing look; another baby drooled, a slender, silvery rope running over his chin and puddling under his ear. Had Mindy known she was pregnant when she stood in the hallway and shared her opinions with the world? Maybe she had seen her own possibilities in each of these tiny faces and was rightly afraid. Kate picked out a baby one row back and two bassinets over, a bald one, indistinguishable from three others. "What a beautiful child," she announced. "Isn't that all the evidence of God we need?" The nurses in the nearby station looked up and smiled.

"Anyone would want to take home such a perfect child," Kate said, and was rewarded by seeing the baby yawn and buck.

"They're all perfect, right, Reverend?" one of the nurses called.

"That's right. I just want to make sure somebody said so." Moving down the corridor to Sally's room, Kate considered the number of times she had visited new mothers and praised the cosmic perfection of their infants. At the moment, she couldn't remember a single one of those babies clearly—only the warm weight, the powdery smell, the vague hands and eyes. Baby. It was a hard concept to hold onto.

But then, everything this morning was hard to hold onto. Her brain felt swamped—she passed nurses without seeing them, greeted patients without hearing her own words. Even though she held her parishioners' hands, reciting prayers over them and waiting through Sally's endless new joke, her thoughts sank back to the pictures in the paper, and Bill-o's long drive, and Ned's weary voice. She wrung out washcloths so hard her hands stung. There was no point in pretending he hadn't sounded doubly weary when he talked to her.

After finishing with Ed, who as usual dozed through her prayer, she retreated to the empty lounge by the elevators. Grieving families sometimes gathered in this room. It was a good place for grief. Its walls were a soft, undemanding yellow, and its small, ergonomically sound armchairs were designed so a person could weep all day. Kate collapsed into one of them and rested her forehead against her knuckles. She wondered whether Ned would have reminded her that the lounge was meant for patients or whether, seeing in her face the face of suffering, he would have pulled up a chair beside her. The echo of his voice had been swirling into her thoughts all morning, but now that she tried to concentrate on that measured rise and fall, all she could hear was the faint buzz of one of the floor lamps and the smooth rubber rush of gurney wheels from the hallway.

A commitment, she'd told Bill-o. That daily, relentless pledge was the clamp that held married couples through the rough spots—the troughs, the sere months, even years, when every word one of them said gnawed on the other's frayed nerves. Commitment was steadier than love, denser, more reliable. Commitment *made* love. Who had taught her that, if not Ned?

She'd known from their first meeting that he was, above all things, good. A good man. His life was an orderly procession of honorable decisions and admirable stands. A Big Brother, a walker against leukemia and hunger, a blood donor. His goodness had stood before her like a reproach. For every afternoon she spent at the homeless shelter, he spent whole weekends there during which he took case histories so that he could spend the following week setting up job interviews and medical checkups. He was a fundraiser and a canvasser; he registered voters and rescued pets. He was living testimony to how much could be done in this world, if only a person tried.

Talking to him, Kate had felt a new spirit singing through her. She saw his self-sacrifice and believed that it led to fulfillment, saw his many acts of charity and believed that such generosity could only come from a full heart. She hadn't yet learned that generosity could come from a stingy heart, or that a willingness to give to strangers was no guarantee against a locked-up heart at home. She thought she had found salvation's outreaching hands, and no crass caution could keep her from trying to clasp them.

She had met Ned on a two-week-long building blitz organized to provide housing for four low-income families, the kind of project that didn't usually include medical students whose overalls held a sharp, ironed-in crease. "Don't you have to study?" Kate asked him as she helped to hold a part of a window frame while he pounded nails. "I thought med students spent all their time learning the names of the bones in the hand."

Ned kept hammering—light, cautious strokes, most of them on center. "Winter's coming. People need to get off the streets. The bones will still be there when I get home."

Kate could imagine them, too, arranged and labeled on his coffee table. Just then a girl, the daughter of one of the families they were building for, called to him: "Hey! You're not a very good hammerer." Kate waited for Ned to respond, but he only nodded and moved on to the next nail. He wasn't so bad, Kate thought. There were plenty worse on the site.

"You're not very good," the girl said again, sauntering over to them. She looked about eleven, with tangled hair and a smoker's brownish, clouded teeth, and had made enemies all around the building team for her habit of offering loud and specific critiques of the work. "I hope you're not planning to put a window right there," she said now. "It looks stupid. It looks like one big eye right in the middle of the wall."

"These were the plans your parents okayed," Kate said. "They've already made their decisions."

"They didn't know what they were doing. They're afraid that if they say anything, you'll quit. They think they have to take whatever you dish out."

"Where do you think the window should go?" Ned said. He left his nail sticking halfway out of the frame, surprising Kate, who had already pegged him as a man of orderly habits.

"Two." The girl gestured at the wall. "Side by side, with a little space in between. The way normal houses have their windows."

"Sounds good to me," Ned said. He dropped his hammer through the loop on his overalls and walked over to talk to the supervisor. He pointed toward the girl and the window. Her timing, as it turned out, had been good; little enough of the wall had been framed in that the plans could still be adjusted, and the team set in openings for two windows, side by side. They did look better, much as Kate hated to admit it. She glanced around to see if the girl was satisfied, but she was off haranguing the plumbing team about bathtubs set too close to toilets.

"It's her house," Ned said, surprising Kate for the second time; she thought he'd been concentrating on his nailing and wouldn't have noticed her watching the bossy girl. "Who knows when she'll have another chance to arrange things the way she wants them?"

"She could learn a lesson about tact. Also about the words *thank you*."

"I'll bet she's already said a lifetime's worth of thank yous. I don't think she wants this new house half so much as she wants the chance to come out and tell people exactly how things should be done."

Kate agreed with Ned there, but in her eyes the desire was a flaw. She looked again at the girl, her skinny legs and big rear end, her dress pulling and riding up under her arms while she pointed at the holes already cut in the flooring for the bathtub's hot and cold water lines. "You have a generous vision," Kate said to Ned, who had turned his attention back to the window.

"I just try to keep my eyes open. Would you like to go for a cup of coffee later?" She smiled, and without looking at her, he smiled too.

He wooed her artlessly, unbalancing her with his perfect ease, which seemed like a kind of wisdom. She began to bring him stories, telling him about case studies discussed in her seminary classes, and about a boy she'd seen getting arrested at the IGA for shoplifting two cabbages. "Cabbages. Not even steak. What was he thinking?"

"He wasn't thinking," Ned said. "Sometimes the only answer to desire is just to take."

"Have you ever taken anything?"

"Not yet." He shrugged. "Who knows?"

Kate replayed that moment when her anxious brain fretted that Ned was a goody two-shoes, a teacher's pet, a Pharisee. Goodness was not unnuanced, but it was simple. It made people uneasy because they saw it so rarely.

She told him about the Siamese cat who lived just below her tiny, steam-heated apartment; it let out a spine-rattling yowl whenever the pipes banged. "Bleed the pipes," Ned said. "Let the extra air out, and they'll stop making noise, and the cat will stop squalling."

"What am I supposed to do, break into the woman's apartment with a wrench?"

"Go down and introduce yourself. When you offer to do things for people, they're usually willing to open their doors." He blew on his coffee and looked at Kate with a mild expression she couldn't decipher; the corners of his mouth might have held the driest amusement, or else he really did go through the world taking people and their requests with impeccable seriousness, helping them when he could, which was most of the time. A person who spent her life with Ned could never slip into bad habits, or lose track of the world she wanted to help build.

He waited until June, eight months after they met, before he asked her out for dinner and a movie. By that time Kate had given up on him half a dozen times, and his phone call left her tipsy with hope, relief, dread. For courage she bought cheap roses, their heads already nodding, from a slight-chinned boy standing outside a muffler shop. The warm evening pooled around her and drew the scent out of even these droopy blooms. When Kate got out of the shower, she spun through the apartment and let her wet hair fling water into the fragrant air. She pulled out a dress she loved, sleeveless and short, with three gauzy layers falling in its full skirt, and raced to the door when Ned knocked, her mouth already full of laughter.

He, wearing a blue sports coat, looked at her and shuffled back a step, out of arm's reach, so he was no longer standing on the welcome mat. "Well, Kate."

"Welcome," she said, opening the door wider and gesturing him in. He had never stepped beyond the front mat, but this was a date, their first, on an evening wrapped around them like petals.

He gazed at her. "Quite a dress."

"Very ooh-la-la, yes?" She twirled for him, but when he didn't answer, she stopped. "No?"

"Yes. But maybe—don't you think—a little much for a movie?"

His awkwardness touched her heart, and she said, "I can change."

"I don't want to ask you."

"But you'd be more comfortable."

"I'm sorry. Guess I'm a fuddy-duddy."

"You just know what you like. Give me two shakes." She darted back to her bedroom and pulled a cotton skirt from her closet, her heart softening at the gentleness of a man who could be made uneasy by a flounced dress.

Six months later, Kate gave the dress away. The gesture seemed to cost little enough. But now she wished she had the dress back, its brilliant blue, its rustle crisp as lettuce. She wished she could remember a single pair of shoes Ned had given up for her. He would give them in a second, she knew, if she'd needed them. He never hesitated in the face of need. But she wished he might just once give her time or money or a pair of shoes that she didn't need. There were all kinds of ways of withholding, all kinds of selfishness. Living with the Bill-o of her youth should have taught her that much. But that Bill-o was gone, and with him any lessons she might have learned.

On the other side of the room sat a little coffeemaker on a low table. The metallic smell of burned coffee clung to the empty pot and cups. Just at that moment she didn't want to look at anything worn out, used or unfinished; she unplugged the pot, picked up the table, cups and all, and carried it to the sink. She waited until the water ran hot before scrubbing down the whole mess, beginning with the sticky tabletop.

After setting the clean cups to drain and brewing fresh coffee, she started in on the rest of the room, straightened magazines and lampshades, gathered crumpled tissues, and used them to dust off the windowsill. A colorless strand of cobweb was stuck high on the wall, and she rolled up a magazine. She was standing on a chair and swatting at the strand when the door of the lounge opened. Kate glanced down. "I think they have people here who are paid to do the cleaning," Mindy said.

"I'm just doing some tidying."

"Like I said. Anyway, a little bit of dirt is a good thing; it equalizes."

Kate jabbed the magazine at the cobweb again. "It's hard to keep the lounges nice. Housekeeping can't barge in here when people are finding out that their father needs heart surgery."

"And that's when people are going to be worried about dust, all right," Mindy said, helping herself to a cup of the fresh coffee. "My aunt told me to come and find you."

"Why? And are you supposed to be drinking caffeine?"

"That equalizes, too. Energy brings balance."

"You sound like you've found some mystical writing."

Mindy shrugged. "I believe in the wisdom of the body." She brushed her hand over her flat abdomen. "Bodies, now."

"Pour a cup for me," Kate said, stepping off the chair. As long as the girl was here, she could try to talk to her, build a little trust. "I believe in caffeine. Probably more than I should. I tried to give it up once, when Dr. Gussey told me that I was addicted. I thought I'd prove him wrong. After two days cold turkey, I fell right to sleep in a church finance meeting. I went home and drank a pot all by myself."

"I didn't use to drink it," Mindy said, dropping onto a sofa and slinging her feet over the back. "I was the only person I knew who didn't crawl out of bed straight to the java. But the baby's father got me started. Now I'm like everybody else." At the words "baby's father," she feathered her fingers again over her flat belly; Kate wondered whether she was practicing the gesture.

"That's two things he gave you: a baby and a habit."

"It's not like I'm shooting heroin. Even though my parents would probably be happier if I was."

"They're worried about you," Kate said. "They're afraid you're going to get hurt."

"Everybody thinks he's scum. They assume he's a drug dealer or a Hell's Angel. 'Why do you think I'd be hanging around some horrible guy?' I ask them. But nobody's paying attention. They're sitting around thinking my baby's father is a convict."

"They're trying to tell you they love you."

"You want to know what they told me? That I'm a little fool. My father's exact phrase. Is that supportive?"

"No," Kate admitted, perching on the end of Mindy's couch. "But people say all the wrong things when they're upset. There are words behind the words. Listen for what people mean."

"I've pretty well figured out what they mean. Now I'll tell you what *I* mean," Mindy said, leaning forward a little, her mouth starting to curl. "I'm going to have this baby, and raise it, and teach it everything I know. If my family doesn't like that, they can go fuck themselves." Her hand shot over her mouth. "Whoops."

"Go ahead," Kate said.

"It just makes me mad. They should be happy! We should be buying baby clothes, but they're too busy telling me how disappointed they are. Nobody's happy."

"Are you?" Kate asked, the obvious question.

"They won't let me be." Mindy's full bottom lip started to quiver, her eyes to glisten. Then she straightened and dashed the back of her hand across her eyes. "Yes," she said.

"Good," Kate said. "Remember that." She picked up Mindy's foot, settled it on her lap and worked off the sandal straps, which had dug into the girl's swollen skin and hidden the toenail polish—an unpleasant color, almost mauve, probably chosen to invite some kind of harmony. After a rigid moment, Mindy relaxed, resting her cup on her stomach and sliding closer so that Kate could get a solid purchase.

"I like foot rubs," Kate said. "Getting and giving. They make me want to go to sleep."

Mindy sighed while Kate probed and knuckled, the tense lines around her eyes slackening, and Kate would have thought the girl was drifting off except that her mouth moved softly, as if she were working a piece of food from side to side.

"So," Kate said, "have you thought about names?"

"Cinnamon Ashley." After a moment she added, "Fern."

"What if it's a boy?"

Mindy shrugged. "Lance. I don't know anybody named Lance."

Kate held up her hand for the other foot. "I always thought that if I had a boy I'd name him Kevin, because Kevin doesn't have any awful nicknames. But I knew a man at seminary whose actual, birth-certificate name was Buddy. And he loved it. Said it meant he was friendly with the world from the get-go. What do you think? Buddy Gussey?"

Mindy kept her eyes cast down, so that all Kate saw were her stubby eyelashes, the color of hay. "I know a Buddy. He wears T-shirts that say HARLEYS RULE."

"Chester," Kate said. "I always thought Chester was a good name."

"For a dog, maybe. *Chester.*"

"I like old-fashioned names," Kate said, handing Mindy her sandals. "When I visit new mothers, I think, well, here's another Scott or Jennifer for the world, and I wish I could just once meet an Obadiah. We had a run on Bruces for a while. I swore fifty times that if I had a baby, I wouldn't name him Bruce."

Mindy glanced up, and Kate knew just what she was seeing: the fine lines like tiny creek beds that were starting to form beside Kate's eyes, the dainty purse of flesh under her chin. In Mindy's eyes, Kate might as well have been sixty. "I'm just trying to tell you," Kate said. "I'm the last person who would make fun. I understand how lucky you are."

"Thanks," Mindy mumbled. She pushed herself further away from Kate. From the corridor outside, they could hear the loudspeaker paging first Doctor Connor, then Doctor Reeve, the gynecologist.

"Are you here for an appointment?" Kate asked.

"I told you. My aunt sent me over to find you. I guess I'm the errand girl now. She said you better come to the church."

"What's happened?"

Mindy shrugged. "A lot of people are there. In the church and out back, too."

"Mindy, for Pete's sake. Why didn't you tell me?" Kate said, standing and glancing around the lounge for her purse and keys.

"I did. Anyway, they don't look like they're going anywhere," Mindy said, stretching out and closing her eyes. Before she turned to face the cushion she asked Kate to close the door on her way out, which Kate did, loudly.

Eight

Kate drove as fast as she could, cutting through two parking lots and shooting in front of a lumbering vegetable truck. At the square, a squinting, brake-riding ninety-year-old tortuously tried to parallel park her powder blue Lincoln, and Kate gunned around her, barely missing an oncoming van. She actually passed the turn onto her own street and had to drive around the block the long way, to come up on the church from behind as if she were sneaking in.

And for a lovely, confused moment, she thought she was sneaking into a miracle. The slender branches of the Bradford pear tree Bill-o had planted, branches that had been bare this morning, were covered from shoulder to tip in white. The tree seemed to have burst into bloom in October, the clusters of blossom luminous as caught stars: the tree radiant, brilliant, arrayed like a bride. Members of Kate's congregation threaded around the trunk and pointed excitedly at the veil of lacy flowers. Kate thought, her heart hammering, that she had been sent a sign, although she didn't believe in signs.

She hurried out of the car. Ellen Phillips called her name and added something that Kate couldn't make out. Her eyes filmed with impatient tears, she hastened to the tree, and was almost close enough to touch it before she could see that the delicate white objects she'd taken for flowers were actually tiny figurines of babies.

Tied with transparent thread, dozens of inch-long dolls, crudely stamped out of a plastic so white it verged on green, dangled from every branch. The little faces were featureless, the hands and feet gluey blobs, but the bodies, hung in groups of three, were still recognizably human. She stared at them, trying to understand, then closed her eyes, ashamed of the disappointment that flooded through her. Very softly she whispered, "Damn."

"I've already talked to the police," Barb said, materializing at Kate's elbow. "They say this might constitute harassment. They want to know if there were any phone calls or threatening letters. Did you hear any unusual noises last night?"

Kate shook her head, listening to Ellen Phillips keen, "What does it *mean?* What are they telling us?"

"I was out for a while," Kate said. "Ned was arrested. Mindy came to stay. It was a big night." And the Sanctuary Christians, too, whom she'd foolishly imagined might confine themselves to a single visit. She started to tell Barb about them, then changed her mind. One look at the tree would fill her in.

"People are waiting for you in the church," Barb said. "Alma, Bob— the usual gripers. They've imported some of the protesters from that business at the clinic last night. Everybody's loaded for bear."

"I'm not surprised. These dolls are pretty gruesome."

"They don't mind the dolls. Bob probably helped hang them up. They want to hear you say that babies are the most important thing in creation, and we should be at home making more of them."

"We should—" Kate began, and just then Ellen rushed over to her and clutched her arm with damp hands, her voice at the edge of a sob. "What is *happening?*"

"Nothing," Kate said. She patted Ellen's shoulder with her free hand. "Nothing that can't be talked through."

"People are saying that you're a bad example. You! And we should keep our children away."

"People sometimes overstate, when they're excited. You can't let them frighten you. As long as we're still communicating, we can still reach one another," Kate said, the sort of idiotic pastor-babble she'd once sworn she would never descend to. Turning her back on the radiant tree, feeling her expression harden into a grimace of pastoral cordiality, she let Barb lead her into the church.

Small groups of people were dotted across the pews, each group engaged in feverish talk. Church members leaned toward one another, their collars loose and faces wet in the hot church, their voices a tense hum. Looking around, Kate saw several of her older parishioners, and strangers in suits who she didn't have to be told were Sanctuary Christians.

Robert Efrim was standing at the front of the church under the stained-glass window of the Good Shepherd, and George Mellot had taken a place by the side door. They had come to choke off her ministry, to plant deep seeds of pitying mistrust in her parishioners. Nevertheless, with their concerned expressions, the men looked for all the world like facilitators of Methodist district work groups—although these men were better dressed. They could have been assigned to write statements on inclusiveness or the environment. In her weariness she momentarily lost track of their purpose and was ready truly to welcome them. Then she began to make out the conversations.

"—torn. And someone whose attention is torn can't give a church the guidance it needs."

"Well, it isn't quite natural, a woman. We've tried to make peace with it, but still."

"—Haven't you always felt something strained in her? Something forced? The way she looks at Ned makes me go cold."

Kate watched them from the doorway until Robert Efrim lifted his head and said, "Why, there she is," in a voice that carried above the murmurous hum and might have been taken for pleasant.

Heads jerked around to look, and she would later think she'd heard, from somewhere, a shout. "Here she is," Kate said, nodding at Robert Efrim. "Welcome to our church. You're not, I believe, a member."

"The Spirit called me here."

"The Spirit has been busy," she said, making a swift head count— thirty people, give or take, better than half of them her own church members.

"People respond to God's call," Robert Efrim said. "It's beautiful to see."

"People respond to all sorts of calls," she said, "as you yourself pointed out. I hope you haven't been waiting here long."

"Waiting?" Bob Peters sang out, his voice gladsome. "We've been waiting for five years. We've been waiting ever since you came here."

"I'm not sure I follow you, Bob." She scrutinized his thrilled face. "I baptized your grandson. I talked to your boy after he lost his job. When did I keep you waiting?"

"How long do we wait for leadership?" he cried.

"Just where do you want to be led?"

Bob rolled his eyes and glanced back at Robert Efrim, who was nodding gravely. "If you have to ask," Bob said.

Robert Efrim gazed at Kate with the same confident expression he'd worn the night before. "It's an unusual church that you lead."

"Is it?" Kate said, feeling herself tighten so that she practically had to chip the words free of her mouth. "We worship on Sundays. Collect for missions and the poor. You'll have to tell me what you find remarkable."

"There are legions not yet born, perhaps never to be born, crying for your help. Won't you help them?"

His gentle voice was as intimate as breath; with his smile he coaxed Kate, and across the length of the church she smiled icily back. What pamphlet had he stolen that speech from? He had misunderstood his audience if he thought she could be swayed by a gooey, borrowed, two-bit oration.

"Oh, please," said Barb loudly.

"She could help them if she wanted," Alma said.

"Won't you help them?" echoed Bob. His face shone, and Alma's looked haughty; she would not be listening to Kate anymore. Kate didn't blame her. Robert Efrim would tell her what she hungered to hear.

Kate said to him, "You folks are the ones responsible for the dolls outside, aren't you? Your visit last night was just a smokescreen. This is your real agenda."

"You held Mrs. Mellot's child. Felt that little girl's whole, living weight. You could help to save other children just like her."

"The police have been called. If I choose to press charges, you'll be lucky to get off with a fine. Frankly, I'd rather see you get jail time."

"You called the police over some plastic babies?" He laughed. "You must be feeling insecure. But I sympathize—your position is insecure, isn't it? Five years ago your church had eighty families. Now you're scrambling for seventy-three."

Kate wondered how he had found those figures and instantly knew that Bob had told him. Bob would blab all of Dove's struggles, but not point out that eight families had left Elite for new jobs, two others to retire in Arizona; Kate had been proud of her ability to retain most of her members, even attract new families. Today's circus was unlikely to help. "Yes," she said grimly.

"People leave when they're confused, when they're lost."

"We need leadership!" Bob burst out. "A leader who is willing to take a stand. Ned was magnificent at that rally last night, I don't mind telling you. And I have to tell you, since you weren't there to see for yourself. Other church leaders protested, but not Pastor Kate. Where was your leadership then?" He waited a beat. "Or were you too busy with your houseguest?"

Someone snickered, and Kate, her mouth flat and her sweat-damp hair clinging to her face, shouldered to the front of the church. She climbed into the pulpit and turned on the microphone. She wished she had gotten around to fixing the speaker; Gabe had dropped it a month ago and now her amplified voice had a tinny jingle. "You've worked up quite a case against me," she said, hearing the anger clip her words. "But I still don't know just what I'm being accused of. You want more protest marches? Or you'd rather see Ned's face up front every week?"

"He's a good man," Bob said. "When there's a need, he goes. No one ever has to ask him. He understands what is important."

No human need ever unsniffed by Doc Ned, the bloodhound for the Lord, Kate thought. "Bob, you're making some big assumptions here. And you're overlooking a few issues. The United Methodist Church believes that each mother is unique, and each mother must make her own choice about every single child. If you can't accept that, then maybe Dove isn't your church home after all." How strange the furious words felt in her mouth. Pastors weren't supposed to send people away. Even to congregants who had baited and goaded and challenged her, she had kept her arms open in outreach. She had forgiven and forgiven and forgiven. The relief that came in finally telling Bob Peters to get lost was enormous.

He took his time about answering, and his frown was puzzled. Finally he said, "Maybe you're right. I never would have thought. But maybe I don't belong here."

The complicated sorrow in his voice punctured Kate's anger like a needle. Suddenly short of breath, she gazed at the rough part in his gray hair, the curling collar of his plaid shirt. Bob Peters. She had baptized his grandson. What had she just done?

In the moment's silence Robert Efrim, standing just to her left, said in a soft voice, "You mean to be steering toward happiness. But your choices keep taking you further and further away."

"You're in no position to make a judgment. And for the record, you're wrong."

"Is your life making you happy now? When we do what we were created to do, we have peace in our hearts. Do you feel that peace?" Robert Efrim asked.

Kate's tongue was heavy in her dry mouth. The stifling church grew still as her parishioners leaned forward to hear her answer. How expertly Robert Efrim had engineered the situation, and how stupidly she kept underestimating him. He tossed out his fat, useless words— peace, happiness—as if they were qualities that could be held in the hand, as tangible as bread, but more unchanging. As if anyone could sail through each day on a smooth pond of peaceful happiness. Who had ever been so confident, so coherent, so lucky?

For a second, Kate almost laughed, and the shadow of that lucky person took shape in her mind. So consistent, so busy with his projects and works, so peaceful. So good. Ned's life was a beam of light in a dark world. And by his light Kate could see her own life: a skein of tangled yarn, a careless pile of sticks. Despite the church's soggy heat, she shivered.

"Are you not well, Pastor?" Robert Efrim asked.

"I'm fine. I'm actually quite happy and glad to be here. It isn't often that I get to witness in quite this way to my congregation."

"And when do we get to be happy?" Alma said. Kate raised her eyebrows. "Have faith, Alma," she said.

"We haven't come here to sow dissention," Robert Efrim said, and Kate thought, The hell you haven't. "We want to give things to you. Fulfillment. Peace."

"Which are yours to give?" Kate said.

"We aren't getting the help we need," Bob cried, and Kate couldn't tell whether his voice vibrated with sanctimonious satisfaction or something closer to anguish. Either way, she was the one who had brought him to this pass, standing in a sweltering church with his gaze turned to Robert Efrim as if the man were Jesus himself. Kate glanced away, to the side of the church, where Barb was staring furiously at Kate and mouthing *Do something.*

Just what did Barb have in mind? Attacks in the church weren't covered in seminary. She looked down with loathing at Robert Efrim; she thought of the pleasure it would give her to blast him and his well-dressed associates out of her church with a fire hose. "All right," she said aloud to Barb and put her mouth back against the microphone. She'd already let him pick the argument, the time and the place. But the pulpit was hers, and should be defended.

"This," she began, "is a Methodist church. It is truly a sanctuary." She meant to ask the Sanctuary Christians to leave quietly, to order them if she had to. But Robert Efrim, perhaps hearing the note of new determination in Kate's voice, turned to face her congregation and lifted his arms. "We have gathered here. Let us pray!" he cried, words Kate had said so often.

"I'll have to ask—" she said, but starting in on the Lord's Prayer at the top of his massive voice, he thundered over her and gestured at his church members to join him. Kate stepped back from the microphone. Even though the man leading the prayer was a manipulative terrorist, she would not let herself be forced into shouting down prayer in her own church. She heard Bob Peters add his voice, then Alma hers, then the Norths from the back of the church.

"Amen," said Robert Efrim, and started in again, more voices joining him. The prayer shot and rattled against the church's pitched ceiling. Kate stood quietly, offering her parishioners dignity, which they deserved, rather than the despair that arced through her. Robert Efrim raised his voice for a third recitation, then marched to the door, his church members falling in behind him, all of them still calling out their prayer.

Kate watched mutely while Bob Peters joined the procession. Bob left, along with his sister Esther, who often brought cookies by the parsonage; Frieda and Jack Anders, who had headed up the last mission campaign; Jess Little, who joked when he was laid up that his arthritis had arthritis. Grief beat high in her throat; she knew she would never see any of these in her church again, and she held her hand on her mouth to keep from wailing as their backs disappeared into the light outside.

"Stop! Oh, stop!" someone called, and Kate looked down, confused to hear her words coming from someone else's mouth. More parishioners remained in the church than had left it—Barb, of course, and

Gabe, Sharon Werth, Sally Plummer's parents, the Norths. Members of the choir, who had entered during the altercation, clustered near the side door, two of the altos fanning themselves and Glenna Phillips, their soloist, wandering fretfully in and out the door.

"I know you love what you do," said Marie Moeller, standing in the center aisle and pressing her hands against her wet eyes. "I've seen how you talk to people."

Kate, her lips trembling, knees trembling, groped down from the pulpit, and putting her hand on Marie's arm, she let the young woman lean into her. "Of course I love my work," she said. "We're not arguing about that."

"I don't know what we're arguing about," Marie said helplessly.

"That's it," Kate said, stroking the woman's damp hair. "I don't think anybody knows what we're arguing about."

"I do," Barb snapped. Her face was scarlet, so slick it seemed to give off light. "This was a camp raid. Collection basket must be getting light at Sanctuary Christian."

"But why come here?" Marie said. "We haven't done anything wrong. We don't worry about seeing Pastor Kate's name in the paper."

"Robert Efrim wouldn't have come if my name was in the paper," Kate murmured, while Barb said, "These folks sniff out churches where people are encouraged to lead logical lives, ones that make sense. Then they dive right for us."

Kate dragged up the trace of a smile to thank her, though she couldn't help wondering where Barb had been all the Sundays Kate had preached about belief in what could not be seen or touched. Soul *and* mind, she always said, though people wanted to hear one or the other. Ned liked to tell her, "It's simple. Just tell the truth," and she liked to say back, "I do tell the truth. And it's complicated."

Perhaps a month ago he had strolled into the living room where she was sitting with a legal pad and the Bible and engaged in her usual battle to write a homily. "What's your text?" he'd asked.

"The extremely irritating Good Samaritan."

"What's wrong with the Good Samaritan?"

"Everybody's heard the story fourteen dozen times. Everybody knows we're supposed to think about all the people we don't want to help. There isn't one new thing left to say." She crumpled the page she'd been doodling on and tossed it in a corner.

"What do you think about when you read the passage?"

"It's a perfect little story, isn't it? Airtight. The stingy priest, the stingy Levite, the charitable sinner. It's so tidy, it drives me crazy. Life never makes things that easy."

"I don't see your problem. Somebody gets beaten up and robbed; you can help him or not. What's so complicated?"

"What if your family needs the money it would take to get the man to the hospital? What if you're already hurrying to your own father's deathbed?"

"You can't just let the man die," Ned said.

"I'd help him—you know that. But I'd also remember, while I was bringing that man to the hospital, that I'd never see my father again. Every action we take has a cost. If you don't calculate the costs, you miss the whole point."

"Pretty dire, Kate."

"Tell me I'm wrong." In the end, she called the homily "The Price of Giving," and pointedly thanked Ned for his help, although he assured her that she had done all the work.

Now she asked, "Does anybody know where these people come from?"

"West of here," Barb said. "Way far. Tiny little country church on the way to Evansville."

Kate nodded unhappily. Ned knew all the silos and turnoffs in that direction, Bill-o had said; Ned went there when he wanted to think. Her legs began to ache, so she let herself collapse in the front pew and felt sweat line the creases under her arms and in the backs of her knees. Her eyes closed on their own; she wondered if she had gotten even an hour's sleep the night before.

"What do we do now?" Marie asked.

"Nothing," Kate said. She opened her eyes, then let them fall shut again. "Nothing different. This part is the real test. If we change now, they've won."

"Maybe they have," someone muttered. Kate shook her head, but she couldn't stir herself to speak.

Eventually people began to wander out of the church, most of them stopping to touch Kate's shoulder and promise their support. "Thank you," she murmured again and again. She heard the rushing whir of the organ being turned on, and then Ellen Phillips—Kate could tell by the shaky touch and missed notes—started going over "Faith of Our Fathers." "It's Saturday," Ellen called, although Kate hadn't said anything. "I practice on Saturdays. Hope you don't mind listening."

"That's fine," Kate said. "I just need to sit here a while." In fact, listening to Ellen was about the last thing she wanted to do. But no phones could reach Kate here, and none of the piled-up office work could spill into her lap; the church was as close to safe harbor as she was going to find. She slouched, stretching her damp legs while Ellen blundered on.

Now was the time to sort out the last, complicated twenty-four hours and ready herself for the next trial, but she couldn't muster even that small firmness of purpose. She let another leaden wave of weariness pass over. She didn't want to sort things out or ready herself. She wanted to go to a place where people had never heard of Sanctuary Christians or Dr. Ned Gussey or pastoral leadership. "I need a break," she muttered into Ellen's plodding chords. "I need a little air. Please. Please!"

Surprised at her own vehemence, she rested her hands on her lap and attempted to quiet the voices that rampaged in her brain. The next thing she knew, Ellen had stopped playing and a hand rested on Kate's shoulder. "Katy? Are you all right? I heard—I thought I'd better check on you." Reflexively smoothing her hair, she stood to face Bill-o, forgetting that she had tried, briefly, to pray.

"What did you hear?"

"I tried calling you in your office and got Barb. She said the barbarians were at the gate."

"She likes the dramatic phrase. It was just a family squabble." Kate turned toward Ellen and nodded. "You can go ahead now," she said. After a reluctant moment, "Faith of Our Fathers" began again with a whole measure of wrong chords.

When Kate turned back, Bill-o said, "You don't want to talk about this, do you?"

"You know, ministers are encouraged to explore their feelings and voice their concerns. Church members likewise. Talking Things Through—that's the model. Meetings and sharing sessions and discussion circles. I'm going to have more opportunities to talk about this than you can believe."

"Then I guess I should leave and let you get a little more shut-eye."

"Wait." She patted the pew beside her. "Please don't go. Stay here and talk to me about your store."

"There's nothing to tell. Nobody's staging a battle in my store. Nobody's even coming in."

"All the more reason to tell me about it. Bill-o, listen to me: If you really want to help, you'll tell me what you got from UPS yesterday."

"Four new cash registers. Two of them don't work." He let himself sit down, although he didn't relax; his head craned as if he was ready to bound to his feet again, and his soft cotton shirt pulled across his shoulders. "We're buying an insert in the Sunday *Bugle*. A unit of shelves came in the wrong color. Look, Kate, I don't want to be shut out. Does whatever happened this morning mean you're going to lose your job? Will you still have a place to live? You've got to talk to somebody. Talk to me."

"I'm talking to you. Didn't you hear? I'm asking you to help me."

"By telling you about my cash registers?"

"I just need a breather," she said and heard her voice break. Though she turned away, Bill-o saw her tears and rested a heavy, hot hand beside her on the pew. His thumb gently rubbed the seam of her skirt. Ellen, who had lumbered to the end of "Faith of Our Fathers," started in on "Jesu, Joy of Man's Desiring," which, to Kate's regular surprise, she played pretty well.

"It was a nightmare," she whispered. "People I know, people I love —they left the church, Bill-o. I pushed one of them out. They left chanting the Lord's Prayer. People—I know their kids. I need them."

"You can't have a church without people," Bill-o said, his thumb smoothing and resmoothing the same patch of cloth in an action as comforting as a heartbeat.

"It isn't just the church: I need *them*. Every one of them. I need Jess Little. His baby girl died of polio."

"Very hard," Bill-o said, shaking his head.

"I need Jess Little, but he's heading off with a minister who's a goon, and I swear to God it's more than I can stand." She punched her leg twice before Bill-o grabbed her hand, and they sat awkwardly twined for an instant before he let her go.

"It's hard to open a garden center in the fall," he said. "People are mulching their gardens, pulling up annuals. They don't want to think about gardening for a while. We have to come up with ways to entice them."

"Opening day give-aways?" Kate asked. "Seed packets? Balloons?"

He nodded. "We do that. Once people are in the store, though, that's the thing. How do you get them to look at rakes or edgers once they've already got their free packet of four o'clocks?"

"Remind them. Remind them that their rake is missing teeth and that grass was getting into their flowerbeds all last summer. Show them pictures. Remind them of what they'd meant for their gardens to look like, before the late rains and then the heat. People want to forget, once things haven't worked out. Don't let them forget. Remind them of what they'd hoped for."

"And what if they go away anyway?"

"You hand out more seeds and balloons," Kate said, her voice rough from tears washing up again. "You pull in people off the street. What does it matter who you've got in the store, as long as you've got somebody? You never know who will decide to go home with a new pair of gardening gloves."

"Is that it?" Bill-o asked, his thumb pressing harder now, almost hurting. "Is that how it works?"

"Anyone will tell you," she said, but the stupid, useless tears still rose. She shook her head and was silent until Ellen finished the last verse and the church was quiet.

"Do you want me to play that on Sunday?" Ellen called shyly to Kate.

"Yes," Kate said, her voice so harsh it surprised her. "It's a hymn of welcome. Play it over and over."

Nine

The next day, a paragraph-long report of the tumult at Dove appeared on the *Bugle*'s middle page. No follow-up pieces appeared. The real story, reported day after day, was the county's unseasonal cold, abruptly following the unseasonal heat. For a week now a stinging wind had whistled straight down from Canada, the air shot through with grainy bits of ice that worked on people's faces like sandpaper. In three hours the temperature dropped twenty degrees, and urgent radio bulletins were issued to farmers about late harvests. Windowboxes that had been foaming with late marigolds and lobelia looked hollow, their displays collapsed into slick, black mats. Maples and poplars dropped green leaves at a steady rate. Kate gave Mindy, who hadn't brought any winter clothes, her extra coat and a pair of gloves.

"I don't usually wear green," the girl said, balancing the shamrock-colored gloves on one hand. "People think it's a soothing color, but it isn't. It leads to disruption, agitation."

"It's thirty-five degrees out there," Ned said. "You're not going to want to walk around with bare hands."

"She can put her hands in her pockets if she wants to," Kate said. "I just want her to have a choice."

"I have to think about things now," Mindy said, and Kate knew that Ned was smothering the impulse to tell her she should have thought of things well before now. Kate was thinking the same thing herself. Still, she took pleasure in watching Ned bite back the words.

"It's good to feel the cold," Mindy said, pulling on Kate's coat and leaving the gloves on the coffee table. "Our bodies need to be reminded of natural things." She swept out the door and left it half-open behind her, allowing Kate and Ned to be reminded of the frigid wind.

"She's going to wish she had those gloves." Ned pulled the door shut.

"No she won't. Her hands could freeze off before she'd wish for green gloves."

"Where does she get this stuff? It's enough to make you want to buy her a whole wardrobe in green."

"Tut, tut, Ned. Where's your renowned kindness?"

"Annoyance is a natural response to an irritant," he said. "That girl is like a rock in my shoe."

"She's serious about her program, whatever it is. The other day I heard her gagging in the bathroom—she was brushing her teeth with salt. I offered to buy her some Colgate, but she said her body wants to get as unprocessed as it can. 'Even if it makes you sick?' I said, and she said, 'Even if.'"

"As if she weren't in there vomiting enough," Ned said.

"It's a natural response." Kate could see that Ned wanted to let the subject go, but she was taking solace in the light talk. It helped ease the ache that had swelled in her since Robert Efrim's descent on her church, the sense that her losses had only begun. Mindy was a distraction, and that by itself was a blessing. Ned, of course, didn't see things that way.

Kate watched him set his jaw whenever Mindy came into the room. She was surprised that his fund of charity could run so short for this untried, pregnant nineteen-year-old. As far as Kate was concerned, a girl who didn't have body odor and left the refrigerator alone was far from the worst house guest they'd ever taken in. "She doesn't ask for much. All she needs is somebody to forage for her, bring her nuts and berries. And salt."

Ned smiled briefly. "Aren't you a joker."

"Famous for it."

"The Joking Minister," he said, and she stiffened.

"We're a laugh a minute. Just ask the ten people who still come to my church."

"You've got a sizable flock," he said. "Didn't you read your own write-up in the paper? Four-fifths of your members are choosing to remain."

"Four-fifths of a flock feels pretty meager in the sanctuary. Not much bleating."

"You'll get new members. You're a celebrity now."

"I'd rather get the old ones back." She almost added, *Starting with you,* but caution or pride—she couldn't tell which—held her back. For all his secret visits to the Sanctuary Christians, he hadn't said a word about leaving Dove, and she didn't intend to make it easy for him. "Anyway, you're a celebrity, too. Battling Doc Gussey, famous all over Elite."

"Nobody's come in for my autograph."

"Robert Efrim will. He'll want it right at the bottom of a check." Ned was quiet, and she bit the inside of her lip. She hadn't wanted to be the one to start the fight. "Sorry. We seem to be standing on opposite sides of a fence."

"The fence isn't that tall. We can talk over the top of it."

"I liked it better when we were on the same side."

"I did too," he murmured, surprising her. But before the moment could take hold, he said, "Well, you've got Mindy to keep you from getting lonely."

"And Bill-o. Don't forget about him."

"He's easy. He isn't demanding berries in October. I'm wondering how long your patience with that child will hold out."

"No break in sight," Kate said pleasantly, as if she didn't feel the sharp edge of a quarrel slicing between them. "It's sort of fun with her here. Who else talks to us about new movies? I can now tell you which songs are in the top ten. It's a different kind of person to have in the house."

"'Sort of fun.'"

"Interesting. Lively." Running out of words, she said, "Her favorite song is 'Love Sugar.' If you would care to hear it, I can give you verse and refrain."

"I told you you wouldn't want this one for seven months."

"She's just a girl in trouble."

"It would help if she acted like she knew she was in trouble. She walks around as if she, all by herself, has the answer to the whole universe."

"Hey, Ned. Now you know what it's like to live with you." The words were out before she could stop them, even though she hated herself when she was like this—needle, needle, nudge, nudge. Of course, he looked hurt.

"Thanks for the support."

"Golly. Support. From the man whose friends invaded his wife's church."

"Not friends, exactly. Fellow seekers, maybe."

"Whatever." Kate looked at the carpet, which could stand to be vacuumed. Robert Efrim wasn't seeking anything. He'd already found every truth he needed.

"Anyway, I didn't send them to your church," Ned went on. "They found you on their own."

"Well, that's fine. But you wouldn't have stopped them, would you? Or warned me."

He hesitated. "People should be able to ask questions."

"Okay, Ned, here's my question for you. When are you going to protest on my behalf? When are you going to act, just for a little while, like you're proud of me?"

"You're able to stand on your own feet. I've always been proud of that," he said, and added, "I'm surprised you have to ask."

Turning away, she found some books to straighten on the shelf. He never lied, ever. "It isn't easy around here," she said.

"You won't let it be. Look, I won't be home until late. Euell Murphy's back in, after that coronary bypass. I want to stay close to him."

"Fine," Kate said. "I'll come and see him in the morning. You know, if you don't come home for dinner tomorrow, either, I'm going to think you're telling me something."

He pulled off his glasses and replaced them with another pair from his pocket—these lenses lighter, riding higher on his face. When he spoke, his voice was disarmingly gentle. "We've been married eight years. Maybe it's time for us to take stock. Sort things out and see where we stand."

Kate pressed her hands, suddenly clammy, against her thighs. "How are we supposed to sort things out if you're staying late at the hospital and I'm here running the Hotel Gussey?"

"It'll be okay, Kate. We just need to align our priorities."

"Priorities. Yes, you spoke to the newspaper about them." She pulled the throw pillow off the couch and slapped it against her flat hand. "Here's a statement to help you prioritize. I've been going along for eight years now thinking that our marriage was your priority—

that I, even, was your priority. You took this vow, you may remember."

He didn't speak until she stopped whacking the pillow. "What about me, Kate? Am I your priority?"

"You have been up till now," she said. "Maybe I need to sort things out."

He said, "A break. That's all. Just a chance for us to catch our breaths and figure out where we're standing. A small realignment."

"Wrong, dear. Big. I just hope you're ready for extensive chassis work." A body-shop metaphor that came swimming back from her first marriage, not that Ned, moving out of the house as fast as Bill-o ever had, paused to hear it.

That evening Mindy came home from work and saw the table set for three. "Who's playing hooky?"

"Dr. Gussey has a patient who needs extra care. He won't be in until late."

"Does this happen a lot? Doesn't seem very nice for you. I mean, you don't always have other people in the house to keep you company." The girl was leaning against the bookcase with one foot pressed up against her thigh, her hair falling in bright wisps around her face.

"When you're married to a doctor, you can count on some nights alone. They go with the territory," Kate said, her voice so genial she practically chirped. "So you see—I'm really very pleased to have you and Mr. O'Grady here."

"I wondered if it was something like that," the girl said and drifted down the hallway toward the bedroom. "Too bad Dr. Gussey doesn't go out in the mornings instead of at night. It's a stampede to get to the bathroom in the morning. That's not an ideal situation for a woman in my condition." Her voice faded away; Kate continued to slice radishes. Whenever Ned was off the scene, she was amazed at how deftly the girl was able to irritate her. Mindy might be a sort of blessing, but Kate hadn't yet managed to give thanks.

She received hourly reports on the progress of Mindy's condition, with new sensations and insights detailed as they were visited on her. When Kate tried to talk about nutrition or ask whether Mindy had found an obstetrician yet, Mindy remarked that now, for the first time, she had a perfect understanding of all her body's needs. A baby implanted its desires in its mother; the union was too profound for language to express. When Mindy and Kate were alone in the house together, the girl floated through rooms, her face wearing a beatific expression to indicate she was engaged in wordless communion with her child. She came up with anecdotes that Kate found unlikely: babies still in the womb who comprehended foreign languages and advanced math; babies who memorized whatever music their mothers listened to and were able to reproduce it, postpartum, note for note.

"That's true," Bill-o said over dinner. "I saw a six-month-old on TV who could whistle 'The Girl from Ipanema.' It was the darndest thing."

"Music is a responsibility," Mindy said. She rested her elbows on either side of her untouched spinach salad. "It's a guide to the spirit. I have to take the time now, every day, to teach my child the music that's important."

"Do you think your child will thank you for making sure it knows every word to 'Love Sugar'?" Kate asked.

"It's a bond," Mindy said.

"Your bond will be stronger if you eat," Kate said, nodding at Mindy's plate. "Babies don't live on 'Love Sugar' alone."

Mindy picked a crouton out of the salad. Bill-o said, "It's remarkable, the stuff that scientists are finding out. They do these experiments and discover that babies are brilliant. Babies *lose* knowledge when they're born."

"Mothers already knew that," Mindy said. "We don't need experiments. All day and all night, mothers are in touch with our babies, giving them food and blood and knowledge. It's a conversation that never stops."

"Is it going on now, for example? Are you in touch with the baby right now?" Bill-o asked. Raising his eyebrows, he nodded at Kate, encouraging her to get in the game. He looked delighted, and she wondered where his common sense had gone.

"Now, absolutely." Kate said. "Believe it. The baby is saying, 'Mother, I'm starving down here. Get me some chow.'"

"Spinach has pesticides," Mindy said. "They can't all be washed away."

"It's worth the risk," Kate said. "There's hardly a better natural source for iron and vitamin A."

"A mother's body can provide everything a developing baby needs," Mindy said.

"I'd hate for you to get off on the wrong foot. Poorly nourished mothers have babies who aren't healthy," Kate said. At the front of her mind was a list of all the baby needs that no mother's body could provide: a stroller, a health plan, a savings account. Looking at Bill-o, she said, "You know about propagating. Help me out here. Tell her that even seedlings need extra nutrients."

"That's true," he acknowledged. "But it's amazing how the tiniest trace elements in the soil will sustain them. And you know what's exciting? Watching the growth, seeing how the parent plant comes to life again in the seedling."

"And that's just a plant," Mindy said.

"Can you tell what the baby's doing right now? Is it moving?" Bill-o asked.

"Oh, yes. It's a little acrobat. It tumbles over and over."

Kate stood and started clearing the table, taking away Mindy's salad. "Tomorrow I'll bring you a book on fetal development," she said. "That way you can keep track of what's actually happening. Right now your baby is still clinging to the uterine wall. It's smaller than your thumbnail. It still has gills."

"I know," Mindy said, and Bill-o slapped the table and beamed.

That night, sleeping fitfully on the foldaway once Ned finally came home, Kate dreamed of Bill-o's gleeful expression. In the dream, his ponderous delight seemed ghastly, and it closed over her face like a rubber mask. Waking up hot and dry mouthed, she laid her hand on Ned's hip, but he didn't waken, certainly didn't turn to her; they'd scarcely touched each other since Mindy had moved in. Kate lay on her back while memories tumbled before her.

Without the least effort she could recall how, twenty years ago, Bill-o had discovered the calendar she tucked in her underwear drawer after her miscarriage. He kept the calendar and refused to touch her on her fertile days, though she'd wept, begged, sunk to her knees and clutched at his legs, not caring that she looked desperate and laughable. "A baby's the one thing I want," she'd cried, and he'd pulled her to her feet, stroked her hair and said, "Well, that's a shame, Katy, because it's the one thing I don't want."

The memory was so clear that she was outraged all over again; by the time dawn cracked across the sky she had her words lined up: "charlatan," "hypocrite," "sadist." But Mindy rose before Bill-o—a first—and wandered into the living room. When Kate and Ned murmured good morning, she held up her hand and pointed to her belly, then took a position near the window. No one spoke until Bill-o ambled in to greet the new day. "I thought I'd join you for breakfast," Mindy said to him.

The girl, who often locked herself into the bedroom when Kate came home and rarely addressed two words to Ned, orbited Bill-o like a moon. She told him what the color of his shirt meant, read his palm and gave him advice on foods and hairstyle, scarcely even left to go to the bathroom, although she was there every five minutes when Bill-o wasn't home. She tapped his elbow, wrist, the back of his hand. Kate wanted to grab Mindy's arm as she zoomed by and tell her to have some self-respect, but who was Kate to talk? At least Mindy wasn't spending mornings enraged by arguments left unfinished in a marriage long, long past.

The rage didn't seep away, either; it fed on every possible fuel—Bill-o's gusto, Mindy's preening, Ned's increasing snappishness. She stockpiled more words, favoring "irresponsible" and "childish." But the words bumped against one another unused; Bill-o's car had only to pull in front of the parsonage, and Mindy would appear and start to chatter before he was all the way in the house. Kate had to wait, her frustration growing daily more sharp toothed.

Her opportunity finally came the night she cut short a strained Council on Ministries meeting—Frieda Anders, whom no one had seen since she followed Robert Efrim out of Dove, still had all the minutes and projected budgets. Kate dismissed the meeting and made it home in time to join Bill-o and Mindy for a TV documentary about primate communication. Ned was adjusting the finicky water heater in the basement—happy to miss this event. Mindy had been talking about the special for days, since she'd seen an ad in the TV Guide showing a chimp mother cuddling her baby. The film opened, though, with two males in a dominance fight, and she squealed and ran for the bathroom as soon as the howling started. Bill-o twitched;

Kate put a restraining hand on his shoulder. "Calm down, Galahad. She knows her way."

"You don't ever worry about her?"

"Women have been having babies a long time. As she will tell you."

"Don't get nasty, Kate. She talks because she's excited. I know it's a cliché, but here it is, right in front of us: the big miracle. Life unfolding before our eyes. If you think about it, it takes your breath away."

"The idea of babies didn't use to give you any trouble breathing."

"Then I've made progress. Anyway, it's not bad for Mindy to want to talk about this baby, all the new things she's feeling. She needs somebody she can share her excitement with." He leaned forward and rested his hand on Kate's knee, and his voice became low and rapid. "I've been looking for a chance to talk to you. You've got to quit coming down on her like a ton of bricks. She needs to talk. Maybe you're just getting caught up in worrying about things, but this girl has a hundred things to say. She needs to talk about how she imagines the baby, what she hopes its life will be like. Here's the biggest thing that's ever happened to her, and you want her to talk about spinach."

"Did she tell you all this?" Kate asked.

"It's not hard to see. Just use a little empathy. If you'd ever been in her situation, you would have wanted support."

Kate opened her mouth and shut it again.

"All that business about balanced meals—come on. She can take vitamin pills. But she's more likely to eat right if there are people around her saying, 'A wonderful thing is happening to you.'"

"I can give her a lot, Bill-o. I can give her a roof over her head. But I can't sit around rejoicing about her miracle of life."

"Miracles are supposed to be your job."

"You think so? I spent ten years married to you and believed that my own miracle would come along to be diapered and burped, but you weren't interested in miracles then. So do you really think I'm all set to ask Mindy how her baby acrobat is doing? Listen, that would be a whole other miracle."

Bill-o frowned at her. "We were never in a position to think about a baby. You knew that."

In a moment of pure disbelief, her shoulders dropped. Then feeling came spiraling back, and Kate's mouth trembled and went loose. "I kneeled on the floor and begged. I promised you things. When I threatened to leave, you pointed at the door."

"It wasn't that bad. You're letting your memory take off."

"Listen to me. There's never been anything in heaven or earth I wanted so much as a baby. Your baby, once."

"We don't need to be arguing about this now," he said, glancing toward the hallway.

"You said you wanted to know."

"Have they finished with the fighting monkeys yet?" Mindy called, sashaying back in with bright pink lipstick and smooth hair. Bill-o shook his head at Kate, who snarled, "Chimpanzees."

"You don't have to bite my head off."

"You're the one who wanted to watch this. You should pay attention."

"I have to be careful what kinds of things I watch. The images I take in get transmitted to the baby. I don't want it to be imprinted with aggression."

"It already knows," Kate said.

After that night Bill-o started to spend two or three evenings a week at the store, to make up for afternoons when he waited in his new house for deliveries and repairmen that didn't come. Everything was a week past deadline now, with the carpeting and furniture still undelivered, his oven still lacking a door, and one of the bathroom taps still weeping. Meanwhile, Ned's patients seemed, all at once, to worsen, suffering more crises, requiring nightly monitoring, so Kate and Mindy, on their own in the house, silently watched TV together, then silently went to bed.

As she lay waiting, past one o'clock, past two, for Ned to come home, Kate wondered what sorts of priorities he was assessing in his empty office. Squirming on the lumpy mattress, she tried to assess some priorities of her own but could rarely force her thoughts beyond Mindy, sleeping in the only decent bed in the house. And although Ned's absence wasn't precisely the girl's fault, Kate's patience thinned to the point of transparency. Watching Mindy spend fifteen minutes every morning forcing down calcium tablets which she'd bought after seeing a TV special on bones, Kate took the bottle from Mindy. "Those aren't for you," Mindy said.

"Pregnancy isn't the only reason for taking calcium," Kate said, shaking out a knuckle-sized pill and washing it down with coffee. "Osteoporosis runs in my family." Which might have been true; in any case, she started taking one of Mindy's tablets every morning.

For the first time in a very long time Kate began to think about how she would act with a baby of her own, an old game of pretend she'd once thought of as practice. Driving to the hospital to see parishioners, she conducted monologues, pointing out a pretty spirea hedge to the invisible child in the back seat, and roaring when she passed the high school football field, home of the Panthers. While Gabe consulted with her over his planned homily, which owed more to the Alcoholics Anonymous Big Book than to the New Testament, she imagined a toddler's face and assigned it features—her own long eyelashes and good skin, her father's dense, wavy hair, her mother's dimpled chin. Ned's long legs, Bill-o's easy walk. Who cared where it came from? A baby.

When she and Ned had first married, she'd thought they had enough time. Kate had been only thirty-five then. Plenty of women had babies at thirty-five without medical intervention, which Kate feared and Ned serenely dismissed. Night after night, the two of them went to the bedroom with a sense of hope that seemed holy, and when disappointing month followed disappointing month, Ned consoled her first with statistics, then in his arms, where hope began to build again.

The months marched ruthlessly one into another. After a year of taking her temperature and making graphs, Kate began to imagine she could hear her body clank like heavy machinery, whistling and sighing with fatigue. She tried to keep her mind fixed on positive images—several of the books stacked next to the bed talked about the importance of imaging—but nevertheless, despite herself, on an evening when Ned began the old debate about baby names that they had taken up in such high spirits on their wedding night, she yanked herself away from him and asked him to shut up, please. "You can make a list twelve names long. What are you going to do with it? There's no baby to name."

"It will come, Kate. Keep your spirits up. We're still young."

"As a matter of fact, we're not. No spirits can rise high enough to let me see twenty-five again. Stop lying to yourself. Or at least stop lying to me."

Ned stood up and walked out of the room, leaving Kate panting as if she'd been on a crying jag, although she hadn't spilled a tear. When he finally came back and pulled her to her feet, she started to apologize, but he put his finger against her mouth. He led her to the bedroom, where he had changed the sheets, heaped up extra pillows and lit a candle on the dresser. "Here," he said, pulling up her sweater and then kneeling to kiss her stomach. He started to stand, but Kate pulled his head back. "You're good to me, Ned," she said.

"You'll be a good mother."

They joined in the warm room that smelled like candle smoke and crisp sheets, and Kate dutifully envisioned her uterus. As the books instructed, she tried to see a blooming rose or heavy clusters of grapes. She willed herself to imagine roundness, swelling, bursting forth. Pressing her stumbling mind along, she pictured a tiny curl of a baby held on all sides by the warm cushions of her body—and then, helplessly, watched as the child, no larger than a comma, stretched, straightened and dropped like an arrow out of her hard womb.

Ned cried out and held still, propping himself up even after he had grown soft again, and when he finally rolled over, kissed her and wrapped his finger in a wisp of her hair, he said, "This time. Don't you think?"

"I'm sorry," she said.

Silent, he lay beside her for a while, then silently got up. Kate stayed in bed, her hips propped up on the pillows long past the recommended twenty minutes, not moving so much as her head from side to side, just in case she was wrong.

She knew that Ned held that night to blame, tracked their childlessness to her loss of hope. They continued to come together by the calendar, but they rarely met each other's eyes in the dim bedroom; Kate could hardly bear Ned's look of resignation. During the day they treated each other cordially, and Kate schooled herself to wear a pleasant expression when parishioners told her that their single greatest joy in life had come through their children.

So now, even though she knew it was unhealthy and that she was causing herself real pain, she buried herself in Mindy's pregnancy. Night after night, dreams came to her of women giving birth to alligators and refrigerators; when she had to counsel young couples, she helplessly remembered every birth defect and complication she'd ever heard of. She stayed up late to read the books on prenatal development that Mindy let fall from her hands and started drinking milk, although she disliked milk.

One afternoon she drove out to the mall and spent a happy hour in Mother-To-Be, holding up pleated blouses, dresses with clever panels, and specially constructed pantyhose. In the end she brought home a smock, which the brisk salesclerk called cute but practical; women often kept right on wearing them even after the baby came. "Is it for you, or do you want gift wrap?" she said at the cash register.

"No wrap," Kate said. She didn't want to make a big production of this, and so when she got home she simply handed Mindy the bag and watched the girl draw back. With great reluctance Mindy touched the mint-green bow at the collar, then murmured a flat thanks and drifted back to the bedroom. Kate held up the smock to admire its lightness and double row of pretty square buttons. Every pregnant woman she'd ever known had complained about maternity clothes—the terrible designs, the shoddy fabric. Now she slipped the smock over her turtleneck. Watching herself in the bathroom mirror, Kate thought the smock looked just fine—mildly stylish, in fact—and she kept it on while she went back to the kitchen and made sandwiches. She woke Mindy up to eat one.

"These naps aren't like sleep, exactly," Mindy said; she yawned when Kate put a plate down on the bedside table. "I have visions. This time the baby was an astronaut, with the big boots and gloves. We were bobbing around in space, patting each other."

"You were an astronaut too?"

"The gloves felt like pillows strapped to my hands. It was fun not being on the ground. I didn't want to wake up."

"Here's what the smock looks like," Kate said, turning around so Mindy could see. "I thought you'd like it better once you saw it on. It's very comfortable."

"Green again. It's a funny color, isn't it? In my vision the baby had all its teeth, and they were blue. What do you think that means, a baby with a mouthful of blue teeth?"

"Tact," Kate said. "Gratitude. This is a gift; say thank you."

"Thanks. But I still wish I could go back to that vision. There are things I'd like to ask."

"You'll be asleep again before you know it," Kate assured her. She waited—not long—until the girl had slumped back down on the pillow before she took off the smock, hung it in the center of Mindy's closet, and picked up an armload of files that needed to go to the church. She slipped out the back door to avoid the noise of the front, even though the back door had become inconvenient, blocked by a foot-high drift of maroon sycamore leaves. Wet from last night's sleet, they clung to her shoes like cellophane. At the door of the church she tried to peel the leaves free, but she missed a few—they flaked off in brittle bits as she walked from room to room.

"Hope you're not planning to sneak anywhere," Barb said, coming up behind Kate with the ancient carpet sweeper.

"People haven't exactly been seeking me out lately. Sorry about the mess. I've got to get that back porch cleaned off," Kate said, brushing half a leaf from the heel of her shoe.

"Put a broom in Mindy's hand. She knows how to use one, even though she won't admit it."

"I don't think that's such a good idea. I'm already playing the wicked stepmother to her Cinderella."

"Cinderella was pure, as I remember. Or at least she wasn't in the family way."

"Mindy believes in the splendid purity of her own spirit," Kate said, then glanced at Barb. "Sorry."

Barb shrugged. "The child makes me want to shake her, and she's my own family. I don't know how you're putting up with her."

"She sleeps a lot."

"You're a saint."

"Tell Bob Peters. Better yet, tell Ned. That would give him a laugh."

"People never recognize saints when they're married to them."

"I think Ned sees the only saint he needs every time he looks in the mirror," Kate said. She glanced out the window at the whiplike branches of the Bradford pear. "You want to know the truth? After living with Ned, Mindy is a piece of cake. She's all wrapped up in herself, but at least she's honest about it. She doesn't pretend to be interested in anything else. She doesn't act sullied when you want to have a conversation with her."

"Yes she does," Barb said.

"Well, not the same way."

"He's not coming home much, is he?" Barb asked. When Kate shook her head, Barb said, "How much longer can you hold onto things?"

Kate looked down at her desk, where she had cross stacked the many letters that needed responses, the questionnaires, forms, and surveys to be filled out, the tall pile of phone messages to be returned. "Not long."

"Tell him to come home."

Kate shifted a letter from one stack to another, and when she spoke, tried to make her voice sound airy. "You know, every time I've tried to make a husband do something, he's gone the opposite direction just as hard as he could. What is it about me?"

"You're not clear," Barb said. "Tell him you need him there. Tell him you want him there."

"I can't do that."

"Why not?"

"I don't want him there. I've already got Bill-o and Mindy to satisfy. I don't have the energy to tend to Ned, too."

"Lie," Barb said. "What's the AA thing that Gabe says? 'Act as if.'"

"We saints can't lie," Kate said. "It's one of the problems with us."

"For Pete's sake, Kate, get off your high horse." Barb picked up the carpet sweeper again and ran it viciously over the rug by the door. "Of course it's easier not to tend to him. As far as that goes, it's easier not to tend to anybody. You're not the first person to figure this out."

"So you're saying that my life is too easy now? I need a little extra challenge?"

"I'm saying your marriage is part of your life, and it's pretty unattractive to see you turning your back on it. You have to try to work things out. The whole point of being married is staying with it. You don't have an option."

"I do, though," Kate said.

"You're not having enough trouble? Kate, you're already pushing people here hard. You want to add a second divorce to your résumé?"

"I have options," she said stubbornly, then wheeled her chair around to look out at the wreck of a yard between the church and the parsonage—fallen branches everywhere, unraked leaves speared on the stems of withered perennials. Any burden that had been picked up could be put down. Any task started could be left unfinished. If free choice meant anything at all, it meant that she had the option, every day, of walking away, a theological verity she was only now coming to appreciate.

Ten

But in the days that followed, Kate didn't walk away from any tasks or put down any burdens. She took on new work, offering to tutor Marie Moeller's oldest boy, who was struggling with arithmetic. She high-fived him after every multiplication problem he got right, relieved to be a part of a helping profession that invited her to dive into the lives of others and escape from her own.

She might have shared the insight with Ned—no one could understand better—but words between them now passed through a narrow channel banked with suspicion on one side and hurt on the other. In the few hours they spent together, they talked about laundry, dinner, the need to get the car serviced. Sometimes at night, jabbed awake yet again by an insistent spring in the foldaway, Kate glanced at her husband and tried to take reassurance from his familiar profile and steady breathing. She discovered she could hold make-believe conversations with him, anticipate his response to every comment, question, remonstrance, or joke. In no circumstance could she imagine him surprising her—except, of course, in the circumstance that had introduced their current, clenched relations.

One night, thinking that touch might let them sail free from the shoals where talking had steered them, she tried to pull him into an embrace. She was thinking also—how could she not?—that it was Thursday night, their usual night. But his muscles locked, and his arm reflexively jerked away from her. She pulled back to her side of the bed although he kissed her and apologized, promising soon, soon, soon. Since then, conversations had withered further, and Ned had spent more time reading medical journals in the living room, the tall stack by his feet testimony to the hours of work that always lay ahead of him.

For her part, Kate pulled out her neglected sewing machine and hemmed skirts that had gone nearly a year unfinished. She added new darts on her favorite dresses; in the to-do of the last month, she had lost weight, and the line of her hip fell away pleasingly under her hand. She started to wear mascara again, and after spending an unscheduled afternoon at the mall, brought home two new pairs of soft pumps. An old spirit was stirring in her, a sense of possibility, and she gave in to it, brushing her hair off her face to make her eyes seem bigger. Barb smiled, supposing, Kate knew, that the softened hair and shapely feet were meant to woo Ned back. But Kate didn't feel like a wooing wife; she felt abandoned and reckless.

Bill-o's furniture and oven door had finally arrived; he'd been slowly moving out of the parsonage ever since, taking three sports coats on one trip, a box of audio tapes the next. Kate could hardly stand to walk past the extra bedroom, which looked like a mouth growing more and more toothless. "You don't have to go," she told him the evening he was clearing out his shelf in the bathroom, packing shaving cream and dental floss into a shoebox. "We're not rushing you out. I'd hate for you to think that you're not welcome."

"He wants to sit up late and watch TV, then eat Doritos for breakfast," Mindy said from the bathroom floor, where she sat with her knees drawn up. Bill-o had to lean over her to get to his toothpaste. "Dinner, too."

"You have to get on with your own life," Bill-o said to Kate. "You've been more than generous."

"We can't help but get on with our own lives," Kate said. "What's the option?"

"Get on with somebody else's," Mindy said.

"I've imposed on you too long," he said.

"Then why quit now?" At least the question got him to stop packing. He looked at her with an exasperated expression.

"You've always been better to me than I deserve."

"I wouldn't say so."

"Come on, Kate. I'm the kid who should get coal in his Christmas stocking."

"You've got a new job and a new house. That's a long way from a sooty stocking."

"One of these days somebody's going to catch on and throw me out on my ear."

Mindy started to laugh. "Oh, you're humble. You're just the meekest thing. You wouldn't dream of asking to get anything for your little, humble self."

"Humility *means* having to ask," Kate said, but Mindy ignored her.

"'Oh, goodness, is this a house? For little me? Look! The cupboards don't close! The floors are uneven! How can I thank you enough?'"

"Mindy, that will do," Kate said.

"Don't forget about the windows. Half of them don't close," Bill-o said.

"And you stand in front of them and say, 'This is great! This is just what I deserve!'"

"When you get to be my age, you learn to take what you're given—" Bill-o said.

"—and be grateful," Mindy finished in chorus with him, then looked up through her eyelashes. "You are unbelievably full of crap."

"Would anybody care to tell me what you two are talking about?" Kate said.

Bill-o's smile looked abashed, which she appreciated. "The other day Mindy told me she didn't believe I was ever young. 'I was young, all right,' I told her. 'Mister Callow Youth.'"

"When were you talking?" Kate said. "I don't remember this."

"Sometimes I come back for lunch, just to get a break. You're at church, but Mindy's here."

"He said he had a flaming youth. So I told him to prove it," Mindy said.

"I drove a Corvair," he said. "Unsafe at any speed."

"Not even in the game," Mindy said.

"I dropped out of school."

"I guessed that," Kate said. An odd, humming nervelessness was ballooning inside of her; with mild interest, she noticed that her fingertips were white.

"I hung around the track, bummed cigarettes."

"Can you get any triter?" Mindy said, twisting to prop her head against the side of the tub. "Hot rods and dropouts. What '50s book did you get this stuff from?"

"Okay, Miss Expert On Today's Youth. Why don't you tell us—" Bill-o began, but Kate talked over him.

"He married me," she said flatly, and the other two stopped talking.

Mindy said, "I've been wanting to ask about that."

Which Kate knew. She'd been saving herself for this conversation, although she hadn't realized it before, and when she opened her mouth the words were right there waiting for her. "You want young? We were babies. We were every reason parents tell their kids not to rush into marriage. We didn't know how to write a check. Bill-o didn't understand how a lease works. My mother had to give him his own bar of soap; he wasn't very clean."

"She gets the picture, Kate," Bill-o said over Mindy's delighted snicker.

"He wanted to be entertained all the time; he didn't have two minutes' worth of patience. He could get bored with a job in a day. One time he quit from an auto parts store after three hours, even though he'd told the boss he'd stay three months. He wasn't much of a promise keeper."

"I've noticed that," Mindy said.

"Everybody makes mistakes," he said to Kate. "You've made a few."

"But it's yours that Mindy was asking about." Kate brushed the hair out of her eyes, which she hoped gleamed. Why should she strive to spare Bill-o's tender feelings? He was leaving. She said to Mindy, "Once he got paid a hundred dollars for a weekend job. We owed money to the electric company and two different credit cards, and he went out and bought a leather jacket. Black, with zippered pockets on the sleeves."

"What happened to it?" Mindy asked.

"I don't know." Kate looked at Bill-o, who leaned against the bathroom door. He stretched his neck gently, but his face was pale, his eyes glittering. Kate wet her lips. She'd thought—he'd all but promised her—that this face was gone forever. A smile she couldn't suppress crawled across her mouth. "What happened to that jacket, Bill-o?"

"I gave it away."

"Why?" Mindy asked. "It was the only good thing you had."

"He gave it to a girlfriend," Kate said.

"Is that what you think, Katy?"

"He must have been different then," Mindy said. "He doesn't give things away now. Not a crummy sweater. Not a ride home from work."

Kate laughed. "You've been angling for presents? From Bill-o? You might as well ask strangers on the street. This man doesn't give away the time of day. You should have come to me; I'd have told you." Kate kept her eyes on Bill-o. "He likes to keep girls begging."

"Only you, darlin'," he murmured.

"Is that what you did? Beg?" Mindy asked.

"That's how young I was," Kate said. "I thought people got things by asking over and over."

Mindy stretched out on the floor between them, her fingertips grazing the tub and her toes reaching into the hallway. Her sweatshirt hiked up on one side to show a narrow slice of skin, rosy as a peach. "What did you beg for?"

Kate waited to see if Bill-o would leap in with an answer. But he only flattened his shoulders against the door and watched her with tiny eyes. She decided to make him talk. "A pot," she said. "One good pot to make soup in. For ten years I cooked everything we ate in a piece of aluminum junk from a thrift store. The handle got hot and came off, and I had to use a piece of foil for a top. It was the first thing I threw away after he left."

Bill-o laughed. "What do you think that makes you, a hero? Kate O'Grady, valiantly cooking for ten years with a bad pot. Give her the Medal of Honor."

"I earned a medal," Kate said. "At least one."

"You know, it's interesting," he said. "I don't remember anything about a pot. It couldn't have been very high up on your begging agenda. I would have gotten you a pot. But your specialty was to ask for way more than I could afford. You wanted to break the bank."

"I'd love to see it," Mindy said. "What did she want, jewels? I'd love to see her begging for a diamond ring."

Although she was asking Bill-o, the girl's face was turned to Kate, who recognized her chance. Now she could remind Bill-o of the child he'd expected her to give up. With Mindy as witness, he would never be able to forget again. But even though the silence was waiting for her, she couldn't wrap her mouth around the words. That lost baby, after all these years, was hers alone, and precious. If she held it up to their view, the baby would vanish.

"I wanted you to stay," Kate said. "If that was more than you could afford, then you couldn't afford much."

Bill-o turned toward Mindy. "I'd look up from a TV show, and she'd be watching me. Come into the kitchen, see her staring at my glass of Coke. She looked at the way I tied my shoes."

"You should have gotten slip-ons," Mindy said.

"I was trying to see what the world looked like through your eyes. You kept secrets," Kate said.

"No surprise," Mindy said.

"You don't think so?" Kate said. "He kept surprising me. But then, my idea of marriage was different. I didn't go on dating other people. I didn't spend money on the sly. I wasn't planning to leave." She let the words keep pouring out, even though once she and Mindy were stuck in the house together, she would regret having tossed away her pride by the bale. The hell with it.

"I wasn't planning to leave, Kate. But you pushed me." He pressed his lips together and stared at the chipped tiles on the floor, his face an icon of wronged regret. Kate stared at him, wondering whether he imagined that those stark, desperate days had been her doing. But before she could sputter anything, Mindy sat up and said, "Bill-o, that is really weak."

She pointed at Kate. "Don't let him get away with that. 'I didn't want to leave, but you forced me.' It makes me want to puke. Admit that you guys split up because he wasn't making enough money or because he had girlfriends or whatever, but don't let him tell you that he walked out because you noticed how he tied his shoes. Jesus God."

Startled, Kate made a noise—part laugh. "There you go," she said to Bill-o.

"My goodness," he said to the girl. "Aren't we stern."

"Just don't play pathetic," she said. "I hate that." She hoisted herself up and walked out, and he went back to the medicine cabinet to sweep what remained—a pocket-sized tin of aspirin, a comb, an old tube of ointment—into his shoebox. When he looked up again, his face was unclouded. "I really can't thank you enough for letting me stay," he said.

"Yes, you can. You're right at the limit." She hoped she looked as unruffled as he did, but she saw her reflection in the medicine cabinet mirror—her face bright with anger, her hair high and dramatic. She didn't so much walk as prowl when she followed him to the front door. "Come back anytime."

"You'll be seeing plenty of me," he said.

She knew better than to believe this. The fabric of forgiveness between them had been a handful of cobwebs. Now that those frail strands had snapped, the old anguish seethed again, and he would slide away as he always had. Nothing had changed. Nothing.

She closed the door to the room she thought of as his, and threw her hairbrush onto the empty shelf in the bathroom. She kept the radio on day and night, and Mindy did not object, though Kate expected her to. She also didn't object when Kate made aromatic lamb stew, a recipe she had learned in the seminary that filled the house with smells of rosemary and garlic. Kate was full of energy; no sooner had she finished the stew than she rearranged the living-room furniture. But the house was too small! There was not an inch of carpet that Bill-o's feet hadn't crossed and re-crossed.

She tried staying longer at the church, where at least her battles were tangible. Three days went to drafting a cautious letter to her district superintendent and her bishop; she explained that weekly collections now were barely breaking a thousand dollars, and she wouldn't be able to pay the heating bill if the district didn't send help soon. "I hope you can see," she wrote in one version, "that this shortfall is not due to any extravagance here, but rather to our recent unforseeable circumstances."

Barb, coming in with coffee and reading over her shoulder, snorted. "Sanctuary Christians? They're about as unforseeable as a tank division."

"We don't see them now," Kate said.

"They're out there," Barb said. "Rumbling."

The trustees called a special meeting, which Kate attended with dread, expecting to be confronted with the long list of her failures. But once the rote opening business was concluded, members of the committee stood one at a time and said, "We want you to know we're behind you"; "Just let us know what you need"; "We support you."

Then Jeff Rankin blinked at her from behind his goggly eyeglasses and waited for her to say something he could support.

"Thank you," she said, her throat sharp with relief. "Next week we can draft a new budget and reassess the building plans. It's good to have hands to hold." She stared at her hands, folded on the table. She didn't have a parable, or motto, or apt, illuminating moment from the life of Christ. "Thank you," she said again. When she went back to her office after the meeting, she found a message pad and wrote, *We must learn to accept strength that is offered, whatever the source.* Dubious theology, worse advice.

Now, two nights later, she forced herself to stay in the office and work on a homily, although she had even less to say than usual. All she could manage were a few stiff phrases crowded in the margins, as if they hoped to slide off the page: Life's hardest lesson is patience, and Cast not the first stone. What about the second stone? Once rocks were whizzing by, why not join the fray? After an hour, she reached for *The Sermon Sourcebook,* which she'd been sent free.

She stared at a random page, hating it: Have you ever had the sense that God was far away? Have you ever prayed without getting an answer? Perhaps you've even gone through periods where you found it difficult to pray.

Oh, can it, Kate thought, pitching the book at the armchair. Those periods were her whole life. And she'd spent enough time talking to church members to know that she wasn't alone; anybody who'd ever tried it knew that prayer was awkward, uncertain, an exercise most often embarrassing. People who prayed found themselves pleading to empty air, and when they finished pleading, the air remained silent. What did the cretin who wrote this book think that faith was, if it didn't involve standing, every week, before a God whose hand none of them had seen and whose nature they could only hope was forgiving?

She should write something about babies and abortion; everyone in the congregation had heard about Ned's appearance at the rally, and everyone saw Mindy going in and out of the parsonage. More than likely, everyone was being contacted by Robert Efrim and asked whether their barren minister could possibly understand the wellsprings of life.

She tapped the page and preacher's words—"patience," "kindness" —presented themselves. Kate wrote them down, knowing that they were not inspired, or even particularly useful. She had always scorned ministers who preached in abstractions, but now here she was, piling mercy on top of patience, restraint on top of charity. Abstractions, at least, made dim sense, which facts did not.

Kate pondered some facts she knew. She knew a family whose daughter had died of septicemia from a self-induced abortion. She knew a woman not yet twenty-five who had five children, two of them brain damaged. She knew the savage joy that transformed the faces of new mothers. These facts shone in her mind like stars, each unaffected by the others. The only pattern Kate could see, a perception she could hardly work into a homily, was that life invited pain, and the invitation could not be refused. Pain awaited everyone, all the time, and if it didn't get a person from one side, it would get her from the other.

Endurance, she wrote. Compliance. Salvation. She lifted her pencil from the page—too late. After months—years!—of seeing through a glass darkly, she was seeing clearly, focusing on what was before her, rather than what she was supposed to see. Ned would be appalled. She put her hand back down.

Life = pain. Death = pain. Show me a day that doesn't hurt. She thought about Chuck Loller, who'd been a church member when she first came to Elite, and a widower. Chuck's sun and moon had aligned themselves around his sturdy, laughing son, his only child. That first fall, when Kate was still learning congregants' names, Chuck took the boy hunting. The boy strayed off to relieve himself, rustling in a nearby bush, and his father, thinking what he heard was a deer, wheeled and shot his child through the head. At the funeral even church members who hadn't known the boy were clutching one an-other's hands and moaning. Chuck held the arm of the pew beside him so tightly that Kate later saw where screws had been worked loose, although he didn't cry, or speak.

She went to call on him the next day, prepared with words about God's sure comfort in times of trial. After five minutes, Chuck got up and gestured her to follow him down the corridor to the boy's room. Two big cardboard boxes stood open on the floor, one holding toys and games wrapped in newspaper, the other half-full with neatly balled socks and folded pants. Chuck reached under the pillow on the bed and pulled out a flannel shirt, green at the hem, but stiff and brown across the collar. Kate, who was not usually troubled by blood, leaned softly against the boy's bureau.

"They kept his jacket at the hospital, but they gave me the rest of his clothes in a bag," Chuck said. "I washed his socks and his jeans, they're in the box, but should I wash this shirt? Doesn't it seem wrong? I ask everybody who comes, but nobody can tell me what I'm supposed to do."

His face was so scoured by grief and sleeplessness that it looked mild—even, horribly, trusting. Kate dropped her eyes for a moment, then patted his shoulder. "This is the hardest loss of all. There isn't a worse one."

"But what do I do about this shirt?" Chuck said. "I can't finish putting his things away until I know what to do."

"Give it to me," Kate said, and he obediently handed it over. She folded the shirt, forcing herself to smooth out the hardened cloth, then placed it on a sheet of newspaper and made a neat package. "I'll keep it for you," she said. "I'll keep it safe at the church. Whenever you want it, you know where it will be."

"You know," he said, letting his glance slide away from her, "when I'm by myself, it isn't the accident I think about or the hospital or the day he was born, it's that blessed shirt. That God-blessed shirt."

It was still in the cupboard in Kate's office, with Chuck's name printed on a tag. He would never come for it, which she had understood when she accepted it. Filled with sympathy for the shattered man, she'd thought she could take his burden away, but instead she'd taken it on—even now she never opened that cupboard, although she needed the space. She was tired of his burden, but no one would step forward to relieve her. Instead, new weight was added every day, new secrets for her to hold and problems for her to attend to: church members' crises of marriage or faith, troubled children, addled parents. Failing businesses, chronic depression, anxieties that rose from no clear source and lingered. Accidents. Disappointments. Betrayals. Love lost and unrecoverable. A ruptured church. A ruptured marriage. *Bill-o*, she wrote, and then underlined the name twice. *Bill-o*.

She had no idea what she would say to him, but she got in the car and drove, craning over the steering wheel to see in the gray light. Around town, streetlights were starting to come on, but not in the Hills of West Elite. There streets were shadowy and absolutely still; the quick tap of Kate's shoes echoed when she got out of the car. Already, seeing the dark windows in Bill-o's house, she felt disappointment starting to pool, and maybe for that reason she grew a little frantic, pressing the bell with one hand while she pounded the door with the other, talking, saying his name, slapping the wood with an open palm until her hand stung and Bill-o opened the door.

His shirt was half untucked and his feet bare; Kate said, "Good Lord. I woke you up."

"Yup."

"Can I come in?" When he hesitated, she let her voice take on an ugly slant. "Or are you entertaining?"

"Nobody here but us chickens," he said. Still, she had to push past him and reach out to turn on the overhead light. In the brightness, she saw his stiff new furniture, dusty green.

"It's early for bedtime and late for a nap," she said. "It didn't occur to me that you'd be asleep."

"It's a good time to sleep. You should try it."

"With you? No, thanks." Kate was trembling, and she turned away to sit in one of the new, low armchairs. The upholstery prickled through her nylons; she crossed her legs, then recrossed them. "I don't have all the time in the world. I have to get back and make supper."

"How are you serving up tonight's spinach?"

"In a cream sauce. What are you going to have, Doritos?"

"And canned bean dip," he said. "Want some?"

"Yes," she said. "I'm sick of setting a good example."

Bill-o sat down across from her. "I guess that's why you're here."

"Partly. Not exactly." She shifted her weight to the other hip; it was impossible to get comfortable on this chair. "I just want to know something. I'm trying to figure you out."

"I'm easy," he protested. "I'm clear as glass."

"Stained glass, maybe. So explain this to me. What did your big Damascus experience add up to? Where's the life change? Do you think a steady paycheck makes you Man of the Year? I keep looking at you, Bill-o, trying to find the big change, and I swear to God I can't find it."

He leaned back on the dull green sofa. "Well now, Katy, that hurts. It really does. Here I am sitting in my own house, living clean. I've gotten an invitation to join the Lions Club. And you tell me all you see is the same old bad boy."

She studied his face, searching for an ironic turn to his lips or the earnest, pained expression that would indicate hurt pride. But his mouth was steady, his eyes clear and unreadable. She leaned forward, squared her shoulders, and made a smile.

"I talk to a lot of people who are making fresh starts, turning over a new leaf. People starting over like to talk to their ministers. They lay out a plan of action. And what I see is that people are either too hard on themselves or too easy. The first ones live their new lives as if one misstep will bring on instant death. They're rigid." She paused. "That's how I used to be."

"Right," Bill-o said.

"The other ones want to go with the flow. If they don't lose that pound today, they can lose it tomorrow. If they're not actually having an affair, there's nothing wrong with flirting."

"But I guess you think there is something wrong," Bill-o said.

"When I run into them a year later, they get an embarrassed look and tell me a leopard can't change its spots. I could have told them. As long as a man's living in a house with two women, coming home for lunch with one and declaring his undying love to the other, he isn't living clean, and nobody's fooled."

"That's what you're here for? To complain that I had a few lunches with the girl?"

"It's pathetic to watch. She's pregnant and twenty years younger than you."

"Kate, this is beneath you."

"I'm just telling you what I see. Friends tell friends. You look pretty shabby."

A grin flickered at the corners of his mouth. "I thought I could count on you of all people to look beyond appearances," he said. "Here's a girl in trouble—lonely, scared. She needs someone to talk to when she eats her sandwich. I would have thought you'd thank me for taking on lunchroom duty."

"Called that one wrong, didn't you?" Kate said.

"Let's go back to those Category One people, the rigid ones, like you." Bill-o rested his elbows on his knees, and his smile sparkled. "Do you always succeed, step by step, straight up the hill to perfection?"

"Drinkers fall off the wagon right into a whiskey barrel. Dieters eat whole cakes. Couples facing bankruptcy go out and buy boats."

"What about the religious ones? The new true believers—what about them?" His voice was sweet, and she had the seductive sensation that she could feel his words moving in her mouth.

"They stop seeing things. They stop seeing meaning. God's hand isn't behind every snowfall or sunrise. Coincidences are just coincidences. A car can run a red light and nobody may get hurt, but not because armies of angels were banked around."

"Is that all? No pacts with the devil?"

"'Is that all?' That's everything. It's as if they lose a pair of eyes. They lose their view of a world where everything that happens is evidence of the good fight."

"Who wants to fight all the time?"

"They're stuck with a world where everything depends on them alone—their energy, their attention. If they want meaning, they have to create it." She dropped her voice. "It's exhausting."

"Everything's exhausting," Bill-o said.

"I know it," Kate said. "I'm tired. Aren't you?"

He reached across the narrow space between them and ran a light finger over her knuckles. Without realizing it, she had knotted her hands into fists. "Who are you planning to fight?" he asked.

She tried to answer him, but no words came. Instead, her mouth ajar, she held up her hands, still clenched, in front of his face. He pulled her out of her chair and onto the sofa beside him, then pressed her fists, one at a time, against his cheeks. She could feel his jaw shift under the doughy flesh as he pushed lightly first on one hand, then the other. "Better?" he asked, and Kate nodded.

"Let me tell you what I think," he said, continuing to press her hands into his face, so that she as much felt his words as heard them.

"I think we start out on our own paths, but our paths keep joining up with other people's. Separations are unnatural. Bonds exist. You can't just turn your back on them."

"A convenient philosophy for a man who's had many bonds," Kate said, and let her fists slide down over Bill-o's throat, then his chest, pressing hard enough to pull his smooth shirt taut. When she reached his waist, he caught her hands and held them there.

"You're going to hate yourself in the morning," he said.

"You haven't been listening. I hate myself now."

"We can still stop," he said. "Nothing has happened. You can trot right back to the parsonage in time to make spinach soup."

"Something has happened—a lot. Nothing looks the same to me anymore. Nothing makes sense. I might as well be seventeen again."

"Meaning what?"

"I want you to touch my breast," Kate said.

He laughed and ran the backs of his fingers lightly up her breast's heavy underside and over the nipple until her heart thundered so hard it hurt. "Pastor Kate," he said. "The right reverend."

"There's no pastor here. The pastor's taking a vacation."

"Oh, you're the pastor, all right. What else could you ever be?"

"A secretary. A grill girl." Kate guided Bill-o's fingers to the buttons on her blouse. "The elephant trainer at the zoo."

"You wouldn't last two days at the zoo," he said, working the buttons slowly. "Animals hate being preached to. But you like to preach. You were born to stand in a pulpit."

"I'm not in a pulpit now," she said hoarsely.

He reached behind her shoulder to loosen her blouse. "We always come back to what we are."

She meant to focus on his touch, the first she'd ever known, but her mind wouldn't be fixed in place; when she closed her eyes and lay back, all she could feel was the strange lightness of his hand, how his fingers brushed over her like feathers. She shuddered and tried to press him against her. Pushing her back with one hand, he pulled her skirt over her hips with the other.

"Turn out the light," she murmured.

"I want to see you. It's been a long time," he said, and Kate twisted her face away. His light hands made every ounce of her breasts' weight press against her lungs; her thighs twitched from the prickly, stiff upholstery.

"I always liked this, right here," he said, stroking the cup of her waist. "No telling how many nights I came home just for this."

"Don't talk," she mumbled.

"But honey, I want to talk. I've never been with an ex-wife before. It's an occasion." He pulled off his own shirt and quickly unbuttoned his pants. "Look at me. Open your eyes; look! Aren't memories coming back?"

"Yes," she said, lying. His thick torso sat so heavily on his pelvis that his hips looked squashed, a dense roll of flesh riding there. The hair on his broad thighs was dark but sparse, the skin beneath the hair, like that on his neck and arms and wide feet, flushed a dull red. As she watched him bend to pull off his shorts, she saw how the muscles across his back still flexed and shifted, but the skin above them was sluggish. Her boiling desire began to seep away, and shutting her eyes, she worked to pull it back.

No use—faster than she would have imagined possible, an unnerving detachment was sliding through her veins, as if she'd been given anesthesia. Bill-o kissed her throat, murmuring words she couldn't make out, and flicked his tongue over her ear so lightly that the touch seemed to dissolve, but the ear seemed not to be connected to her, and his voice was like something overheard from another room. They might have been characters in a predictable movie, and already she wanted to cut to the next scene. When he licked the inside of her thigh, she let out a cat-like cry, meaning to make him hurry. Instead he laughed and worked his tongue in tiny circles, each touch as light as a petal. She twisted and whimpered beneath him, finally grabbing his hips and pulling them down to hers.

"So greedy," Bill-o said.

"Yes."

"Are you sure? I don't have any protection."

Kate reached out to guide him into her, but Bill-o batted her hand off—"I know the way," he said. So she wrapped her legs around his damp back and pressed her hands against his neck. She had been the one who'd started this; she'd been the one to drive five miles with her fist jammed against her teeth. Now she raised her hips to his and closed her eyes, wishing she could find her way back to that blind hunger. Instead, immediately, an image swelled in her mind. While she bucked on the strange couch, undefended, with Bill-o's wet weight pushing into her, she saw a baby.

A fat baby, tumbling, clutching toes that were round as peas, it sailed over lakes and channels, spun in tidepools. Kate felt herself cupping protectively around it. While Bill-o murmured words and rank promises, she rocked under him and saw a baby riding like a rajah in her cushioned, perfumed chambers. Bill-o's sweat pooled between her breasts and ran off her belly. Together they crawled up the awful sofa, the rough upholstery scraping at Kate's skin, though she hardly noticed. The baby was clapping its tiny hands. Its mouth was an O.

"Oh yes, Katy, you've wanted this," Bill-o was saying. "How could you ever do without this? You wanted it and want it and want it." He was thudding against her, and Kate tried to adjust herself—"Come," she murmured, shaking her head. "Now." But he delayed, lightly bouncing his hips over hers and shimmying until the baby squealed with glee, bobbling like a round-bottomed nursery toy. Against her will, Kate felt a slow surge beginning, like a gathering-up of waters, and as it quickened she said "No!" Bill-o clutched her shoulders and bore down. Too fast the waters crested and shattered into white foam, and she saw the baby riding joyfully at the top of the wave. Then Bill-o himself made a wordless noise and pulled out of her, roaring, frantically working with his hand until he groaned and came across her breasts, already so wet she hardly felt him. He fell back at last, panting and slick, his mottled-red belly quivering. Kate closed her eyes, then opened them, but she wasn't quick enough—the baby was gone.

"Shh, now," Bill-o said, pulling her for a moment into his drenched arms and rocking, so that all she could smell were his sweat and crotch. "No need to cry. Stop now, Kate. Stop crying."

After a while she stood and reached for her clothes. She didn't open her mouth. Although he offered to get her a towel, she put her clothes on quickly, not looking at him, sprawled on the sofa and watching her. Her coat still unbuttoned, her mouth still a hard line, she left with his sticky semen gumming her blouse to her chest.

Eleven

The more distance Kate put between herself and Bill-o's house, the more powerfully her mind, suddenly ruthless, replayed images — Bill-o's thick, trembling legs, spongy belly, his hot skin damp as meat. Every time she shifted or moved her hand, his stinging scent flew up and clung to her face, until finally, even though the temperature outside was twenty degrees and dropping, she rolled down her window, leaned into the shocking air, and panted like a dog.

No words could describe what she had done, she thought, then caught herself. Certainly there were words, and lots of them: adultery, betrayal, fornication. Not to mention stupidity beyond belief. What no words could capture was the anguish that coiled through her, the sense of total, unrecoverable loss. Half-uttered words broke apart in her throat until she had to pull over and grind her hands against her face.

She rocked her forehead on the steering wheel, her eyes squeezed shut. Even so, she could see the mangled pieces of her life arrayed at her feet — two shattered marriages, a fraying ministry. She stared at them until she heard car wheels crunching behind her. A patrol car had pulled up, its blue light silently whirling, its officer approaching deferentially. "Reverend?"

She blinked and then recognized Dick Gibbs, who came to the church once a year to talk about F.O.P. fundraisers. Now he stared at her from behind his hat and padded jacket and scarf and heavy gloves. She leaned toward the gearshift in case he could catch Bill-o's smell.

"This is no night for open windows. And no place to pull over; you're lucky you haven't gotten sideswiped. Are you all right?"

"No," Kate said. "But I'm sorry about stopping in a bad place." Now that he had her attention, she realized that she'd put herself on the outside of a hard curve, where unruly honeysuckle sprawled into the shoulder, a place not even safe to walk. "I wasn't paying attention."

"I can see that. Why are you crying?"

"It has been a *heck* of a day."

"Reverends get those too, eh?"

Kate swallowed and tried to pull up some membrane of self-control. "I haven't been drinking," she said. "I know I showed bad judgment here—," she swallowed again, "—but it's just been a real, real bad day."

"Anything I'm going to be hearing about tomorrow?"

"I hope not."

"You know, people don't realize it, but police officers are trained to watch for all kinds of things. Unusual, erratic behaviors. It's called proactive policing. We want to stop the crime before it's committed."

"Are you giving me a warning?"

"I'm just telling you," he said. "It's the kind of thing people ought to know." He lingered another freezing, searching moment before he told her to watch her speed and strolled back to his own car. Her fingers stiff, Kate rolled up her window and pulled back onto the road. She drove precisely thirty-five miles an hour the rest of the way home. Dick followed her every inch and idled on the street outside the parsonage while she let herself into the dark front room and flicked the porch light to let him know she was safe.

Safe? She was as safe as the robbery victim after the jewels are gone. She was like the dazed survivors of car wrecks on the late news, who shook their heads and said, "I'm just surprised to be alive."

Mindy, off at work, for once had remembered to turn out the lights before she left. Now Kate turned on every light she could find, including the grimy bulb that buzzed and flickered over the stove. She wanted to shower—she wanted to work herself over with bleach and a Brillo pad—but first she needed to see what she was doing, and she lifted shades off the lamps in the living room and bedrooms.

Only after the parsonage was blaring with light did she take her shower—scrubbing at her breasts and between her legs until the skin felt raw, and then scrubbing more. But she couldn't scrub away the sense that the part of her she'd thought long dead—drowned, crucified, buried with a stake through its heart—was not only alive but hungry, and on the prowl. She fell asleep on the living room couch with her hair still wet and every light burning.

The knocking at the front door seemed to start only an instant later, but it hauled her out of sleep that was like a velvety well, and she groaned and pressed her face against the cushion. That would be Dick, operating on a policeman's proactive hunch. She was so prepared to meet him that when she saw Frank Speckler, Janelle's forty-year-old son, bracing himself against her doorframe, her mouth still said, "Dick." Frank didn't seem to hear.

"We need you. Mother's gone."

"Come inside," she said, stepping forward and pulling him gently into the house.

He started talking even before she helped him to sit down. Janelle had slipped away so fast that no one caught on. When Frank stopped by to see her before dinner, she was dozing. An hour later, when she was alone, her heart stopped. Everyone was caught off guard. "I know I shouldn't think this way, but I feel like she sneaked away from us. Even though I know she was never sneaky."

"Not her," Kate said.

"She was the best woman anybody ever knew. That's what one of the doctors said. He was crying."

"It's unusual for a doctor to cry. It's a tribute to your mother."

"I can't make anything register," he said. "My brain keeps shooting around. If Mother wasn't the sneaky one, who was? Who set me up?"

"You're hurting. You want to blame someone." Smooth with long use, the words spooled out of her mouth. Privately, Kate thought he was asking a fair question.

"The doctors told us that by the end she wouldn't recognize her own family, so I figured we'd all know when the end was coming. We could get ready. But she was never unconscious a minute. It was still sudden. She might as well have been hit by a truck."

"It seems unfair."

"I'm not supposed to think like this," he said, blinking and shaking his narrow head as if he could throw the thoughts off. "Mother would hate it. I'm not even sad! I just keep feeling like I'm forgetting something."

"You're shocked," Kate said. "Reactions haven't set in yet." The sadness would come—more of it than he wanted. "I'm so sorry, Frank. I loved your mother."

"I wasn't asking for miracles. I knew she was going to die. But it never occurred to me I wouldn't even get a chance to say good-bye."

"It doesn't seem like much to ask," she said softly, looking at the man's ravaged face and longing for real comfort.

"You need to help me with this. I've gone for a long time counting on the idea that comfort would come when I needed it. But I'm high and dry here, Reverend. Please." He stared at her as best he could manage, his red-webbed eyes wavering and blinking, and she realized that all the light in the room was hurting him, so she reached toward the table lamp beside her and turned it off.

"Suffering's the thing no one understands," she said, feeling as if she were offering a drowning man a rotten life preserver. Frank was nodding, his mouth slightly open. She could see that he thought her words were nothing but preamble; any moment he expected her to move on to the good news. He thought she had some explanation he could put on like a pair of glasses, and it would show how there was goodness in the fact that he hadn't even been able to kiss his mother good-bye. A fresh wave of self-contempt swept through her.

"—Suffering," Frank prompted.

"And this is the greatest suffering of all. Your comfort and security gone."

"Things keep coming back to me," he said, looking at his reflection in the black window. "When she got sick the first time, I asked her what I could do, and she said she wanted to see me every day. I didn't have to stick around—she just wanted to lay eyes on me. Not much to ask. But I didn't go. She was in the hospital for so long; sometimes I'd let a week go by, and I was just at home watching reruns. Then I'd go in and she'd say, 'Nice to see you,' and I'd get so mad I'd let another week go by."

"You were scared," Kate said.

"I was selfish," he corrected her. "And mean. That's why I didn't get to say good-bye, isn't it? I didn't go to see her when she asked me. So I got what was coming to me."

"No, Frank," she said, appalled.

"That at least makes sense," he said, nodding fiercely. "I brought this on myself."

"Punishments don't work this way."

"It adds up," he said. "It makes sense. We get what we deserve."

"You've got to stop. I know you're looking for an explanation, but there isn't an explanation—at least not the kind you think." She talked faster. He was staring at his shoes in the way people did just before they got up to leave.

She said, "The whole point is that we *don't* get what we deserve. What we deserve is unspeakable. What we deserve is to be brought to our knees, and not in worship, either. But we're promised that we'll get better than we deserve. Our job is to believe in the promise." Leaning across the coffee table toward him, she could see how he kept twitching, as if she were delivering tiny blows.

He cleared his throat. "Just like that?" He snapped his fingers. "Just believe?"

"I didn't say it was easy."

"Can you do it?"

"Sometimes."

He didn't say anything. Watching him, Kate ransacked her brain, trying to come up with some new promise. "All right," he said finally.

"Do you see?"

"I'm worn out. Listen, people are meeting at my sister's house."

"I'll come."

"Things need arranging."

"I'll take care of them," she said, standing and resting her hand on his shoulder. The smile that he gave her in return was faint, but unexpectedly kind.

"Thank you for talking to me. It helps. You see things straight," he said.

"The court is still out on that," she said after he was too far away to hear.

Although she would have liked to sit down and mourn Janelle herself, she changed her clothes, and left a note for Ned. A death in the church always rearranged her life. Visits needed to be made to the family, and then the viewing, the funeral, the burial, the ham sandwiches and potato salad and pie provided by the United Methodist Women at the fellowship hall. The words of comfort offered again and again, never enough.

She shook hands with Janelle's many family members, who arrived in carloads from Paducah and Louisville; she embraced the women who turned their streaked faces to her. One of Janelle's sisters told Kate, "She was the best of us all. She was a purely sweet woman. She's in heaven now?"

"If anyone's in heaven, Janelle is there," Kate said. The line gave her solace, so she repeated it for two of the nephews.

Janelle's sister, saying Kate was like kin, asked her to stay with them, and Kate did so gratefully. The family's fond, wandering stories held her attention and prevented unsettling words from crowding into her mouth; she smiled when one of the nephews told how Janelle had presented him with store-bought cupcakes on a plate when he came for a visit. No one else ever let him eat store cakes, and for years he thought it had been a special treat. Not until after he was married did Janelle confess that she'd gotten them out of desperation; three batches of her own had gone wrong. She was a terrible cook, the women agreed, wiping their eyes. Her cakes collapsed and her canning jars didn't seal; out of six girls, she was the only one who couldn't learn her way around a kitchen. Still, the boys had been crazy for her.

"Really?" Kate said. "She never told me she was a belle."

"She was as sweet as sugar," one of the sisters said. "You can buy cupcakes at the store, but where are you going to buy a nature like that?"

"God doesn't make but a few of those," another sister said.

Kate nodded, thinking that the lack of Janelles in the world was another example of a divine nature that revealed itself as stingy and malicious to anyone who bothered to look. She leaned forward and asked to hear more about Janelle's bad cooking.

But the new suspicions closed in on her as soon as she left Janelle's family. In bed that night she thought indignantly about Frank, who had deserved one last visit to his mother. Just as Janelle had deserved a better death, not one that force-marched her through months of spiraling pain and left her eyes stained a faint, frivolous yellow. And Kate herself deserved stoning, disfigurement, dismissal and disgrace. But none of them received what they deserved.

Her eyes aching and her mouth filled with the taste of clay, she gave up trying to sleep, turned on a low light and tiptoed to the bookcase. A full shelf was devoted to crises of faith, books written to help pastors counsel church members whose belief in God was splintering. *The Dark Night, Questioning Faith, Help Thou Mine Unbelief.* They were the wrong books. Kate had no trouble believing. Daily deepened her intimacy with a God who allowed hearts to be broken, who permitted hideous collisions of action and intent, who brought back Bill-o and took Janelle. What she needed was a book to teach her to believe with less deep, dreadful assurance. She took down a famously dull volume on church history and read thirty pages, but retained none of them.

Because she didn't trust the workings of her brain or the savage flex of her heart, she used a standard eulogy at the funeral two days later, studding the sermon with modest references to the Girls' Club picnics Janelle had sponsored and her annual Christmas stockings for orphans. "In her long years of suffering, she didn't complain," Kate said. "Her gentle nature inspired everyone who knew her." Then she sped right on to the resurrection and the life, before anyone could ask her how this sweet-natured woman had merited such suffering.

Kate lingered at the back of the church after the coffin was carried out; she always made sure that every mourner had a ride. As she struggled to pull her coat over her robe, Ned approached her. He was wearing his best tie and a somber look. "May I ride with you?" he asked.

"Where did you come from?"

"The hospital, just a few minutes ago. Do you have room in your car?"

"Of course. Janelle would be pleased to see you here."

"She—" he began, then shook his head. "Never mind. "Let's go." Silently, they crossed the parking lot, and only after Kate pulled out of the driveway did Ned add, "I wish I could have heard your eulogy. People were talking about it; you comforted them."

"I hope so. I kept thinking I wasn't doing Janelle justice." And then, not wanting to sound churlish, "Thanks."

"No one expected her to go so fast. She didn't make it past the halfway point on her Masterpiece Theatre show."

"I was wondering about that."

"I couldn't get it off my mind," Ned said—imagining, Kate supposed, Janelle and a few other interested souls gathered around the celestial TV set for the rest of the series. When he spoke again, his voice was soft. "You look good. I haven't seen much of you lately. You've been busy, I know."

She glanced at him, but his expression was smooth. If he meant to test her, his face gave no clue. She said, "I've been spending time with Janelle's family. They're kind people. They miss her. I'm going to miss her."

"Me too." He reached across the seat and rested his hand on her wrist, a touch that should have burned her guilty flesh like a brand. But it was only Ned's hand, after all, cool and dry, and he lifted it after a moment. "I've hardly had a minute to think about Janelle. Things at the office have been a mess. I'll have to go straight back after the burial—appointments right through."

"So you won't be home for dinner again?"

"I thought maybe we could go out tomorrow. We haven't been to the Coachlight for a while. I made a reservation."

"You're asking me on a date?"

"I thought it might be nice."

Kate focused on the road. She wished she could talk about icy patches or resurfacing, but everything became a metaphor. "What about Mindy?"

"She can't expect you to make her dinner every night," he said. "I'm worried about you. It can't be easy, living with another woman's pregnancy."

"It could be worse. At least she's impressed with the importance of her condition."

"I hate to see her preening around, lording it over you."

"Well, Ned. Thank you for your concern."

"Naturally I'm concerned. You're my wife."

"You sound like you're getting used to the idea."

"I am," Ned said.

Fear shot through her like pain, and along with it, a desire to confess, which she knew was wrongly timed, weak, panicky. He said, "I'm remembering, figuring out who we are. We've drifted away from ourselves, Kate. We're doing things we never meant to do."

"Like what?"

"We don't recycle." He waited. "That's a joke."

"I know." They did recycle, most of the time.

"We've lost our way to each other. So why don't we start a few steps back? Get re-acquainted. How do you do; I'm Ned Gussey."

He held his hand out and she stared for a moment before she realized he actually expected her to take it. The light touch usually came more easily to him than this, and she wanted to both protect him and give him a shove. She shook his hand. "I'm Kate, Kate, big slug bait." Her father's old chant.

"Too pretty for slug bait."

"Ned, honey—stop. You don't even like me right now, do you?"

"I don't know you."

"I know how that feels." She brought the car to a soft stop right at the cemetery entrance. "I wish," she said, "I truly wish we had one thing in our lives we could actually hold onto. Just one thing to hold us safe. I am tired of closing my hands on water."

When he asked, "How can a minister say such a thing?" his voice sounded small, as if he were speaking to her from another room.

"I don't know." She saw Frank and one of his sisters start to pick their way down the cemetery driveway as they gestured and called to her. She waved back and held up her hand, meaning to indicate one minute, but they kept coming.

"We can't just sit here," Ned said. "Are you all right to do this?"

"Sure. They taught us in reverend school: It doesn't matter how a person feels, it only matters what a person does. You could have taught a seminar in the subject." She squeezed his hand, then drove to pick up Frank and his sister, who were halfway down the driveway. From the back seat, they directed her to the gravesite. There the mourners were gathered and waiting, their hands jammed into their pockets for warmth, and they looked grateful at her approach, gratitude that Kate intended to live up to.

❧

She began trembling halfway through the burial. At first she thought she was merely cold. Her hands shook while she held the prayer book, but everyone's hands shook in that frozen air. Wind sliced across the hillside, and the ground was so icy that her feet, in delicate-soled black pumps, throbbed. Even when she was home that night, wrapped in her heavy bathrobe and tucked into a corner of the couch, the quivering made her teeth knock together.

Kate toured the TV channels, skimming past a racy nighttime drama and two sitcoms. She paused at what might have been Janelle's show, a scene of two attractive women trading moody, clipped accusations, but the memory of Janelle made her eyes sting again, and she pressed the channel button blindly, landing at a public-access debate about property taxes. "All these so-called politicians say we won't be able to afford trash pickup and streetlights," a woman was grousing. "These people all know each other, and they know where the real money is. The real issue is about information: They have it, and we don't. And there isn't a thing we can do."

"Not one thing," Kate agreed. Without a funeral to distract her, the understanding that had been trying to force itself on her all afternoon rose up unfettered. Not only had she betrayed Ned like a streetcorner whore, not only had Bill-o made her skin shimmer as if he were creating it anew, but Ned might already know every detail.

The scene played like something out of M-G-M: Bill-o, his face cloaked in histrionic penitence, dropping by Ned's office to share a piece of information; Ned nodding, balancing a pencil between his fingers. Quietly, all by himself, he would decide that the act was over and forgiven, for reasons that he would believe were charitable. If she tried to tell him that charity wasn't secretive, he would look at her with hurt bafflement, the look he always wore when the world misinterpreted his many good intentions. Sometimes remembering that look was enough to annoy her, but not now.

Closing her eyes, she thought of her hours with tear-stained, desperate church members. "Is the affair over?" she had asked. Now she flinched as she had seen them flinch. The question proceeded from a faulty premise; the affair couldn't be over. She and Bill-o were wrapped by cords she had tried to sever, snap, gnaw through, and every time she'd thought herself free, she found herself bound more tightly. Even if she never saw him again, he would always be the man to whom she had given her life twice, once in ignorance, once in despair. She drove a fist into the couch and then, embarrassed, smoothed out the dent.

After a while the trembling slowed, and she stood up. In the kitchen sat half a pot of cold coffee, left over from the morning, not too burned. She set it in the microwave and glanced at the table, where she had left the notes that had sent her kiting across Elite. *Show me a day that doesn't hurt.* She ripped the page free and buried it deep in the garbage, under the cottage cheese. Then she picked up a pencil and wrote on a clean page: *We try to walk, but we only have a dim ray of light, a pinprick. Sometimes even that tiny light goes out, and we stumble. We walk into dead ends and blind alleys, but God must expect that. God has watched us walk in the dark, and knows how badly we do it. If God didn't expect us to walk into walls, we'd have light all the time.*

By midnight she had fifteen pages, far more than she would be able to use, and her pencil continued to hurry over the lines. The more she wrote, the more words rose up, phrases rounded and balanced, as if they had long been rehearsing themselves. She remembered Frank Speckler's frightened, yearning face, a face that needed to hear these words, and wrote faster, though he missed church more often than he came.

She finally went to bed after one o'clock and slept dreamlessly, awakening like a TV housewife—energetic, her hair barely mussed. Mindy dragged herself into the kitchen to watch Kate slot the fold-away mattress into the sofa frame and plump the throw pillows. "You're very peppy."

"There's a lot to be done. Time's a-wasting."

"I hardly slept all night. I finally dropped off around dawn, and then I heard you out here making coffee."

Kate tossed the pillows onto the couch. "Mindy, believe it or not, I try to accommodate you. But this is actually my house, and every day I have things to do."

Mindy drifted into the kitchen, poured herself coffee and loaded it with milk, then dipped her finger into the cup and sucked on it. "It was easier when Mr. O'Grady was here," she said. "I wish he'd come back."

"He won't," Kate said.

"I thought he was your friend."

"Since you're already up, I'll go ahead and take my shower."

She thought she heard sounds while she was scrubbing her hair—slammed doors, the hard *whap* of a book hitting a wall, but her ears were full of water, and once she turned the shower off, the house was still. She pulled on a trim skirt and blouse and hurried to the office, where she could type up her notes. If she was lucky she'd be able to finish before she had to leave for the district meeting in Elletsville, an hour and a half north.

But the notes took longer than she'd hoped, and her ideas no longer seemed so clear, although she supposed they would be clear enough. At 10:45, already late to get to the noon meeting, she stood up and brushed her ankle against the rough edge of the desk; a run streaked up to her thigh. Muttering, she hurried back to the parsonage, her steps crunching on the unraked leaves, and let herself in the back door. She hoped Mindy wouldn't be in the bathroom, where Kate stored her extra nylons.

She was in luck, if she wanted to call it that. Mindy was sitting with Bill-o on the couch. Their talk stopped and they swiveled their heads to watch Kate come in. She thought of deer with their wary, liquid eyes.

"What are you doing here?" Kate said to Bill-o.

Mindy giggled. "See?"

"Let me guess," Kate said. "I'm the Gestapo."

"Not that bad," Bill-o said. "The D.A., maybe." Kate wondered if he had looked so flushed before he heard her key in the lock. She could feel the blood in her own face. Had Mindy not been in the room, Kate would have suggested that Bill-o move to a chair. Ned sat on that couch every night.

"I just came over to visit," Bill-o was saying. "We were talking about Mindy's baby."

"Make any decisions?" From under the corner of the couch poked something white, probably a napkin gone astray. Kate automatically pulled it out, then looked at what she had: panties, still warm. The girl's giggle shot around the room. "I guess not," Kate said.

"I don't think I need to hear what comes next," Mindy said. Kate handed her the panties and said, "Go get dressed." The girl did not; she went as far as the bathroom and closed the door.

"Aren't you even embarrassed?" Kate said to Bill-o. How could she not have recognized that moist reddening across his mouth, that sheen on his cheeks? She must be some special, willful kind of idiot. "Or is this where you tell me it's not what I think?"

"What do you think?"

"That you're punishing me. You haven't lost the knack."

"Brace yourself, Kate. This isn't about you." His face glistened. Kate could hardly bare to look. "I was getting somewhere in my life," he said, "making headway. Now I'm at the bottom of the hill again. And you're still the only one I can tell who will understand."

"Nope. I don't understand."

"You have to. You're standing here with me."

She was aware of anger filling up a broad space in her brain, some place locked away. She wondered what would turn the lock. "Mine is a different hill. It's covered with broken glass. I don't know what yours is covered with."

"Oil," he said. "I keep sliding down."

"And then you slip over to me and ask to be forgiven."

"Who else would I ask?"

Pressure inched across the back of Kate's skull. In a moment it would be real pain. "Don't ask me anymore. And please—don't talk anymore about all the headway you made."

"Do you think that I'm proud of myself?" he said.

"No. But I don't think how you feel makes any difference."

"Then what does make a difference?"

"Search me."

He dampened his full lips; she could see him choosing his words. "You were the one who started this. You owe me a little more."

"I didn't start this." She gestured down the hallway.

"You don't think so?" His face, which might have looked mocking, wore a searching look—soulful, a word Kate resisted. "Has being a minister made you start fooling yourself, or are you just forgetful? The only thing that beats getting to the top of the mountain is falling off of it again."

"I'd rather stay at the top. I'd rather glimpse the top, just once."

"Do what you want. But you're the one who taught me. The point of going up is to zip back down. It's what we're made to do. The biggest lesson you ever taught me, but a good one."

For an instant her brain seemed to be sheeted in white, and she opened and closed her mouth soundlessly. Perhaps this was how prison escapees felt, frozen in a searchlight, immobilized even though they were frantic to scurry into safe darkness. When she managed to speak, her voice was barely audible. "So what comes next?"

"Start climbing again."

"Just like that."

"Where else is there to go, once you hit bottom? You push off and start again."

She nodded. "Do your climbing outside of my house. And don't see Mindy anymore."

"Kate, when are you going to learn to see what's right in front of you?"

"I wish I knew." She braced herself beside the bookcase until she couldn't hear his footsteps crunching through the frost-covered leaves. Then she took a quavering breath. The living room smelled like Mindy's perfume, as sugary as bubble gum. Kate unlatched the window and let the hard air tumble in.

In the bathroom Mindy lay curled beside the toilet, her forehead pressed against the cool ceramic base. Kate silently helped her up, rinsed out a washcloth and wiped the girl's lips and damp forehead.

"Did he call your name when he came to the door?" Kate asked, keeping tight control of her tone. Now more than ever, she had to do right by the girl. Mindy shook her head. "Did he say he was looking for me? Did he make you think it was all right to let him in?"

Mindy would only shake her head. "You need to tell me," Kate said. "I have to know what happened. I may have to call the police."

"I wanted to let him in."

"You have to show some judgment. You've got enough problems on your hands, and Bill-o isn't going to be the one to help you."

"I needed to see him."

"He can make a person believe anything. But he won't help you, no matter what he says."

Mindy's whole face twisted. Kate hadn't known a face could do that. "He was right all along; you don't see what's smack in front of you. Whose baby do you think this is?"

"Jesus," Kate said slowly. "Jesus, Jesus Christ." She sat down hard and stared at the back of Mindy's head for a long time.

In a voice that was rough and ecstatic, Mindy started talking. "We've known each other for almost a year. When he was still a rep for NaturWise he'd come by the Ben Franklin to check stock. After the first few months he'd wait until I was off work. We'd get coffee. He called me at the store when he was on the road. We spent hours just talking. You don't believe that, do you?"

"As a matter of fact, I do. He likes to talk."

"It wasn't some sordid thing," Mindy said, a quiver entering her words. "We love each other."

Kate flattened her hands against the impulse to slap the whine out of the girl's voice. Mindy pointed her finger at Kate. "I only came here because there was nowhere else. Do you think I don't know about you? When you leave the house with your collar on, I have to close my eyes to keep from laughing. Don't think you can run off now and tell my family anything. I can tell them a few things, too. I won't have to say much; people already have their doubts about you."

Words slipped into Kate's mouth like wine. "You're nineteen years old. You're knocked up. You don't have a husband. You don't have a decent job. Honey, you don't have jack."

"I have an interesting story to tell about my pastor."

"You think they'll believe it? From the girl who went for the first traveling salesman who came along?"

"Then I'll have Bill-o tell them. Or don't you think they'll believe him, either?"

"Yes, they will," Kate said slowly, not sure yet where she was going. "Everyone always believes Bill-o."

Still shaky but wearing a sharp, triumphant smile, Mindy pulled herself to her feet. "You can expect to start seeing more of him around here. And you'd better just leave us alone. If you want to keep your job." She leaned toward the mirror for a moment, tracing the line of her cheekbone with a light finger. Kate stood up too.

"No," she said.

"You don't have any choice. I'll tell them the truth, or have Bill-o do it."

"You can tell people," Kate said. "Maybe you should. But I'm not going to let this parsonage become some kind of safe haven for you and Bill-o because I'm afraid of what you might tell people."

"What are you going to do when you get thrown out of your church?"

"I know how to find jobs. Maybe I'll get a job in a plant store. Maybe I can get on at the NaturWise."

Mindy's head rocked back as if Kate had slapped her. "You know what Bill-o says about you? He says that every place a woman should be soft you're hard as sheet metal."

"He used to tell me that, too," Kate said. With elaborate politeness, she stepped into the hall. But the girl hesitated, then hunched over in a single, absurd motion, covering her face with her hands. "You're no actress," Kate said. "And you know where the phone is. Start calling."

"I'd leave here if I could," Mindy said from behind her hands. "I'd be gone already. But I'm trapped."

"Go home," Kate said. "Tell your family."

"I'd never see Bill-o again."

"Doesn't that tell you anything? Good grief, this is the oldest game in the book. He may be coming around now, but I can promise that you won't see him after your baby is born. *Promise.*"

"I thought you believed in people changing and making new starts."

"I thought I did too," Kate said. "And here's the thing, Mindy, here's the absolute kicker—I thought Bill-o was proof that people could change. I sat there while he told me about how he wanted a new, clean life, and I believed him. I rejoiced. All he had to say was 'new life' and there I was, cheering him on like a pom-pom girl."

"This is a new life," Mindy whispered, cupping her hand over her flat belly.

"Then the best thing you can do for it is to keep it away from Bill-o. Get out of Elite. Go to Australia and hope that you don't ever meet another man who says he wants to hear you talk."

"You didn't."

"And look where I wound up—providing a love nest for a man who walked out on me better than ten years ago. But he won't walk through my door again. And it's time for you to go home."

"I can't."

"That's your choice."

Mindy dropped her hands and trained her eyes on the baseboard. "Look, I'm sorry I said all those things. I'm sorry I threatened you. I wouldn't really tell anybody. I get so tangled up; Bill-o says things and they stick in my head until I can't remember whether they're my ideas or his. I'm glad you've been letting me stay here—I mean, I'm grateful. Can't I have another chance? I need a chance. Please."

The girl's voice was reedy and plaintive, so immature Kate wanted to snap that she had as much business bearing a baby as she did bearing a kangaroo. Strumpet, slut—the girl had deceived her at every turn. No one, not even the endlessly forgiving Ned Gussey, would blame Kate for setting her out on the sidewalk. Bill-o's little bit on the side. And then the galling follow-up thought: Kate's lover's little bit on the side.

She dug her fingernails into her palms and gazed at Mindy, who resembled Kate in no way. Nevertheless, the two of them made up a sorority—they were hazed and pledged, bound to each other. Never would Kate be able to feel lonely again, now that she had a sister who knew her hopes and hungers. As Kate knew Mindy's. Already, when Mindy needed a second chance, she knew exactly whom to ask.

The air between Kate and the girl seemed to vibrate. Kate took her time. "Clean your room," she finally said. "The parsonage is getting filthy. It would be nice if you vacuumed. And turn down your radio when you play it. These walls are very thin."

She turned away at Mindy's sour thanks and listened to the girl's flat-footed exit from the bathroom. Going to the sink, she wet a washcloth and scrubbed first the scummy sink, then the mirror—rubbing at the traces of water and toothpaste until the shining glass was clean.

Twelve

She waited in the bathroom, leaning close to the clean mirror to pluck her eyebrows while Mindy opened and slammed drawers, jangled clothes hangers, and finally heaved the front door open and banged it shut behind her. Kate didn't know whether the girl was going to work or to see Bill-o, but it didn't matter. Mindy was nailed to Bill-o now, and anything Kate said or did would only nail them tighter. She dried her hands on a washcloth, then tried to rip it in half. The cloth was sturdily woven and wouldn't give.

In ten minutes the meeting in Elletsville was scheduled to start; if Kate hurried, she could arrive by the time things were breaking up. She looked at her blasted expression in the mirror. To her own eyes, nothing about her looked as hard as sheet metal. All her eyes could see was flesh. Tender, still lightly pink, longing to be touched. *Trapped,* Mindy had said, but she was too young to understand the meaning of the word.

From the front porch, Kate heard cautious footsteps and a low cough. She palmed back her hair and went to the door, but there was no knock, and when she opened the door no one waited; only footprints shone in the frosty grass. A brown velvet ring box rested on the mat, and she picked it up, supposing it was meant for Mindy and held a cheap ring or—who knew?—an expensive one. But when she opened the box, she found a plastic baby doll, moon colored, both of its fragile arms broken off, as perfect a symbol for impotence as Kate had ever seen.

Snapping the box shut, she ran out onto the grass and strained to see up and down the street. Nothing moved; at midmorning, midweek, the quiet sidewalks looked as if they had been sucked clean. Nevertheless, she strode to the furthest part of the yard and craned around the yew hedges, clenching the ring box, trying her best to crush it. She would not allow herself to be terrorized by a pack of wheedling bullies who strewed plastic babies as if babies had only one meaning.

"What are you doing out here?" Barb called, picking her way over from the church. "You're supposed to be in Elletsville. The secretary at the meeting called, hoping you hadn't been in a car wreck, ha-ha."

"Ha-ha." Kate held out the ring box. "This was delivered to the parsonage."

Barb looked at the doll, and her features tightened. "Just when you thought it was safe to go outside."

"Left on the front step like a love offering. The box was a nice touch, don't you think? For a second there I thought I had a swain."

"Have you called the police?"

Kate shook her head. "I ran out here as soon as I heard somebody at the door. Whoever left it couldn't have gotten far."

"Get on the horn, then. If you hurry, the police might be able to do something."

"I'd rather handle this one myself. Robert Efrim's bound to sneak back around, see how his gift went over. I'm in the mood to have a conversation."

"Well, you can't wait out here in your shirtsleeves. At least go inside and get a coat."

But Kate, invigorated by the icy air scraping at her throat and hands, wouldn't move. Her blood seemed to surge with new purpose. "Do you suppose this is some kind of fundamentalist voodoo?" she said, opening the ring box again to see the featureless face and flat torso, a machine-made ridge ran along the doll's side. "Is Robert Efrim sending me a warning?"

"I wouldn't be surprised if the thing has 666 microscopically engraved on its forehead. He's letting you know what he thinks of you."

"Like I needed to be told." Kate studied the doll. Armless, and with misshapen legs pointing away from each other, it looked like pictures of a mangled fetus, the kind of gruesome picture that some protesters blew up to poster size and carried in demonstrations. "I really don't think I've earned this."

"They want to scare you," Barb said. "They're trying to gain your immortal soul."

"They can have that for a bargain rate."

"I wish you would call the police. You can't let this kind of thing go without a response."

"You're right." Kate dropped the box in her pocket. "it's time for a response. Robert Efrim has called on me; it's my turn to call on him."

"The *police*," Barb said. "Responding is their job."

"This harassment is spiritual, not criminal," Kate said, already hustling back toward the parsonage for her coat and keys, while Barb trailed behind her and told her for God's sake, to watch her back. Kate pulled her coat on without bothering to button it and backed the car out without running the engine to warm up. Only one state road out of town headed west, straight downhill, and when she turned onto it, she mashed the accelerator.

She shot past empty fields littered with broken, brown tassels and shucks of feed corn, past maples and oaks patchy with withered leaves. Zooming on the tight roads at twenty miles an hour over the limit felt better than anything she'd done in weeks, and she wondered whether Robert Efrim knew anything about the raucous pleasure of driving fast. She drove faster. Of course he did.

If he was true to form, he also knew she was on her way right now. As soon as he saw her he would start in on the parable of the lost sheep, and for once Kate could be ready. "Threatening behavior," she said aloud. "Terrorist tactics. Intimidation." She imagined herself standing in the pulpit of his church, denouncing him who stood wordless and shamed. The scene was too much to hope for, but Kate didn't let that fact stop her from relishing the scuff of leather as his parishioners turned to leave.

After twenty miles, the hills gave out, collapsing into a flat plain that reached to the gray horizon. Even in November, this land looked better than the land around Elite. Here soil lay in light ridges instead of packing into yellowish, asphalt-hard troughs. Lines left by the combines ran as straight as comb marks through wet hair and never encountered a single stone or root. Plants thrived here, Kate thought absently. Crops produced record-breaking yields; even a small garden center would be hard pressed to keep up with demand. If she'd been Bill-o, she would have requested a site down here instead of Elite.

No sooner had she conceived the thought than she knew Bill-o hadn't asked for Elite. He'd been given it. Elite was a lousy location, a money pit, a dump where management wouldn't want to bury its best talent. She was surprised she had taken so long to catch on. But she was slow to catch on to everything with Bill-o, who believed that she was the one to pull him downhill. There was not one word she could say to refute him.

She drove more slowly, noting which fields had been planted with winter rye to add nitrogen to the soil and which had been just recently cleared. On some of the farms, the dark dirt looked rich enough to eat, and Kate fought a mild urge to pull over and have a taste. She let her speed drop further and made out the Sanctuary Christian Church sign from half a mile away.

The sign, tall and wooden, its raised letters outlined in red, looked more substantial than the church at the end of the drive, a vinyl-clad structure the size of a triple-wide trailer. It perched on the site as if it had been dropped there, without a single potted flower or shrub to soften its glaring lines. Kate supposed the starkness was meant as anticipation of the end times—if the final trump was about to sound, there wasn't much point in landscaping.

As she got out of the car, two women stepped from the church to greet her; one of them wore a plain brown dress and tennis shoes. Kate recognized the other woman as Mrs. Efrim, who had stood in Kate's yard and pointed out every hardship faced by a woman in ministry. Now, as then, her mass of silvery-blond hair was piled in a trembling mound, making her head look backlit and enormous.

She clasped Kate's hand between both of hers.

"Welcome. Welcome! At last."

"Thank you," Kate said. "I'd like to discuss a few things. Is Robert Efrim in?"

"You're the answer to our prayers! We prayed for this day, when you'd come," said the other woman, the delight in her voice so genuine that Kate stepped back.

"Perhaps not this specific day," she said.

"Oh yes," the blond woman said. "Mr. Efrim and I have held you up before the Lord.""

"Very kind," Kate said. "But I haven't come to worship. Mr. Efrim —is he in?"

"Come into our house," said the other woman, who wore her thin brown hair pulled back in a pink barrette. A tooth was missing from the right side of her mouth, and when she held out her hand, Kate smelled the chalky odor of cigarettes. "It's warm in the house; we have tea. Won't you have tea with us? Please?" She smiled, covering the gap in her teeth with her finger, and Kate was softened.

"That sounds nice," she said. "Thank you."

Mrs. Efrim led the way around the church to a small frame building in the cleared field behind it, while the other woman, dawdling, introduced herself as Miss Rudell and took Kate's hand. The artless gesture startled Kate, but Miss Rudell kept chattering about the tea that was waiting inside—good tea, fresh, it smelled like flowers. When she squeezed Kate's hand, Kate squeezed back.

"Is this the Efrims' house?" she asked, nodding at the tiny structure.

"This is the house for us all," Miss Rudell said. Catching Kate's expression, she added, "We don't all live here. But we can all come here. It's our house."

"A safe house." Kate spoke louder than she'd meant, and Miss Rudell nodded happily.

"Very safe," she said, leading Kate through the door to join Mrs. Efrim, who was already seated on a persimmon-colored couch. She stood when they entered and clasped Kate's hand again. "It is joy to have you here," she said.

Kate curved her mouth politely, disconcerted less by the greeting than by the collision of brilliant colors in the room. Light blue walls were covered with crude watercolors—swirling rainbows, lipstick-pink wings, orange flames. Wobbly clay doves and crosses painted green and blue clustered on low tables that were covered with stop-sign red corduroy cloths. The colors were vivid in the truest sense, nearly alive, the paintings and statues and tables all but quivering, as if they could barely contain their own chromatic exuberance. When Kate blinked, the room swam out of focus.

"We've been waiting to welcome you. Here we are always in fellowship," Mrs. Efrim was saying. She raised a yellow teacup. "Sugar?"

"Thank you," Kate said. "Is Mr. Efrim in?" The two women shook their heads in unison, Miss Rudell beaming at Kate, who smiled back at her, feeling as if she'd suddenly been dropped into the nineteenth century. When she spoke, she made sure her voice was drawing-room gracious. "You know, I hadn't planned to sit with you, although I'm happy to do so. Fellowship between us is—called for. But I came today because I have a question to ask Mr. Efrim. When will he be in?"

"You can ask Mrs. Efrim your question," Miss Rudell said. "She'll know."

"That's a nice thought," Kate said. "In real life, husbands and wives don't actually know everything about each other."

"She'll know," Miss Rudell insisted.

Mrs. Efrim said serenely, "We are one."

Kate turned her daffodil-colored teacup between her hands and searched for a response that was neither insulting nor plaintive. Finding none, she took the ring box out of her pocket and opened it. "Why did he leave this for me?"

Miss Rudell drew back with a shocked expression, but Mrs. Efrim leaned forward and, with great tenderness, stroked one tiny stump. She said, "This is not Mr. Efrim's."

"I understand that someone else might have actually left it on my doorstep. But why did he want it put there? Truly, hasn't he pursued me enough?"

Mrs. Efrim shook her head, making her hair softly quake. Beside her, frowning with confusion, Miss Rudell shook her head, too. "You still don't understand. This is not Mr. Efrim's," Mrs. Efrim said. "This has nothing to do with him."

"I'm sorry; I can't believe that," Kate said. "He's left dolls like this before. If I called the police, who else would they suspect?"

The woman's pure, unlined expression didn't shift. "This is not his." Beside her, Miss Rudell ticked her head back and forth, her disappointed eyes locked on Kate.

"You're very sure of yourself. Don't you ever—" Kate began, then stopped, arrested by Mrs. Efrim's untroubled eyes, as clear as water. The woman had absolute faith. Nothing had taught her that faith could be wrong. She had no concept of her vast vulnerability. Unexpectedly, with a feeling like the unfolding of wings, Kate's heart opened to her.

She began again. "I came here because I knew you would tell me the truth. So, please, let me tell you another truth, one you need to hear. Spouses can surprise each other. I don't mean to sow dissension by saying this." She grimaced, hearing Robert Efrim's words come from her mouth. "No one needs to intend any harm. Someone might be absent-minded, forgetting to mention a little event, a chance encounter, an idea. Someone might take an afternoon. Lives drift away more quickly than you can believe."

Miss Rudell shifted closer to Mrs. Efrim and held her arms over her chest like a shield, but Mrs. Efrim only smiled. "You don't understand. We are one."

"I do understand," Kate said doggedly. "Every night, over supper, the two of you discuss everything that happened that day. There's nothing that you wouldn't tell him. But people are mysteries. They have dreams they themselves don't realize. We never know all they are capable of."

"'For I am fearfully and wonderfully made,'" said Miss Rudell.

"You have come to us, nowhere else," Mrs. Efrim said, nodding to acknowledge Miss Rudell's contribution. "Why? Because you long to learn. You've been married twice, but never truly married."

"I have been truly married. That's what I'm telling you." Kate felt her pulse beat a little harder, hollowness spreading through her like smoke; she felt like a terrible prophet. "This is the truth, rock solid, to build your house upon. I'm telling you in fellowship." She glanced at Miss Rudell, who cowered against Mrs. Efrim as if she expected a whip of flame to lash out of Kate's mouth. "I'm telling you out of love."

"Much evil disguises itself as love," Mrs. Efrim said.

"In this case, love wants to know," Kate said. "Do you know where your husband is, right this minute? Could you go to him and put your hand on his arm?"

"We are one," Mrs. Efrim said, and Miss Rudell echoed, "The two become one body." Her face alight, she rested her chapped, chewed fingertips on Kate's knee.

"There are many wrong marriages," she said.

"I know," Kate said.

"Wrong marriages don't make one body."

"No," Kate said. "The two remain two."

Miss Rudell nodded at Kate, encouraging her. Kate needed only to take the smallest logical step to see, as Miss Rudell did, that Kate had lost track of two husbands because they were separate bodies, able to stray from her without the riving of flesh. Kate shook her head. "It's not that simple. Even one body will develop cracks. That's what it means to be married. What you'd thought was unified divides, and then divides again, until you can't count the pieces at your feet."

"You yearn for something better," Mrs. Efrim murmured.

"Of course I do. My God, who wouldn't want to stop sweeping up pieces every day?" Kate bit down on her lip, wishing she could call back the words, or at least the passion that had made them ring out so. To her relief, the woman only leaned forward to freshen Kate's tea. Miss Rudell stood and crossed to Kate's sofa, sitting close beside her and smoothing Kate's hair with a light hand, murmuring, "Pretty."

After a moment, Kate said, "This is an interesting room. Did you decorate it yourselves?"

"It's the old church," Miss Rudell said. "We worshiped here until we could build the big church."

"It's very bright," Kate said.

"In the kingdom, there will be no darkness." Miss Rudell leaned closer and said in a pleased murmur, "The walls in the big church are pink."

"That must be quite a sight. Perhaps you can show me on my way out," Kate said.

She meant to take only a quick glance and then leave before she could blurt any other scalding truths of her marital life, but another fifteen minutes went to the tour of the big church. Like the other building, it was arrayed with brilliant watercolors and statues, its pink walls barely visible behind the art. Miss Rudell explained each shade of symbolism by quoting scripture, which Mrs. Efrim twice softly corrected. Mrs. Efrim also showed Kate the registry of marriages, an apricot-colored notebook listing names, dates, and sentiments the happy couples had felt moved to include—"What God has joined" most of the time, and once, more revealingly, "The race is not to the swift." Kate smiled and nodded, trying to edge toward the door. The room's insistent colors crowded against her brain, muscling aside any subtle understanding or quiet hope.

She waited until they had returned to the frozen, neutral landscape outdoors before she said to Mrs. Efrim, "Ask your husband about that doll when he comes home. Just to satisfy yourself and prove me wrong."

A slight shift occurred in the woman's expression, no more than a flutter of her lips. Then Mrs. Efrim said, "We look for the day you will celebrate with us. We will pray for you."

"And I will pray for you," Kate said, enjoying the tiny jolt that crossed the woman's face. "Be sure to tell Mr. Efrim."

She took special care in backing out the narrow driveway. Only once did she look up to see them watching her, Mrs. Efrim with a gracious, mirthless smile, and Miss Rudell pumping her arm up and down in farewell. Kate waved back, then stepped on the gas.

As soon as the church was out of view, she slowed down to trolling speed. Mrs. Efrim would certainly discuss Kate's visit over the dinner table that night, telling Robert about Kate's wrong beliefs, her heart of stone. But might Mrs. Efrim look at her husband and wonder, however fleetingly, where he had lunched that day, whom he had talked to? Might Kate herself have introduced the first crack in the Efrims' one body? Was she once again dragging someone down? She thought of Miss Rudell's joyful face and wished she'd never opened her mouth.

Preoccupied, she drove carelessly. Twice she veered onto the highway's rough shoulder, and five minutes later a car wailed past, only inches away, and she saw with shock how far she had drifted into the oncoming lane. She turned off at the next exit and pulled to the side, her tires skating on loose gravel.

The near-miss had left her body flooded with tingling panic, her heart whapping like a loose shingle. "Sorry," she said to the air, since she couldn't apologize to the driver she'd terrified. Once the word was out, she relaxed her grip on the steering wheel, and said it again, feeling what was left of her good cheer give way. Sorry. Sorry.

She was sorry she had missed Robert Efrim. Their showdown still awaited her, and she would rather have been the one to choose the time and place. She was sorry she had spent so much time at his strange church, and sorry to think that Ned might find comfort there.

More to the point, she was sorry she hadn't known Ned would be drawn to such a church, sorry she hadn't understood his need, sorry he remained a stranger to her. She was sorry she had married him, sorry she hadn't been able to see how they would disappoint each other, their one body become two. She was sorry her life had arrived at such an unpleasant pinnacle, from which every possible descent involved concession and failure. And she was sorry above all that Bill-o had come back and pried up the top of her new self, which she had thought so bright and good, to show her the coiling worms within.

She whispered, "Is this what I deserve?" The words whined nakedly, and she closed her mouth and looked out the windshield, squinting to see Elite, though it had to be invisible from here. The town sat on the far side of a line of dark, irregular hills that reared up from the valley floor, hills locally renowned for their steepness. Kate had seen cars and sheds tied to trees to keep them from slipping in rainstorms. Farmers still told the story of the man who planted his west-facing slope. Caught on his tractor in a cloudburst, he slid, along with his soybeans and topsoil, seven hundred feet downhill before getting trapped in a culvert.

He was one of the lucky ones; after a month he was out of the hospital and getting around well enough to sell his tractor and his farm. More commonly, once or twice a year, some driver missed one of the road's hard turns despite the metal restraining bars, the signs, the reflecting strips, and rows of crosses erected by grieving families. Kate had conducted a funeral just a year ago for two liquored-up boys rocketing home from French Lick on roads they had known since they were babies. Their car had bounced all the way to the valley floor and crumpled like a cigarette pack. The undertaker had been able to straighten out their bodies but could not quite erase the wildness of their mouths.

Bending her head automatically, she began to murmur the prayer that asked for blessings on the boys' families, but the words blurred into shapelessness, and she sputtered to a stop. Her mouth was overfilled with prayer; prayer's scummy residue coated the back of her teeth. Prayers before meals. Prayers before meetings. Prayers before the women's club fashion show, the youth fellowship soccer tourney, before bed, before rising. "Pray," she had advised church members. "Even when you don't feel your prayers do any good. Especially when you don't feel your prayers do any good. You need them most then."

When she began again now, she half shouted, to make sure the words got out. "Bless Bill-o! Grant him light. Help him prosper." Fighting the desire to suggest that Bill-o be taught a lesson or two and, just this once, be made to see that the world wasn't his to warp and interpret, she closed her eyes. "Bless his store. Bring spring early and mild for his sake. Create new plants that will thrive in Elite."

She had prayed at bedsides for the disappearance of tumors that spun intricately around spinal cords. She had sat between ashen-faced parents and prayed for the return of children who were sliding needles between their toes and whispering suggestions to strangers behind buildings. She had learned charity, or its dutiful appearance. She could pray for Bill-o. "Bless his house," she said.

From him she moved without pausing to Mindy. She asked that God protect her, strengthen her, give her insight and fortitude, which she would need. Kate couldn't keep herself from imagining how the girl's dimpled, golden face would look after ten years of numbing jobs taken to support a child whom, some nights, Mindy would look at and bleakly hate, but she prayed on: "Come to her aid. Keep her from milk leg, peritonitis, indigestion. Drop good fortune in her lap, while she still has a lap. And bless her child, when it comes—fill it with the spirit that knows and worships you." That, Kate knew, would drive Mindy nuts.

She prayed for Bob Peters, Alma Vyrie, and, at some length, for Robert Efrim and every member of his brightly colored church. To close the circle, she asked for blessings on Ned, who struggled and suffered to serve. "Surround him, cloak him, and grant him the joy that he doesn't really believe in, though he thinks he does." She thought of Ned's face, so often wrinkled with the exertion of his goodness, and wondered whether a divine hand could wipe all those furrows away. Her hand couldn't. Ned didn't deserve the lines her hand traced.

She shifted her foot on the brake pedal but didn't lift her hand to the gearshift. Sheepish, she lowered her head and murmured, "Bless me. Bless me. Please. Bless me." She listened to the car engine's steady churning and the long wind outside until those sounds began to fade, and she heard the heavy silence that surrounded them. The stillness seemed to grow as she listened, overwhelming the puny noises that rode on its surface. When she inhaled, she took the silence in.

Gradually, breath by breath, the many voices in her brain and memory receded. Nothing took their place. Kate felt suspended—above what, she couldn't say. She imagined she could feel blood lapping through her veins, cells placidly dividing. Never had she been so conscious. She felt nothing at all—not comfort, not dread, not heat or cold, not hope. The outline of her body seemed to press on the air that held it, and silence opened inside her, a well of silky darkness. She waited. Her patience was greater than patience; a perfect stillness held her, without thought or memory, emotion or intention. She took one breath and then another, listening to nothing until, smoothly, the world returned—the car and the wind and her familiar, noisy brain. She wanted to weep at their return.

Several minutes passed before she cautiously shifted the car into drive and signaled to get back onto the road. Chastened, she pondered the silence. "When you pray," she had told her parishioners, "don't forget to listen. When you're finished asking, wait and listen for an answer." But she hadn't told them what to do if the answer was a great stillness, which might have been the presence of God and might have been a gaze into the abyss. If there was a difference. She pondered that idea, too, then turned on the radio and listened to farm reports the rest of the way to Elite.

By the time she got there it was past three, an iron-colored afternoon. The lunch she'd packed that morning, which she'd planned to eat during the Elletsville meeting, was back in her office, so she hurried from the car straight to the church, then stopped in the foyer when she heard Barb's voice ringing down the corridor, talking about her.

"—kind. Too kind to press charges, which she should have done. They'll be back again. They're a long way from done with her."

"Kindness isn't the same thing as wisdom. She sees some things, but she doesn't have the big picture." Bill-o. Kate pulled her coat so tightly around her that she heard one of the seams crack, and she let out a shaky sigh. Why was she even surprised anymore?

"She's got more of the picture than anybody else around here," Barb said sharply.

"I'm not trying to run her down," Bill-o said. "I'm just telling you what I've noticed."

"She wants to let folks think about things. She has an open mind."

"But you're the one who has to deal with the phone calls later, once people are done thinking and want to complain about what her open mind has let in."

Barb laughed. "I tell her about the screamers. We set up a scale, ranking hysteria and loudness."

"Shouldn't you get a salary for being the minister's flak-catcher?"

"I don't think there's room for me in the budget."

Bill-o chuckled, then fell silent, and Kate crept a few feet closer, although she was having trouble moving; all her joints seemed to have locked up. Barb finally said, "What's happening now—this is typical. She tries to see every side of an issue."

"I've always admired that about her," Bill-o said.

"And she's no Pious Pete."

"No, she's not like that."

"The only thing is—I've been here through four ministers now. All of the others talked about right and wrong. There wasn't this constant 'On the other hand.' At least Ned is willing to say what's what." Kate heard the warmth in Barb's voice, and wondered how close Bill-o's chair was to hers, and whether his expression denoted Concern, or Worry, or Sorrowful Acceptance. Whatever he said would be partially true. That was his secret.

Barb went on, "People ask her what they should think. And all she tells them to do is listen with an open heart. That doesn't help! People are asking for guidance, and they're not out of line to expect their minister to provide it. Sometimes I wonder if she has any beliefs at all. Oh, I shouldn't say this."

Bill-o let the pause between them deepen. "It's important to face the things that are bothering you," he said.

"Every once in a while, when she isn't here, people wind up telling me what's going on in their lives, then asking what they should do."

"And what do you tell them?" Bill-o asked softly.

"Just don't leave. We can't take any more losses." Kate heard the catch in Barb's voice. "I should trust her," Barb whispered. "But sometimes it's not easy." The phone rang then, and Kate pictured how the two of them must have stared at it through four rings before Barb picked up, barely beating the machine. Kate took the moment to make herself edge back down the corridor; once they started talking again she would be unable to keep herself from sidling closer and closer, ravenous for each razor-edged word.

Outside, the air was a sheet of bright cold. She balled up her bare hands in her pockets, then set out to the north, where houses quickly thinned out and skinny, excitable dogs in flimsy pens shrieked as she stormed past.

"Wrong. Unfair," she said aloud. "Vicious." Not that there was anything surprising about Bill-o undermining her. He wouldn't be content until her world was reduced to rubble, the only thing he understood. The shock had been delivered by Barb, her friend, who wondered whether Kate had any beliefs at all.

Barb had typed agreements that Kate had brokered between warring families or neighbors. Barb knew about decisions Kate had made for church members who trusted a minister more than they trusted the law, who brought their accusations of theft and infidelity directly to Kate.

Barb had been helping Kate finish a district report the night Will Vyrie banged on the door, his whimpering, white-faced daughter Janie beside him. Will jerked his thumb toward his truck, where Kate and Barb could see his older girl, Florence, glaring at them from the cab. "Flo's been stepping out with Janie's fella."

Janie was sixteen, Florence easily twenty-two. The younger girl was gulping now, stammering, "She doesn't love him! She's just after hurting me. Three months ago, she didn't even know his name."

Kate did—Dennis Shortley, an unfinished-looking seventeen-year-old who worked, sometimes, at a body shop on the edge of town. When he dropped out of youth fellowship, he made a point of telling Kate that a man had better things to do with his time.

"Now Flo's in the family way. And the boy says it's none of his doing," Will went on. "Janie here wants him back. Though I know some dogs who'd be better bets."

"I love him!" Janie wailed, and Florence, from the truck, imitated her sister with ugly precision.

"Come in," Kate said, and then raised her voice so that Florence could hear. "Come in. We need to talk." Will had to start walking toward the truck before Florence moved, and Barb got a steno pad.

Talking helped nothing; the girls sat rigidly at opposite ends of the room, answered Kate with shrugs and mutters, and Will stared, waiting for her to make a judgment. "What does Dennis think he should do?" she asked.

"He'll do what you say," Will said grimly. "Don't you worry about that."

"I can't just point my finger and choose. Three lives are concerned here. Four," she amended, looking at the sneering Florence. "I can talk to you and counsel you, but I can't make your decisions for you." Barb busily writing, her face neutral.

"They'll do what you say," Will said.

"I say we need to start a conversation."

Will sighed so loudly he might as well have cursed. But for the next three weeks Will delivered Dennis and the two girls to Kate's office, where the boy swore the baby was none of his. At the third meeting Kate said, "A blood test, you know, would clear this question right up," and he dropped into sullen silence. Florence smiled. No one said anything more until Janie keened. "It isn't fair! I did what I was supposed to do. I made him wait, said, 'Only after we're married.' And then Flo came whoring along."

"I told you I didn't want to hear that word again," Will snarled.

"She's going to get him! It isn't fair!" Janie wailed.

"Nobody's going to 'get' anybody. This isn't a competition," Kate said, but it was. Florence had won. They soon left, Janie sniffling noisily. Kate could see they wouldn't return. "Want some coffee, Solomon?" Barb had asked.

Not watching her feet, Kate stepped squarely on an empty soda can and wrenched her ankle. She rocked for a moment, sucking air through her teeth. She should have told Will to take a strap to the little shit, or done it herself. The boy still smirked and slouched around Elite, not one bit changed, although she longed to change him, rearrange his mouth so that a smirk would slide off it.

From all the counseling she'd done, all the conversations she'd had, what good had emerged? She had sat and watched bitter couples decide to go home and battle some more. She had held secrets about drug addiction, theft, grinding meanness. She had believed in people's right to guide their own course and had stood on a safe ledge when they slid slowly downhill. Or not so slowly. The other word for her splendid temperance was cowardice, as Bob Peters had been trying to tell her.

And yet she truly hadn't known what Janie and Flo should have done, or the shivering boy who had dreams about handsome men, or the several wretched couples. She had lacked the wisdom, just as Bill-o told Barb. Only now, finally, was Kate facing a dilemma about which she was uniquely well informed. Now, finally, had come her time to step forward.

Grace or luck had kept Kate from carrying Bill-o's child. But neither grace nor luck were shadowing Mindy. "I guess you think you're going to be my savior?" Mindy would almost certainly say once Kate started talking.

"You bet," Kate would say. "Get ready."

Imagining the conversation, she walked to the top of a rise, from which she could look back and see most of Elite. Forlorn houses trailed to the south edge of town, and Olsen's paint factory stood like a wall at the west, gray from this distance even though up close the buildings were a dirty white. The town never looked worse than it did in late fall, and it was hard to think that there was anything worth saving there. She jerked her chin up. She had a responsibility. It was silly obtuseness that had kept her mouth closed for so long.

Thirteen

Kate had planned on coming home early from her and Ned's dinner at the Coachlight. She could drop him off at the hospital and make it home before nine, plenty of time to start talking to Mindy. But Ned's patients got in the way of her plans. Everyone was stable, there were no new admissions at the hospital, and Ned was looking forward to a night at home after dinner. He was getting hungry for the domestic comforts. Kate stirred the potatoes on her plate. "Right now our home is not all that comfortable," she said.

"No intercom, no cafeteria food. You don't know how good you've got it."

All through dinner he set the chatty tone, told anecdotes from the hospital, asked questions about Mindy and the church. Kate could see him fitting her answers alongside his stories, assembling the mosaic of their lives, and counting the number of tiles they still held in common. She was doing the same thing.

The parsonage was dark when they got back—Mindy must have been given late shift. Kate and Ned hadn't entered an empty house together in weeks, and the rooms suddenly felt expansive.

"Shoot. We should install an atrium," Kate said.

"A ballroom."

"I've been wondering where to have those state dinners."

They were planning the concert hall when Mindy got home; she stopped short in the doorway, letting the cold air in. "Hey," Kate said, and watched the girl's eyes dart from her to Ned, side by side on the couch.

"Come in," Ned said. "Close the door."

"I'll make my own dinner," Mindy said.

While the girl rattled pots Ned turned on the TV, settling on a show about ancient Egypt. According to the unctuous announcer, Pharaohs were buried with goods for the next world—utensils, money, and food to make the journey. Archeologists had found traces of wheat beside the gorgeous sarcophagi. "A stalk of wheat," Ned said. "Pretty dry eating. Even you might balk at that, Mindy."

"Wheat is not a desirable grain. It pulls from the earth. That's impure. Rice pulls from water. It's a pure food," Mindy said, stirring. "Even rice from a box. It works through the system and creates balance."

"It's starch," Ned said. "It works the enzymes in the stomach."

"We have broccoli," Kate said. Mindy was silent, and Kate added, "In the crisper."

When the rice was done, Mindy heaped a plate, added a broccoli floret and melted back to her room. "So much for our company," Ned said.

"We're too old for her."

"We're old, all right. And she was afraid we were going to start making out in front of her. I was on the verge of telling her we don't usually go public with that. You want some coffee?"

Kate nodded, fear once again freezing her mouth. Guilt is its own punishment, she had told so many philandering parishioners. But she hadn't begun to understand her own words. To look at Ned now, his clean hands and shambly legs, hurt, physically *hurt* her.

"I'm still hearing what a good job you did with Janelle's funeral." Ned set a cup in front of Kate. "I stopped by to see Frank. He said you pulled him through."

"I'm glad he thought so." Catching Ned's look, she added, "I wasn't at my best."

"How could you be? Considering everything that you were doing."

Kate closed her eyes. Once again, the desire to confess crashed through her, and she knuckled her eyes. Every expert counseled contemplation and prayer before confessing infidelity; many counseled not confessing at all. "Remember the pain that will be inflicted on the blameless party," one textbook warned. Even so, Kate might have blurted out the truth to Ned here and now, except that Mindy was in the bedroom, listening through the thin walls, and Kate would not humiliate Ned where Mindy Leaf could hear.

Now she felt his cool hands on either side of her face, massaging her temples and hairline. "Kate, she's running you ragged. You've got to find some other solution."

"I ask her to clean the bathroom sink, and she remembers, sometimes. She'll do the laundry if I ask her six times and remind her how the washing machine works."

Ned snorted softly. Kate said, "There's only one real solution, and Mindy's not willing to even talk about that. Although we're going to start." Gauging by the even pressure of his fingers, her words shocked him less than she'd expected.

"If there's anybody who could make abortion look like a solution, she's the one," he said.

"This time it is a solution. It's the only one I can see."

"Well, keep looking."

"I do, Ned," she said sharply. If he had been the one to stumble in on Bill-o and Mindy, he wouldn't be so certain. "I look every day, but there's not a simple answer. Anything I'm able to see for that baby is pretty darn grim."

He stopped massaging. "So what are you saying?"

"Mindy's parents aren't talking to her. I'm the one who has to get her to think about what she's doing. I have to look into her future."

"Her future starts when the baby comes."

"That's what Mindy thinks. But things have already started. And if she doesn't do something soon, her future's going to be a room with no windows and no doors. She's got to be almost three months gone. If you can find some other escape hatch, you tell me."

Ned walked into the kitchen, where he turned on the water; he let it run noisily for a minute, enough to get hot, then shut it off again. "You know, there are plenty of things between you and me that aren't easy. I've been thinking about this. I know something about rooms without windows or doors. But if you help this girl to get rid of her baby, that will be the end. I don't mean to sound dramatic here, but there's only so much I can take."

He turned the water back on, so when she said, "Slow down, Ned," she nearly had to shout. "Please. What isn't easy for you?"

"I don't want to get into all of this now. I was hoping this would be a pleasant night."

"Me too. But we're into it. Come on, Ned—I feel like I got a post card: 'Dear Kate: Have contracted fatal disease. Details to follow.'"

Even then, he didn't answer right away. "I was reading the other day about pathogens that mimic antibodies. I wasn't looking for a metaphor. But I started thinking about the process of mutation, and how anyone would think a kind of intelligence was at work to allow a disease-bearing cell to disguise itself as a healthy one. Does the cell even feel a change taking place, or does it just find itself performing a different function?"

Kate sat dumbfounded until he said, "Say something, Kate," and she had to clear her throat.

"Every time," she said, "every time I think I know just how much I've disappointed you, the floor falls out again. Every time I think I've hit rock bottom, I drop some more. Will there ever be an end to this, do you think?"

"That's what we're finding out," Ned said. He turned on the noisy water and filled up the sink to wash pots that couldn't go in the dishwasher, including Mindy's rice pot. Kate dried. They finished the job in fifteen minutes, and Ned went to the armchair in the living room, where medical journals were stacked up.

A little before ten o'clock he pulled out the foldaway, then went back to the chair. She watched the news with the sound off and wondered how much longer they would share a bed, even this horrible one. He had delivered his ultimatum, as was his right. But for once Kate had an ultimatum too.

The next morning she lay still until Ned softly let himself out of the house. Then she moved softly herself, trying to keep from waking Mindy. She wasn't ready to be talking to anyone. At church she would make Gabe greet any visitors. Even if she couldn't take a day off, she could take one that wasn't quite on.

But in her office waited a message from the bishop's secretary, instructing Kate to call the bishop as soon as possible. Kate listened to the message twice, then pulled out a pitcher to water the plants.

Everybody else in the North-Central jurisdiction called the bishop Killer Joe. Action, not tolerance, was his long suit. After the pastor of a Jasper church brought pizza to a pretty congregant's door on a night the woman's husband was out of town, he soon found himself leading a tiny congregation in Cloverdale. Remembering, Kate double-checked the oxalis in Barb's window. She watered the big palm, too, which took two quarts. When she finally dialed the bishop's number, the office air was rich with the smell of damp soil. "I think I know what this is about," Kate said when she heard the bishop's quick voice.

"I didn't call you when I got the first letter, or the second letter. Would you like to know how many letters I have now?"

"No," Kate said.

"They're fond of referring to you as the woman at the well."

"I've heard that one myself. We've been doing John's gospel in Sunday School."

"How much deeper do you want to dig yourself?"

"I don't think I'm the one doing the digging. It's just that I get up every day and find that the floor's an inch lower."

"Then you better start jacking it up again. Kate, I don't usually have to call ministers and remind them that they're only permitted one spouse at a time. Dove has enough problems without you causing a scandal."

Grimly, Kate started to laugh. "That's for sure. But I guess the letter-writers didn't want to tell you that my ex-husband has moved out. I'm now providing a home for an unwed mother-to-be. I am living a life that's above reproach."

"You'd better get the word out," he said. "People are still finding grounds to reprove you."

"What am I supposed to do? Have tours of the parsonage and let folks stare at her penitent face?"

"Yours is the penitent face they need to see." Impatience tightened his voice. "Use your head, Kate. You can't go backwards, so show that you're growing from all this business. Let people see you and Ned forging a stronger marriage. A good ministry can be made even with significant error, if the church members see real change in the minister."

"You're right. Of course," she said. But as soon as the bishop hung up her anger flared, and she thought that if he knew the kind of real change that was taking place in Ned, he wouldn't be so hot about forging a stronger union.

A little before noon, she went back to the parsonage and knocked on Mindy's door. Mindy answered, "What? Who?" and yawned stagily.

"It's me," Kate said, turning on the light as she entered. "Who did you think? I wanted to make sure you were awake. Sleeping round the clock isn't good for you or the baby." She snapped up the window shades.

"I'm tired," Mindy said. "You don't know how tired I get."

"I have a pretty good idea. It's time to get out of bed. I'm going to make lunch, and you can help."

"I'm not hungry."

"That's fine. You can sit at the table and keep me company."

Mindy, lagging and yawning behind her, took five minutes to negotiate the short hallway to the kitchen. She slumped at the table while Kate blended tuna and mayonnaise. "Your tiredness should have passed by now, you know," Kate said. "At this point, you should be feeling energetic."

"Well, I'm not."

"And it's a good thing your strength is coming back, because you've got a lot that you'd better think about. For instance, where are you and the baby going to live? You know you can't stay at the parsonage indefinitely."

"Thanks for the reminder," Mindy said. When Kate put a plate with a sandwich in front of her, she pushed it away.

"So, where?"

"I don't know yet. I'll need east-facing windows and at least one south-facing door."

"Mindy, would you try to be realistic? There can't be more than twelve apartments in town that you could afford. You need to be making inquiries. Not every place will let you come with a baby. Have you started asking around?"

"For a minister, you're a real interrogator." Mindy fingered her hair, isolated a small section and made a quick, messy braid, then another. "Of course I'm making plans. What do you think?"

"I think your plans have gotten about as far as yesterday."

"I'll find a place, all right? Do you want me to leave right now? Is that what this is about?"

"Nope," Kate said. "I just want to help you get your ducks in a row. What are you going to do for money? You should be seeing a doctor every two weeks. Have you paid attention to how much obstetricians charge?"

"I have a job."

"Let's just add a few items up," Kate said, sliding a pad of paper over from the telephone. "There'll be hospital costs and then all the clothes and blankets and a layette and a stroller—the basics. You'll have to start budgeting for diapers. Most apartments will want first and last month's rent, plus a deposit. The way these numbers add up, Mindy, working the cash register at Ben Franklin isn't going to cut it."

"When I finish school I'll get a better job," she said, her voice tight.

"Of course, that introduces some other costs," Kate said, drawing a line under the first column and starting a new one. "You'll have tuition, books. And then you'll have to pay for day care whenever you're in class. Assuming you can get the baby into day care—it's often hard, especially with infants. Have you got your name on any waiting lists?"

"Stop it!" Mindy swept her fork onto the floor. "You're not trying to help me. You're jealous, and so you're trying to make me miserable."

"You're right. I am jealous. And let me tell you, if I was pregnant, I'd be getting things ready, so my child was tended to from the second it arrived. I'd be prepared."

"I'll be prepared."

"Show me." The girl pressed her lips together in a ferocious line and closed her eyes, one of the expressions she used to indicate communion with her baby.

"Give it a rest, Mindy. I know what you're thinking. You're cherishing tender images of Bill-o bringing flowers to your hospital bed, kissing your hand and reaching out to coochy-coo the baby. Let me just ask you something. Has he ever said one word about raising this child? Suggested names? Talked about kindergarten or Little League?"

"It's early to be thinking about Little League, don't you think?"

"Parents who plan to watch their kids grow up start imagining graduations and weddings before the child is even born. They tape pictures of the ultrasound to their refrigerator doors, name it and quarrel about whether that blob of cells will play forward for IU or Duke. If you and Bill-o aren't having these conversations now, when you're caught up on your sleep and there isn't a real baby with a dirty bottom, I don't think it's likely you'll be having them later."

"People change," Mindy said. "Once they realize they're really parents."

"You know what I think?"

"Gee. Tell me."

Kate smiled sunnily. "I think Bill-o has realized about as much as he ever will about parenting. I think he's got a kid in half the counties in Indiana. And you know what he calls those kids? Mistakes."

Mindy was quiet then, her eyes fixed on her plate; Kate expected the waterworks again, but when Mindy did speak, her voice was clear and her eyes dry. "He might," she said. "It wouldn't surprise me. But the thing you don't understand, the point you haven't gotten from the start because you're so busy hating him, is that I love him. And if you love somebody, you believe in him. It's as simple as that. I love Bill-o, and he loves me, and I believe that he'll be there for me. For us," she added, flattening her hand over her belly.

"That's a stupid belief." Kate bit the end off a pickle spear. "If you're going to go to all the trouble and risk of believing something, believe in something that's worth your while. Be like Gabe—believe in a Higher Power. Believe in angels or astrology."

"Nice talk, Reverend."

"Crystals," Kate went on. "Numerology. Anything you come up with is going to be a better bet than Bill-o."

"He's all I've got."

"Then find something else," Kate said.

"Are you finished?"

"No."

Mindy pushed her chair back and left the table; in a moment, Kate heard her running water for a bath. She exhaled. "Mercy."

She was amazed at herself. For once words were jumping to mind the moment she needed them, along with examples, justifications, rationales. She felt as if she had discovered herself to be an ace skier or crack shot, possessed of skills she hadn't imagined. Words were falling from her mouth as if they had been waiting, all Kate's life, to be said, and she believed every one of them. She was speaking without shades or ambiguity. She was preaching. If a hot bead of self-loathing now lodged in her stomach, it was offset by confidence, so new to her.

Mindy's lunchtime sandwich sat drying on the table when Kate came home at five, and Mindy claimed, through the bedroom door, that she didn't want dinner. Kate went back to the kitchen to poach chicken and boil noodles. After squinting at the recipe from an old United Methodist Women cookbook, she even fished out her double boiler and made a heavy, eggy custard. When the food was ready, she made up a sickroom tray, garnishing it with a sycamore leaf, and went back to Mindy's door. "The mountain comes to Mohammed," she said and let herself in.

Mindy was lying in a peculiar position, and it took Kate a minute to realize she had her radio in bed with her, under the covers, pressed up against her stomach. "Sit up. The baby can stand a station break."

"I told you I wasn't hungry."

"You have to eat, whether you want to or not." Kate bent to help her sit up, and Mindy scrambled against the headboard, avoiding her touch. Without comment, Kate went back to the kitchen. She gave Mindy a half-hour. Predictably, the girl had slid back down under the covers, but the empty plate on the bedside table glistened.

"There'll be dessert, once it chills."

"I'm not hungry."

"You know what happens when mothers don't take prenatal nutrition seriously? They get low birth-weight babies." Kate pulled up a chair. She'd heard Ned give this lecture to chain-smoking, pole-thin girls; it was one of his best. "They get irritable babies who are slow to develop, babies who are always a little behind the other kids their age. Is that what you want, one of those drippy-nosed kids who's always whining and stumbling around your feet?"

"Thank you for your tremendous sensitivity."

"I'm trying to get you to wake up. Your right to eat whenever you felt like it went out the window when you got pregnant. I'm assuming," she added, "that you want a baby who's got a fighting chance. It's a full-time job, trying to put up with a slow baby that's always fussing. It's a hard baby to love."

Mindy's eyes flooded. Lying on her back, tears drizzling toward her ears, she looked like a child, and Kate struggled against her impulse to take the girl's hand and promise her that joy was so near she could taste it. Mindy said, "I'm doing my best. I haven't had a chance to do anything yet. I talk to it every day."

"But you don't plan. You're carrying a mortgage on the future there in your belly."

"You make having a baby sound like owing money to Visa."

"That's how it feels to girls who aren't ready. Wouldn't you rather think about these things now, before it's too late? You're in deep, Mindy. When you're in this deep, there's only one way out."

Mindy flipped her eyes open. "You won't stop at anything, will you? You've never felt what a mother feels. You wouldn't be able to say this if you'd ever carried a child. But you haven't."

"No, I haven't." Kate stood and smoothed her blouse. "But I'm an adult and a wife, and that puts me ahead of you. You better understand what you're letting yourself in for. Should I go get your custard now?"

Mindy groaned and curled under the covers, but the nausea of the first months had passed, and both she and Kate knew it. She wiped away tears. "You have a hundred ways of getting your little revenge."

"Tardy development. A difficult child, a slow one," Kate said. "A lot is at stake here." She left the room, closing the door on Mindy's teary hiccup.

Later, when she returned with the shiny, firm custard—she hadn't made it in years and was pleased to see she hadn't lost the knack—she started in again, glancing away from Mindy's red eyes. The money, the plans, the youth slipping daily away. She talked until ten o'clock, when she told Mindy it was time for sleep. The next morning, after silently seeing Ned off, Kate woke Mindy by talking about statistics for juvenile delinquency in children from one-parent homes.

She hammered, chiseled, and filed at the girl's defenses, and the shards dislodged by her argument settled in heaps around the parsonage. By the third day, Mindy was crying more or less around the clock, and Kate reminded herself that tears were appropriate, overdue, a sign that reality's cool winds were beginning to blow through the chambers of the girl's overheated brain. She didn't bother to analyze the tears that leaked sourly from her own eyes when she awakened, but she made sure Ned didn't see them. She and Ned weren't talking to each other; they were hardly looking at each other, and Kate lectured to Mindy every moment she could, crowding the ulcerous thought of her husband out of her mind.

"You've seen the girls who jump into motherhood without thinking. You know the ones I'm talking about, freezing in cheap jackets at K-Mart with three kids howling in the shopping cart. I know that's not what you mean to be. But that's right where you're headed. You won't be able to give the baby the attention it needs. And do you know where the kids who don't get enough attention from their parents end up? In jail, Mindy, or in crack houses. Where will this child of yours end up?"

The girl, her back to Kate and her body pressed against the sofa's beige cushions, had given herself up to sobs. Kate said, "I know you think I'm forcing you. Maybe I am. But I'm doing it for your own good."

"Thanks," Mindy whispered, and Kate was relieved that the girl wasn't too far gone to muster a little sarcasm.

Hair dull and flattened, tiny eyes blinking like a rabbit's, she looked pummeled, all the more wretched because for the first time her condition was beginning to show. The sweet line of her waist had barely softened and her stomach was only the tiniest cup, but overnight she had started to wear the postures of pregnancy, using her hands to ease her hips when she stood, sitting with her legs set sturdily to support a belly that didn't yet exist. In three days she seemed to have gained five months—grinding months, miserable ones—and Kate, dropping her eyes, kept talking.

Morning after morning, night after night, she seized every moment that Ned was occupied or away. Four days. Five. Mindy's tears stopped and her face turned blank, and Kate wondered whether the girl was even hearing Kate's waterfall of words. "No father," Kate said on day six, "an overworked mother. Where will we find your baby?"

"In a pan," Mindy said. She set down the piece of toast she'd been gnawing.

"A what?" said Kate, all her backed-up words skidding to a stop.

"A plastic one. Doctors don't use metal anymore, which is good. Metal drives away, petroleum products attract."

"Do you understand what you're saying?"

Mindy rearranged her expression, but it remained ambiguous, the mouth straight, the eyes watchful. "Where else am I going to go? What else can I do? It's sad, but like you keep saying, I'm not ready for this."

"Mindy, wait. Make a decision, but make a good decision." Kate had been ready for a slow, reluctant crumbling. This rockslide was too sudden, and felt untrustworthy.

"The wrong time, the wrong chance. I have to change my direction now. It's the only thing I can do. And you keep saying you want to help me. Okay. Help me."

"How do I know you're not going to shift again in ten minutes?"

"If you're not going to help, then get out of the way," Mindy said, standing and walking out the door.

After an uneasy moment, Kate called the office and asked Barb to hold down the fort. Then she hurried to pull on a sweater and slacks. The girl was already settled in the car's passenger seat.

Mindy didn't ask where they were headed when Kate got in, even though they turned north, away from the Elerette County clinic. The next-closest facility, as anyone who read the protesters' statements in the *Bugle* knew, was in Indianapolis, two hours away. Kate had secretly looked up the address and tucked it in the glove compartment. She was sorry to be so cloak-and-dagger, but she had her reasons. She was making sure, if such a thing was possible, that once Mindy got to the clinic she wouldn't have to confront a Sanctuary Christian, or Ned, or any other certain, certain soul.

Fourteen

On the way out of town Kate stopped for gas and a box of Kleenex. Mindy showed no sign of tears yet, but the long drive ahead left plenty of time for mood swings and changes of heart. Kate was ready to console, rouse—whatever was called for. She had a speech prepared about sacrifice that she intended to re-use as a homily.

For the time being, though, the girl showed no need for a speech. She made periodic, mild remarks, reading the price of squash from the IGA sign and pointing out the new coat display in the window of Aldrich's, which Kate hadn't noticed.

"I'm glad it's almost winter, aren't you?" Mindy said.

"In some ways," Kate said cautiously.

"Things always seem clearer in the cold. Sharp."

"Yes," Kate said, turning onto the state road that angled northeast —not the quickest route, but the safest. The fields on either side of the road had been harvested so recently that smashed bean plants still lay in their shallow furrows, not yet set upon by deer or raccoons. Those fields should have been cleared better. Animals who raided the gleanings in November would be back in May, nibbling the soft new shoots down to the ground.

"We just moved all the Thanksgiving merchandise to the front of the store," Mindy said.

"Ceramic pilgrims?"

"Baskets sell well at this time of year. We got some dried gourds in; people like to arrange gourds and bittersweet on their tables. You can make a pretty centerpiece for under five dollars."

She went on to describe table runners and coordinating napkins, and Kate made herself listen. Mindy was describing table linens as a kindness, a shield of small talk to protect them. Kate appreciated the gesture, but she wondered if the talk had to be quite so small. However annoying or silly or grand Mindy's conversations had become, they'd never been boring. Now Kate heard how every year Harvest Gold napkins outsold Autumn Sunlight. She snaked a Kleenex from the box and blew her nose. Ragweed got to her in the fall.

From the inventory of Thanksgiving goods, Mindy went on to discuss the store's new no-credit policy, upsetting to longtime customers, then settled on a description of Christmas fabrics, a topic that held her until the radio towers on the southern edge of Indianapolis poked into view. At the sight of them she fell silent, her hands flat on top of her thighs, her face locked into a studied, bland mask.

"We still have a ways to go," Kate said. "Another twenty minutes, easy. We can stop, if you need to. Take a bathroom break or get a cup of coffee."

"I'd rather go on and get there."

"I'd understand if you needed to take a minute."

"I'm ready," Mindy said. "Let's go."

Kate glanced over; Mindy nodded and made hurry-up motions with her hands—"I mean it." So Kate gunned the car up the hard arc onto the interstate, heading north, past downtown with its dingy statehouse buildings, past the airport, the nice section of town, two malls, and Speedway, marked by an old tire factory on one side of the interstate and the vo-tech, stained and square and four blocks long, on the other. When Kate was a child her mother had commented, every time they passed it, that the building looked more like a penitentiary than a school. Kate would gaze at the wire-covered windows and imagine yearning faces pressed against them.

"You drive fast, for a minister," Mindy said.

"Sorry." Kate slowed a little. "These are my old stomping grounds."

"I like going fast."

"Still," Kate said, and then, "I'm traveling down memory lane here. The neighborhood I grew up in was just beyond that overpass. The interstate was practically the first road I learned to drive."

"I didn't drive on an interstate until I was eighteen. Even then, my mother wouldn't let me go by myself, and she kept yelling that trucks were coming over."

"Tell your mother that the interstate is safer than the roads around Elite."

"You don't think like a mother," Mindy said. "You have to do this." She flattened her hands on the dashboard, stiffened her arms and legs, and opened her mouth to imitate a prolonged wail. Kate laughed. In a month of sharing a house, the girl had never hinted that she might be capable of clowning. Dropping her hands, Mindy turned her attention back out the window. "I don't think like a mother either."

Kate bore down to get past a semi, and she was gripping the steering wheel as if she meant to throttle it. This trip would be easier if Mindy were teary and regretful, or if she were still reeling out smug observations about the life accreting inside of her. But the self-contained, faintly ironic persona was new, and Kate had the unsettling sense that she was chauffering a full stranger to an abortion clinic. Barreling down the fast lane, she almost missed their off ramp; only by veering through two lanes could she make the turn. "Sorry," she said again.

She drove warily on Indianapolis's rough surface roads, signaling every turn and threading down one-way streets. This part of town wasn't connected by boulevards or four-lane thoroughfares. Every street seemed little more than an alley, walled in by sagging bags of trash and dented, colorless cars, obviously long abandoned. The whole area had a gasping, kicked-in air, insufficiently industrial, halfheartedly retail, a neighborhood where no one seemed to live or work. Looking at the drivers she passed, Kate wondered if she also appeared furtive and immediately knew that she did. She made two quick turns, operating off the directions she'd been given, and came out beside a strip mall featuring a closed optician's office and a pizza restaurant with a happy chef painted on the front window. At the mall's far end, behind a chainlink fence, stood the clinic.

"Land ho," Kate said.

"Why do they make them so ugly?" Mindy said. "Never mind; I know. Let's go."

But Kate could only inch forward. The fence that wrapped around the small parking lot opened at a gate barely a car's width across, and beside the gate stood a handful of protesters wearing neon green posterboard signs and carrying immense flashlights. Kate had read about them—the Life Lights. They traveled around a three-state area; protesting first one clinic, then another, they depended on coverage in the local press, which they could count on if news was otherwise slow.

All of them women, they clustered around a card table where a thermos, Styrofoam cups, and a bakery box had been set out on a tray. One was telling a joke that involved lots of hand motions and shrugs. She had swiveled halfway around before she noticed Kate's car idling in the turn lane. The women funneled toward the gate, drummed their flashlights on the hood and chanted "Life, not death! Don't kill! Keep!" standing so close that the car brushed their hips as Kate nosed it into the lot.

"I hate these people," Mindy said calmly.

"They return the favor," Kate said, concentrating too hard to remind Mindy that a week before she had been, at least as far as her own situation went, on their side. The protesters pressed their faces against the fence once Kate squeezed through the entrance and chanted even louder as she helped Mindy out of the car—"What if your mother had come here?" one woman kept shrieking. Kate muttered, "Let's *go*, let's *go*," trying to hurry Mindy inside before whatever switch that had been flicked in her brain snapped back again.

But Mindy patted her hair and smoothed her coat. She nodded at the screaming women. She might have been walking into a bank. When she and Kate came to the metal-detection check behind the steel security door, she surrendered her purse as if she did it every day, leaving Kate to be the rube when first her keys, then the stainless steel pen she'd unthinkingly tucked in her pocket set off the alarm.

The waiting room, its walls pale green and its stiff vinyl chairs a stale brown, was half filled with young women hunched over forms or magazines. Two of them had come with men, who fidgeted on the hard chairs. They all let their glances skate across Mindy and Kate, then skate away, then back. Although a radio played softly from the receptionist's desk, the room seemed silent to Kate, its sounds crowded out by the quivering of hurt feelings, indecision, disappointment, fear.

"You'll need to sign in," the receptionist called. Still fumbling to close her purse, Kate watched Mindy glide between the chairs of tense

women and murmur something to the receptionist.
her seem glamorous, and Kate found it difficult to kee,
at her. She held up the long consent form and skimmed it
ballpoint pen. With difficulty Kate resisted the impulse
form out of Mindy's hands and go over it herself, slowly.

A half-hour passed before a nurse called Mindy's name ʌor the
obligatory counseling session, another half-hour before she was
called for the procedure. Mindy nodded at Kate. "Can she come in
with me?"

"Your mother?" the nurse asked.

"My minister."

The nurse's eyebrows flew up. Kate could already imagine the din-
ner-table conversation that night. But she rested her hand on Mindy's
shoulder and kept it there as the nurse led them to a cubicle that had
an examining table with steel stirrups, a sink, a single round stool and
a poster of a seagull on the ceiling. The nurse—a tiny woman, smaller
than Mindy—silently recorded weight and temperature and blood
pressure, taking Kate's hand off Mindy's shoulder as she adjusted the
cuff. She checked to see that Mindy had signed the consent, and stared
at the signature for a moment, as if she doubted the name there. Then
she asked Mindy the date of her last period, and whether she had any
history of miscarriage, ovarian cancer, or venereal disease. Her voice
was toneless. Mindy's was bright, which Kate found unsettling.

The nurse glared at her chart again, then rummaged in a drawer,
coming up with a sample pack that held two tablets in the clear plastic
blisters. "Take these. If you'd come in two days later we would have had
to run an IV. Undress from the waist down; here's a drape. The doctor
will come in a little while." She smiled, an obvious effort. "Just relax."

She gathered her charts and pencil, and Mindy already had the
tablets down before they heard the nurse going into the next cubicle.
"Pills are easy," Mindy said. "I'm glad we came today."

"This means you don't need a general anesthetic. We're still early
enough."

Mindy nodded and let Kate hold her hand while she looked at the
seagull poster on the ceiling and the words riding over its wings: YOU
HAVE TO FLY HIGH TO FIND JOY. Kate sighed.

You don't like that, do you?" Mindy asked.

"It doesn't seem very sensitive. It could make a patient at a place like this feel worse."

"I like it," she said dreamily. "I think it sends the right message."

"Well, sure. These posters always send the right message. But it's a good idea to think about which right message you're sending, and who you're sending it to. People may not be in a position to hear it."

Mindy reached for the drape and unsnapped her pants. The sedatives must have been taking hold quickly; up until now, the girl had maintained an orthodox modesty, shutting the door even if she only had to change her socks. Now she wiggled out of her tight pink jeans without even turning aside, and Kate glimpsed a line of faint brown hair tracing from her navel down to the top of her flowered underwear before she dropped her eyes.

"You certainly seem confident."

"I am confident. The people here do this every day."

"I'm not talking about the people here; I'm talking about you," Kate said.

"I'm in their hands. At this point, I don't have to do anything."

"Oh yes, you do. You're acting out a major decision, and you don't seem to be aware of it." Kate stared at the speculum, forceps, and plastic syringes lined up on a tray. She picked up the speculum, opened and closed it like a nutcracker. "You've made a one-eighty turn. You spent the entire last six weeks talking about your baby astronaut and the importance of imprinting 'Love Sugar.' Now you come sailing into an abortion clinic as if you were going to have your teeth polished. I'm not sure you really know what you're doing."

Mindy grinned. "So you're saying you'd be happier if I was sobbing."

"Not happier. But more comfortable. There's a phrase that I learned in pastoral counseling: 'appropriate affect.' You haven't got it."

"You're a hard person to please. Didn't you want me to stop crying and take responsibility? Here I am, eyes dry, taking action, and now you criticize me for not being more miserable. I don't know what you want."

"I want to know that you won't be sobbing tomorrow."

"Oh, no. Not a chance." Her voice was so bell-like that Kate turned to look; Mindy sat swinging her legs loosely from the examining table, the drape resting on her lap like a napkin. The skin of her abdomen shone like hammered gold. "I'm on a path. Decisions are part of the path. And sometimes we have to decide against taking one path today so we can have another, better path tomorrow."

"Philosophy. This is new," Kate said, struggling to keep her voice neutral.

Mindy held up her empty hands. "I've always been on a path, but I haven't always known it. Now I can make decisions that will take me where I want to go."

"And where is that?"

"To happiness. Fulfillment. The life I've wanted, all along."

"Oh, Mindy," Kate said. "What are you thinking?"

"Lots of paths can take a person to happiness, but each person needs to learn to stay on the path that is hers. When a person's distracted, she makes the wrong choice, and she loses her happiness."

"By which, I guess, you mean Bill-o?"

Mindy lay back on the table, her hands behind her head. "It isn't that he doesn't want a baby; this just isn't the time. Soon, maybe, but not now, with so much still up in the air. A baby now would bring us unhappiness. It's the same thing you've been telling me. He said that I should listen to you—you've been trying to guide me to my happiness. The way he explained, I could see that."

"So," Kate said, exhaling raggedly. "You're here because Bill-o sent you."

"I agree with him." She smiled, happy with herself, and Kate's stomach clenched. She knew that smile. She had worn it herself.

"Mindy, are you sure about this? Are you sure Bill-o didn't just wear you down? Did he keep talking and talking until you couldn't argue anymore?" Seeing herself, of course, following Mindy around the parsonage, badgering, nagging, bullying, too consumed with thoughts of Ned to realize she was using every trick Bill-o ever taught her.

"It may not seem like it to some, but coming here is our stake in tomorrow," Mindy was saying. "He said I could think of it as the path to our future."

"I'll bet he did. Mindy—look. Put your pants back on." Kate went to the doorway and glowered down the corridor. "Nurse!" She turned back to Mindy, who hadn't moved, picked up the girl's underwear and pulled her feet through the leg openings. She tugged the garment up as far as Mindy's knees; then Mindy pressed her thighs against the table.

"I'm not a doll for you to dress. I'm staying here. I know what I'm doing."

"No, you don't. If you knew what you were doing, you'd be crying now, hating me. You'd be hating Bill-o, too, or at least you wouldn't be loving him. You need to wait. You need to remember what you're doing."

Just then the nurse, looking irritated, pushed aside the curtain in the doorway. "It's too soon to begin the procedure."

"We've changed our minds," Kate said, prying up Mindy's left leg.

"No, we haven't," Mindy said, trying to push the underwear back down. Kate batted away her hand. The sedative, getting its grip, made Mindy sway on the table.

"You signed the form," the nurse said, pointing at the clipboard hanging on the door. Kate took the clipboard and ripped the long page in half. "What form?"

"Oh Christ, I should have guessed," the nurse said, and cried, "Security!" Mindy, slumped back on her elbows with her underwear still riding cockeyed up her thigh, giggled.

"There's no need to call anybody," Kate said. "We've just changed our minds." Shoving at the small of Mindy's back, she slid the girl off the table, finished tugging up her underwear, and reached for the jeans, wishing she had told Mindy to wear a skirt.

"Do you want this woman removed?" the nurse asked, gesturing at Kate. Behind her in the doorway, two men appeared, their bony faces frightened and resolute.

"For pity's sake, put these on." Kate tossed the jeans to Mindy, who tried to wrap them around her hips. Woozy, she lost track of the ends, and one leg hung down in front.

The nurse said, "We can make her leave," at the same time that Kate said, "Don't think about what anybody has told you. Think about how you feel."

"I know what I'm doing," Mindy said, but her voice was full of air. She dropped her eyes and flapped the dangling pant leg.

"You. Get out of here," the nurse said to Kate, pulling her by the arm. The men outside the door were already reaching for her, and

Kate almost gave in, seeing the three of them squared off. But in the moment before she might have gone quietly, she glanced back and saw Mindy's frustrated, fuddled expression, and how her hands ineptly re-arranged her jeans, trying and failing to cover herself better.

"She needs help," Kate said to everyone in the room, and set her feet. "Mindy, have you forgotten?" She strained to find useful words, persuasive ones. "This is your baby. You've dreamed about it. You know its touch. Are you really sure about this? Sure?"

"There will be other babies," Mindy said.

"Maybe. But there will never be this baby again."

"Get her out of here," said the nurse, yanking Kate into the hall-way, where the men clamped their hands just above her elbows.

Bracing her feet against the wall and leaning hard, Kate managed to get her head back into the cubicle. Finally she knew what she wanted to say, the absolute, rock-bottom truth. "He'll use this against you," she cried. "He'll see you looking at other babies, and he'll remind you. Don't give him another way to hurt you, Mindy."

The girl's hand moved vaguely, as if it could brush Kate's voice back, and then the men pulled Kate away; she practically had to run to stay on top of her feet and demonstrate that she wasn't resisting anymore.

They wouldn't let her stay in the waiting room, although Kate tried to explain that she was finished now. Wordlessly the guards quick-marched Kate beyond the exterior, reinforced, triple-locked door. Pushing her onto the building's shallow wooden porch, they slammed the door behind her so hard the boards shivered under her feet.

At the sound of the banging door, the protesters on the sidewalk shrieked that she was a criminal, a murderer, a creature unnatural and evil. One woman stepped forward like a soloist, shone her flashlight at Kate and cried, "What will you say when you face that baby in the next world? What excuse will you have then?"

"I did my level best," Kate muttered, her jaw tight. She bolted to the car, her hands shaking, and dropped her keys twice. Even when she was in the car the women kept chanting. "Your place in hell is al-ready reserved," one woman yelled. Kate nodded miserably, turned on the ignition and tuned the radio to a rock and roll station, pushing the volume up so high the bass line went fuzzy.

She rested her head against the back of the seat and closed her eyes, trying to stop her jittery tears by focusing on every note sung by some sincere vocalist whose very life would end if he didn't have love. "Don't you wish," she said. The song chewed through chorus after chorus, close to five minutes before it finally sank its teeth onto a final chord. The DJ was skillful; his seam into "Love Sugar" was almost undetectable, and Kate started tapping out the rhythm on the steering wheel before she recognized the song.

You've got what feeds me,
You've got what pleases me,
You are the sweet shore
I'd travel the world for.

Probably Mindy would be humming the deathless words when she went to see Bill-o tonight. He would be tender, his arms full of solace and sweet promise. Only after he had kissed her hands and her breasts and she was dropping into exhausted sleep would he murmur, "Most women can't sleep after doing what you did."

She leaned forward and spun the station dial, hoping to find an oldies station, a symphony, anything. But she got herself trapped in some kind of nest of radio preachers, their theatrical, hectoring voices rising in concert with the chanting outside the car. "For whosoever—" Kate heard, and turned the dial, "—but they did not repent—" "—nothing less than our whole lives—" "—a righteous and perfect sacrifice—" She finally fixed the dial on a rowdy ad for a pizza chain, then glanced up to see Mindy standing on the porch, watching her. The girl wobbled and waved, her pink jeans back on and a peculiar smile playing across her mouth.

She swayed there while Kate hurried over, and the chanting of the protesters rose like baying. Kate concentrated on steering Mindy, who was fully sedated now and walked as if she were boneless. Her liquid ankles and knees swerved into Kate with every step, and her free arm waved toward the women at the gate. "Murderers!" they screamed. "How will you greet your murdered child?"

"Good morning, child," Mindy said, her voice loopy. "Time to get up."

"No joke," Kate snapped.

"No," Mindy murmured obediently.

At the car, Kate balanced Mindy with one hand while she unlocked the passenger door. "Killers! Cold-blooded killers!" cried the women, and Mindy turned to face them.

"Wrong," she sang back. Kate, who had the door open, put her hands around Mindy's waist to help her in, but Mindy grabbed the ledge at the top of the car and held on.

"You people don't know much," she called to a woman who stood with her eyes closed. The woman was screaming, "Destroyer! Enemy of the innocents!"

Mindy leaned across the top of the car. "Would you just shut up a minute and listen? I'm keeping this baby," she bellowed. "I walked out of the clinic and believe me, they didn't make it easy, but my baby's alive. So would you please quit screaming at me? I've already had a hard day."

To Kate's surprise, they actually fell quiet, the woman who'd been calling Mindy "enemy of the innocents" rubbing her hands over her Choose Life sign. Finally another woman asked, her voice respectful, "How did you know you had to leave?"

Kate pulled at Mindy's elbow, but the girl held on, gesturing toward Kate with her head. "Do you see this woman? She explained things to me. She's a minister."

"She brought you here!" cried the woman, outraged, and Kate called back, "And I'm bringing her home again," managing to dislodge Mindy's fingers from the top of the car and settle her inside. She took an extra minute to fasten the girl's seat belt, a process that felt like putting a seat belt on a fish, and by the time she closed the door she was sweating. When she came to her own door she paused for a moment to clear her head.

Just then a woman from the group at the gate ran into the parking lot; she was crouching and scurrying as if she expected enemy fire. She darted up to Kate, one hand groping in her oversized satchel. "Is it true?" she asked. "Are you that young woman's minister?"

"Aren't you supposed to stay off of clinic property?" Kate asked.

"I'm not here to protest," she said, proffering an Indianapolis *Star* card from her shirt pocket while her other hand came up with a small camera.

"We're not tonight's news. Go away," Kate said, banging her knee on the side of the car; at the sound Mindy, who had unlatched her seat belt, opened her door again and spilled onto the blacktop. The protesters cried at her to be careful, didn't she know she had to be careful? and Kate raced back around the car to pick her up, muttering while she cradled her that she was going to chain her in. Mindy smiled. The other woman followed close behind, her camera snapping like a castanet.

The story, with pictures, ran in evening editions that night, and by the morning was on the inside pages of newspapers all across the state, including the *Bugle*. After Kate finished reading it, she brought the article and a cup of decaf to Mindy, who had started crying weakly on the ride back from Indianapolis and hadn't stopped. "Your baby's famous," she said; Mindy closed her eyes.

The phone rang and Kate left her with the newspaper. She supposed that the girl would read the story eventually; for now, Kate had done almost all she could. Later she'd bring in the comics page, and later still go out to buy one of the astrology magazines that Mindy liked, as well as some ice cream. Chocolate chip, her favorite. Kate would ask whether it was the baby's favorite, too, and whether the baby had a sweet tooth, the questions Bill-o might have asked a month ago, and wouldn't ask again.

Fifteen

Without discussion, in the days that followed, Kate and Mindy divided telephone duty. Kate called Bill-o's store, where she left messages with grunting teenagers who laughed when she gave her name. Mindy dialed him at home; she would call late and let the phone ring for ten minutes at a stretch.

Kate suspected that the girl had been going out to Bill-o's house, too, probably leaving him notes there. She crept home to the parsonage long past her Ben Franklin hours—her conversation prefabricated and her expression brittle. "I just want to talk to him. I need to talk with him." She twisted her hands, leaving long red marks. "He thinks I want to talk about the baby. But I just want to talk to *him*. If he knew that he wouldn't be hiding out."

Kate didn't answer, thinking wearily of all Mindy still had to learn. If Bill-o had wanted to be found, they would have stumbled across him at stoplights and on the front porch, as unavoidable as a shadow. But Kate went out to the NaturWise only to discover a building that looked as though it had been abandoned for a week—merchandise stood on the sidewalk in warehouse crates, cash registers sat blank and unstaffed. Marie Moeller reported that a week had passed since Bill-o had come into her IGA for chocolate doughnuts and a fritter. "He might have gone out of town for a meeting. Some sales thing," Ned said.

"Not Bill-o," Kate said, shaking her head. "He doesn't do corporate. He's sliding."

"He would have told us if he was in trouble."

"You've seen him on the way up. But he can fall back down again." *Bringing everybody he can reach with him,* she nearly added, but she didn't want to linger around this topic with Ned. Acting on a superstitious hunch, she went out to the Bradford pear tree and bent one of the skinny branches. It curved, full of dormant good health, and Kate let it snap into place. Back in the house Mindy, one hand supporting her lower back, was dialing the telephone again.

"Ring. Ring. Ring," Mindy said.

"He might be out of town," Kate said helplessly.

"Lights go on at his house. Shades are pulled up and down. The mail's picked up. There are crumbs around the toaster."

"The man can't wipe a counter to save his life," Kate murmured, hating the thought of Mindy peering so closely through his windows she could make out the crumbs.

"He's not even trying to fool me. I wish he would; if I thought he was out of town, I wouldn't keep calling. But he's right close by, listening to his phone ring."

"If that ridiculous story hadn't shown up in the paper—" Kate began.

"It wouldn't make any difference. He would have backed off anyway; he was already starting. Now I'll bet he looks forward to coming home and sitting next to the telephone. This is the happiest he's ever been."

"Then it's time to stop calling," Ned said.

"Like that makes any difference," Mindy said, pressing and letting up on the cutoff button, then dialing again.

At ten-thirty, Kate let her take the phone into the bedroom with her. She knew that Mindy would dial his number all night and was warmed by the thought of Bill-o kept awake. She helped Ned pull out the foldaway, turned off the light and dropped into a flickering, gauzy sleep that dissolved, minutes or hours later, at the sound of Mindy's voice. Kate sat up and strained to hear, then threw back the covers and edged down the corridor to hear better.

"—that really is killing me? You listened. You asked questions; you made suggestions. After a while, nothing I did seemed real until you told me what to think about it. And then your words started to come out of my mouth. Your words were all over my brain. Isn't there some disease like this? That travels to the brain and stays there? That's what you're like." Kate had never heard the girl sound so sure and sorrowful—so adult. The words might have come from Kate's own mouth.

"Mindy," she whispered. "Honey. Stop it."

The girl didn't even look at her. Hunched over the receiver, she went on, "At first I thought I'd die if you never touched me again. I thought that was the thing. But guess what. I can touch myself. I can't talk to myself, though. Or I can't listen to myself, and I can't hear you talking back to me. I need you to do that, and it isn't much, but you won't do it."

"Stop," Kate said. "He isn't there."

"This helps," Mindy said into the phone. "It isn't hurting anybody."

"It's hurting me. And it's not doing you any good. He—" She swallowed. "You don't want your baby to hear you talking this way."

"The baby isn't listening. Babies talk. 'Want this, want this, want this.' The baby doesn't hear what I have to say."

"Then I'll listen to you. Talk to me, Mindy. Don't talk to an empty phone. My God."

"There's a lot to say."

"Don't I know it," Kate said, closing the door behind her and pulling up a chair. She listened straight through the night and into the next day. Every word Bill-o had ever uttered, every near-promise and half-vow, his jokes, his ambitions, his complaints and observations. The words swirled and made drifts; three times Mindy told Kate about the afternoon she and Bill-o had been driving, miles into the country, when he stopped to whistle over a golden retriever running beside the road. He let the dog in the car and started talking to it. He shook its paw and asked how it planned to vote in the next election, then drove all the way back to town, even though Mindy pointed out he wasn't home enough to look after a dog, and she was allergic. He parked at city hall and walked right into the mayor's office with the dog and Mindy trotting behind him. A sharp blond secretary looked up, smiled at Bill-o and said, "Oh, Duke. When are you going to learn to stay home?"

Back in the car, Mindy kept asking Bill-o how he'd known the dog had belonged to the mayor, and Bill-o asked how it could happen that she didn't know her own mayor's dog.

"He didn't even live here then," Mindy said. "How could he have known?"

"He's a scholar. Or a detective," Kate said. "He finds things out."

The girl talked pitilessly, hour after hour, and Kate moved her chair closer to the bed. Story by story, phrase by phrase, Mindy's words conjured Bill-o until he seemed to stand before them, a bright package of joy and malice, a force as coaxing as the sun. Kate leaned toward the bed as if she could warm herself on Mindy's words. "Keep talking," Kate said. "I'm right here."

Well past eight o'clock the next morning, when Ned had already left for work, and sulky gray light seeped between the plaid curtains, Kate finally stood and eased her stiff back and legs. "Do you want breakfast?" she asked. For the first time in hours Mindy fell silent, so Kate tiptoed from the room. It was Friday, Mindy's day off; the girl could sleep. But a half-hour later Mindy was talking again, remarking that no matter what time Bill-o went to Hardee's for coffee, he always knew the name of the girl working the register.

By that evening, her voice had acquired a rasp. While Kate made dinner, the girl described and enumerated the shoes in Bill-o's closet; she hadn't changed out of her nightgown, or combed her hair.

"Every time a pair of shoes looks a little worn, out they go. 'You don't want to look like a hobo,' he says. 'And if you have to make a get-away, you want good shoes on your feet.'"

"Sounds like advice he would give."

"We used to go into my manager's office when I had breaks, and he'd wrap up my shoes in chintz or corduroy the store had gotten in. He'd fold up fabric squares and make me veils to wear. He called me the goddess of the Ben Franklin."

"I hope you demanded that he worship you."

"I should have, shouldn't I? I should have made him kneel down."

"That's never been his posture," Kate said, picking up the telephone and strolling back toward the living room, where she paged Ned. "Mindy won't sleep," she said. "She's on a talking jag. If you write a prescription to calm her down, I'll come get it."

"I can't do that, Kate. She's not my patient."

"She hasn't slept for twenty-four hours, and she won't eat. Think of her baby. It's had enough trauma lately."

After a pause, he said, "I'll see what I can manage." Twenty minutes later he arrived at the front door, the briefcase that usually carried only papers bulging with a stethoscope and blood-pressure cuff. He poked the stethoscope back in place. "You'd think I never made a house call."

"I'm sorry you have to. But you'll see; she can't settle down."

"I'm happy to do this for you, Kate."

"I'm grateful," Kate said. "She's in the bedroom."

She stood near the door while Ned propped Mindy up, listened to her lungs, and asked questions that she talked through. "You're over-excited," he said. "You may not realize the strain you're under." Kate couldn't tell whether Mindy heard or believed him; she described a TV movie about Jackie Kennedy that she wanted to see. It was in three parts: Wednesday, Thursday, Saturday. She kept talking when Ned shook two tablets out of a bottle and handed them to her, promising that the pills were mild, and wouldn't hurt the baby. "What you need," he said, "is sleep."

"It isn't that I don't want to sleep. I just can't imagine doing it."

"Don't think so much."

"Ha! Nobody's ever told me that I think too much," she said.

He coaxed her to lie back down, then joined Kate in the doorway. The two of them watched the girl's lips move as if she were sucking on tiny seeds. "She'll be all right," he murmured. "She's just exhausted. You two put in quite a day up in Indy. Kate, I'm proud of you. You did a fine job."

"Thank you," she mumbled. Everyone in town had an opinion about her trip to Indy. The trustees would have preferred that Kate keep Dove out of the national news, and someone had Xeroxed the UMC statement on abortion—solidly pro-choice—and left it taped to the church's front door.

"It's delicate work," he said. "Nobody could have done any better. I don't mind telling you I was surprised."

"I surprised myself."

"That's just how it works, isn't it? All of a sudden a new way of see-ing things opens up, and before you know it, you're walking in a dif-ferent direction."

"I don't know about that," Kate said, wincing at the eagerness in Ned's voice. "I may hate myself next week. But for about a half-hour there I was sure I was doing the right thing. Or at least I was sure Mindy was doing the right thing."

"She'll thank you. Every time I deliver a baby, the mother thanks me."

"Ned, you know that's not true. When Lucille Oppen had her last girl, she wouldn't talk to anybody for two weeks. A social worker had to come in."

"She thanked me later," Ned said. "She told me that that little girl was the most precious of all. Even though she never did name the father." He glanced at Mindy. "We should tell her this story."

"Didn't you know?" Kate said, lowering her voice. "I thought you must have heard by now. It's Bill-o."

Ned took off his glasses and rubbed his pinched nose. "Well, blow me down."

"First she wanted the baby because she thought it would give her a hold on him. Then she wanted an abortion because he told her that would give her a better hold."

"And now?"

"Maybe she's finally figured out that nothing will get a hold on that man."

Ned fished up a shirttail and started polishing his glasses. "I guess I shouldn't be surprised. But there were times he could have told me."

"He wasn't going around confiding. I came home and caught them in a natural act."

"You could have shared this."

"The lines were down."

"You could have sent up a signal flare." He paused, then laughed a little. "Bet that was a messy scene."

"You don't want to know."

Mindy made a soft, light sound, her ruddy mouth as sweet as a child's. Ned said, "How could he?"

"I tried to warn you."

"Yes, I recall. Are you going to make me eat crow?"

"I would have a month ago."

Together they gazed at Mindy. Ned said, "This doesn't make our situation any easier."

"Was anything ever easy? Remind me."

"I thought our life was, once."

"It wasn't, dear."

Kate touched Ned on the wrist and said, "Are you home for the night?" He nodded, although another minute passed before he sighed and walked into the living room.

The next morning she and Ned rolled out of bed together, early—the foldaway discouraged lolling. Since it was Sunday, Ned beat eggs with cinnamon for French toast while she showered, brushed back her hair with its new flip and pulled on a skirt she loved, its soft wool the color of smoke. Before she left the bathroom, she scooped Ned's razor blades and some old antibiotics into a plastic bag for him to get rid of. Barb had agreed to look in on Mindy a few times through the day, but Kate was still worried about what options the girl might embrace once she woke up.

Kate smelled bacon when she came back into the living room, which meant that Ned had stopped by the IGA on his way home last night and felt festive. "Woo," she said. "Nitrite heaven. Doc Gussey's cutting loose."

"And he's taking you with him," he said, handing her a loaded plate. He had already set the table, lit the squat candle that usually sat on the mantel and placed it beside the syrup bottle.

"Candles for breakfast?"

"When else? We can't have them with dinner." This was Mindy's doing—her first week in the parsonage, she had told Kate that flames drew down darkness.

"Anyone looking in will think we're giving ourselves airs."

"Anybody who's shocked to discover that the minister has a little romance in her life shouldn't go looking in windows." He held up his orange juice for a toast. "Here, let's give them a real shock."

"We don't have much time."

"To my woman, my pastor, my wife," he said.

She lifted her glass to his, then set it back down without sipping. "Does this all mean I'm not a pathogen anymore?"

"I had to back up a little to remember who you were. Who we are together."

"I guess my business up in Indianapolis figures into this."

"I looked at the picture in the paper and thought, 'That woman is capable of anything.'"

"Ned, I love you," she said harshly, which was true, but incidental. He didn't seem to have the slightest idea that he wasn't the only one reviewing their marriage and that the review was not over.

"I love you too, Kate. Always have. Now eat or your stomach will growl on the pulpit. What are you going to preach about?"

She nibbled at her third piece of bacon. She loved the salty, smoked taste more than was good for her, as Ned well knew. "Darkness. I was going to give this homily last week, but then I thought I'd better wait a little after Janelle's funeral."

"Good idea," he said. "But when are you going to talk about Mindy and the clinic? I think it's an opportunity."

"I've already got the homily typed." She stood up and carried her plate to the sink. "Sunday School starts in half an hour. I'll go make sure the room is set up."

"Just think about this. If you tell people what you did at the clinic, you can solidify church membership—maybe win back some people. The bishop would like it."

Ned was partially right, Kate reflected as she buttoned her blazer. The bishop, big on trustworthy leadership, would encourage her to talk honestly. He would call on her to share her thoughts, hopes, fears. He would encourage her right up to the point at which she actually began to tell people the truth.

Crossing the yard to the church, she saw that some kind of small fair was setting up in the park across the street, the sort of little festival sometimes put together by environmental groups, although not usually in such cold weather. So far all that had been erected was a red and yellow striped tent with yellow banners snapping on either side of the entrance. She headed over, ready to sign a petition protesting toxic waste disposal.

While she was halfway across the street, a knot of people wandered out of the tent. Someone gave a happy shout, and the whole group turned and surged in her direction; Kate recognized Robert Efrim's immaculate crest of hair and George Mellot's clublike jaw. They were calling her by name. She could hear Miss Rudell's thin, delighted voice, although she couldn't see her.

Robert Efrim broke away from the pack, strode up to Kate and rested his hands on her shoulders until she stepped away. "Pastor Gussey," he said. "This is a happy day."

"Let's hope so. Do you have a permit to set up a tent on civic property?"

"A happy day," he repeated and reached out again to clasp her shoulders. The others, catching up, crowded and jostled her, eager to touch. "We're happy to be near you."

"The city council won't let you set up a church in a park. This is against two laws that I know of." For the second time, she tried to twist away, but he held firm, his hands pressing down on her shoulders.

"Reverend, I know you don't like to quote Scripture," he said and kept talking over her angry response, "but sometimes there's no other way to say the truth. The stone that the builders rejected has become the cornerstone!"

"Rejected!" called several voices, and, less ecstatically, "Cornerstone." Shifting his position so that he stood by her side, one hand still clutching her shoulder, Robert Efrim began to walk with Kate toward the tent—its interior, she could see now, was the color of lilacs, and there was brilliant green artificial turf underfoot. How many collection plates had this little traveling show required? But once Robert Efrim escorted her through the opening, the other Sanctuary Christians pressed so closely behind her that a belt buckle cut into her hip, she stopped thinking about money. "Oh, no," she said.

A thick cable ran, head height, across every side of the tent, and from it hung posters, photos, and blowups of newspaper articles. Between a sixteen-by-twenty photo of a mutilated fetus and a poster that read LIFE ISN'T A CHOICE, articles about Kate's trip to the abortion clinic were suspended, enlarged so that she could read them from across the tent. The picture of Kate cradling Mindy beside the car got a poster to itself; Mindy's head, grainy in the photo, dangled heavily, a grapefruit held by a twig.

"Our actions give us away," Robert Efrim said, nodding toward the poster.

"Believe me, if I'd known that reporter was there, I'd have taken different actions," Kate said. She reached up and lifted his hand from her shoulder, but she couldn't back out of the tent; the others had swirled in behind them and now stood on every inch of the false grass; those nearest Kate fondled her hands. Though she tried to edge away, they shifted closer, and she felt someone pet the back of her neck as if she were a cat. Her lungs felt tiny and tight, and when she said, "It was a peculiar situation," the words came out high.

"You infiltrated," said a woman's serene voice. Glancing to her left,

Kate could make out the cloud of Mrs. Efrim's bright hair rising behind a man's shoulder. "You're working on the side of the angels."

"Nothing angelic happened at that clinic."

"I knew! I knew when we started praying for you!" Miss Rudell sang out from her place beside the poster, the corner of which she thumbed affectionately. "I could see the light shining in your eyes." She beamed at Kate.

"You're blowing this thing way out of proportion," Kate said, trying again to move away from the hands that cupped and clasped her. "You're claiming a victory where there wasn't any. The girl changed her mind and wanted to go home. So I drove her. That's all."

"'After trying to block the doctor's access to the patient, Pastor Gussey was forcibly removed from the clinic,'" Robert Efrim quoted. "You saved a life. That's a victory."

"I only did what she wanted," Kate said stubbornly.

"When we hunger for what is good, we eat good food," Mrs. Efrim said. "You were drawn to our home. You've become my sister, my own hands and voice."

"I'm not!" Kate said. "Look—you people are opening yourselves up to major embarrassment. I happened to talk the girl out of the clinic. It was an accident, and the circumstances were very specific. I'd never do it again."

She had thought her words would make the Sanctuary Christians stop crawling all over her. Instead, they leaned even closer, flattening their hands on her shoulders and across the top of her head, pressing on her chest and the full length of her back. Even her calves and feet bore the press of their hands, and the more Kate struggled to break free, the closer they held her. A woman behind Kate said, "You should accept. Happiness comes when you accept." Kate yanked away before the woman could start up about the grain of wheat having to die, but then Robert Efrim said, "You've been called. If you turn away from the call now, you'll spend the rest of your life running from it."

"I see you're now willing to believe in calls," Kate snapped. "You've told me what you have to say. It's time for you to shake my dirt from your shoes and go."

Robert Efrim was already shaking his head; a tender expression softened his mouth and eyes. "How could I walk away from you? I love you."

"You call this *love?*" Wrenching an arm free, Kate gestured at the bright canvas walls around them. "What am I supposed to think, when you set up your satellite church across the street from mine? You've already come here once to make trouble. Is it your recent increase in membership that allowed you to come back with a tent?"

"We received a generous gift," he said in a voice heavy with significance.

Such fury raced through her that she lowered her own voice to a near-whisper. Otherwise she might have shouted. "It was Ned, wasn't it? Ned bought you this."

"Not at all. William O'Grady left a donation. He was a great help; he arranged for these posters to be made. He asked me not make the gift public, but then he said that he didn't mind if you knew." Robert Efrim smiled at her, so close she could smell his minty mouthwash.

With great distinctness, she said, "Well, God damn." Then she turned and forced her way toward the tent opening, ramming past the hands that meant to hold and bless her. She could hear Miss Rudell crying, "No! No!" the woman's voice a small pit of grief. Lowering her head, Kate shoved back out into the cold morning, across the street and back to her own church.

None of the Sanctuary Christians followed her—she glanced back over her shoulder to check—but she still kept whispering, "*God* damn, *God* damn." When she burst into the church, Gabe was arranging the hymn numbers on the board, and Ellen rehearsing "Rock of Ages." No Ned. "I'll be back," Kate called and sped over to check the parsonage, even the garage. But the only sign of Ned was the breakfast dishes, washed and draining, and she hustled back to the church to straighten her hair and slip on her robe. There, at five minutes before ten, she found Ned, who whistled with relief.

"Where have you been?" he said. "Everybody's waiting for you."

"Where have you been? Have you looked outside? You've got to get rid of those people."

"Kate, I want to ask you a favor."

"I don't care if you have to call the police. But please get them gone."

"Kate, they'd like to come to my Sunday School class."

"Come again?"

"They promised not to ask questions; they understand that they're guests. I told them that I have a lesson planned, and I expect to teach it. But they're ready to listen, Kate. Bob Peters is here. We can get him to come back to Dove."

"By any chance, does your lesson have to do with Mindy?" she said.

"This is our chance. We can turn them away, or we can help ourselves. And them."

Kate touched her head behind her ear, where the bone felt too tight. Ned was wearing the same expression he'd worn shortly before Janelle died—engrossed, confident. She said, "You're making lemonade, is that it?"

"God handed us Robert Efrim."

"I'd just as soon hand him back."

"We should take this chance, Kate. How many do you think we're going to get?" He held out his hand and she took it, allowing the twenty members of Dove Methodist Church and the fifteen or so Sanctuary Christians gathered for Sunday School to see the Reverend and Doctor Gussey walking hand in hand to greet them.

Ned began the class with a passage from Isaiah and some questions; Kate fixed a quiet expression on her face and surveyed the visitors. True to their word, they held a respectful silence, though several, including Jess Little, caught her eye and sent her shining smiles.

Ned leaned forward to answer a question Kate hadn't heard. "Let me tell you something. A man I know has fathered a child, a baby not yet born. He calls the baby a mistake and wants the mother to kill it. He swears he won't support them, and I believe him. He says, 'I'm pretty despicable, aren't I?' I think, 'Yup, you sure are.' He says, 'The world doesn't need any more mistakes like me.'"

Ned paused and tapped the table while Kate wondered how he had gotten from Isaiah to Bill-o. Ned said, "He's right. The last thing the world needs is any more like him. But the same child isn't born twice. This baby might be what brings that proud father to his knees. The people we give up on are the ones who save us. I learn this every day."

Kate was startled to think that Ned, who never gave up on anyone, had given up on her. Now he was discussing the stone that the builders rejected, a theme apparently inescapable today. He said "rejoice" and "salvation." He sounded like a bad TV minister, reaching for holy-sounding words, turning everything into some kind of hooray for God. She only snapped to attention when she realized he was saying lines that had, up till now, been hers.

"All we can do is embrace what comes to us. We can't pretend to know where our roads will lead. What was right yesterday looks wrong today. The path that led downhill turns up. Sometimes the road brings us back to the very thing we'd left behind. I've seen it happen. A woman supporting abortions yesterday can find herself leading women away from abortion clinics today. New roads!"

He leaned over and kissed the top of Kate's head. She mugged, opening and closing her mouth like a fish.

"Ned, may I say a few words now?" she asked once the chuckles died down.

"Of course," he said and mouthed something at her—perhaps "Don't," perhaps "More." She nodded. It would be easy now to say the right words, the ones that would win Bob and Jess back again. But before she could attempt to woo anyone, a few things had to be set straight.

"At the service this morning I'm going to preach about how God sometimes makes us walk in darkness. That's what I've been pondering for the last few weeks. But sitting here with you this morning, I'm thinking about some special applications."

Ned moved very slightly away from her, which suited her fine. "Let's face it. We always walk in darkness. We can't see one inch in front of us, and the only proof we have of God's presence is the fact that we don't pitch into a chasm. It isn't much."

Bob Peters looked stone faced, and the other Sanctuary Christians had lost their fellowshippy smiles; her own church members hadn't been smiling to start with. Kate wet her lips. "Ned here was talking about mistakes. Mistakes? You bet we make them, every one of us. We may not make the same mistake twice, but that just means we're inventive about new ones. So our duty is to cushion one another as we fall." From the side of the room a Sanctuary Christian woman said "A-men," and Kate turned to face her.

"I guess you all know about my trip to the abortion clinic. You need to understand. I didn't go to intervene. I went because the young woman wanted to go, and I brought her back because she changed her mind. As far as I'm concerned, both her choices were bad ones." No one said amen to that.

"She's looking for a choice that will make her happy. She'd like me to tell her what that choice is—I'm supposed to give good news. And the only thing I can think of to give her is a sandwich."

Ned murmured, "Feed the hungry."

"I've tried to find God's face in her situation. But the harder I look, the more I see only human faces, my own among them, making mistakes."

Ned's face, when Kate glanced at him, had taken on a dusty cast, and she inhaled hard, whether out of confidence or pugnaciousness she couldn't tell. "Things aren't going to change. We'll go right on bumping into one another, stumbling over messy human mistakes when we'd meant to find some clean, whole answer. And you know what I say about that? Be glad if you can't find the perfect answer. You're being forced into the world. Be glad if you're asked to help one woman make a wrenching, unbearable decision. You know what that struggle is? It's *holy*."

Kate stopped. No other word came to mind; she could only hope she'd said enough. At the moment she wasn't exactly sure just what she'd said. Ned asked if anyone else would like to speak, and none of the Sanctuary Christians volunteered, a small point of surprise and satisfaction. After some final comments, Ned let the class go, early. The Sanctuary Christians filed out while the Dove members chatted, two of them thanking Kate for her talk. "I knew those pictures in the tent were wrong. The people there kept pointing and saying, 'This is your pastor. This is who leads you,' but I knew you couldn't have just yanked that poor girl out of the clinic. That wouldn't be like you," one woman said.

"I'm afraid not," Kate said.

"I got into a little squabble with my husband last week. 'It's not that simple,' I kept telling him, and he kept telling me that I sounded just like Pastor Kate."

"Oh, dear."

The woman laughed. "I told him we could discuss both sides of the issue over dinner, and so he took me out. Worked pretty well."

"Glad I was a help to you," Kate said, and the woman touched her on the arm and turned away. A moment later, Ned appeared at her side with a cup of coffee, which she sucked down.

"Barb called the police," he said. "They're making Robert Efrim strike the tent."

"Robert Efrim's done what he came here to do. Did you know that Bill-o underwrote that side show?"

"I'm not surprised. He's been going out to their church for Bible study. He told Robert that he wanted to learn what they could teach him."

"New roads," Kate said bitterly. "Sorry—I wasn't criticizing you. You surprised me. You had some new things to say."

"You likewise."

Kate looked at him, his eyes made small behind his glasses. She saw the rough patches on his cheeks that appeared when he slept too little, and the long lines that framed his mouth. No other face had ever been so clear to her. "You know me pretty well," she said, then added, "You look tired."

"I am. I can't take that fold-out bed any more."

"Me neither. We can break the bad news to Mindy when we get home."

"Tell her that new beds attract new chances."

Kate smiled unevenly and reached out to touch one of the lines beside his mouth. He covered her hand with his, then turned; moving lightly, he confident, she tentative, they walked through the crowd.

Sixteen

By the time Kate returned to the parsonage that night after Bible study and the youth group meeting and an unscheduled discussion with three of the trustees, it was after ten o'clock, and she found that she had been reinstalled in the parsonage bedroom. Ned had changed the sheets, transferred clothes, set armloads of Mindy's magazines and pillows in neat stacks on the guest room bureau. He had even vacuumed, a task Kate hadn't gotten to for weeks.

"Gosh," she said, watching him pull a sweater of Mindy's from the bookcase. "You're like a white tornado."

"It feels good to get things taken care of."

"Where's Mindy?"

"Barb took her out for dinner. She's still trying to find out who the baby's father is." He combed his fingers through his hair, hardly rearranging it at all. "Mindy's parents will take her back, if she just tells them."

"We can't make that decision for her."

"I know. But the house would be ours again. You can't say it isn't tempting."

As a matter of fact, Kate could. No more pronouncements about the universe? No more odd, occasional jokes? Never again to hear a word or inflection and know Mindy's thought exactly as she knew her own? When the girl came home that night, she was wearing Kate's green gloves. Kate took her into her arms. Mindy looked at the re-arranged clothes and trinkets and said, "So I'll be sleeping in the little bed now."

"You may like it better," Ned said. "The mattress is very firm. It should give you more support."

"Well, that's probably good; yesterday my back hurt all day."

Kate frowned. "Why didn't you tell me? I could have put a board under the mattress. We've been meaning to do it."

"I didn't want to bug you. You seemed to have enough on your mind," Mindy said. Ned looked surprised and nodded approvingly. He nodded again when Mindy offered to wash the dishes—a first—even though Ned shooed her away and said he'd tackle them himself.

The girl drifted into the living room and back out. She lit on the arm of the couch and fiddled with the sleeve of her sweater. Kate said, "Mindy, you're welcome to stay here as long as you need to. Just because we've moved you into the guest bedroom, don't think you have to leave." She pitched her voice low, under the racket Ned was making with the dishes.

But Mindy's response was clear and social. "I appreciate that," she said. "Thank you. How did things go for you today?"

Kate peered at the girl; never before, not once, had she asked about Kate's day. "One service, one youth fellowship meeting, and a hundred and sixty-four people who want me to call them. Not bad, for a Sunday."

"Are the people with the tent coming back?"

"Probably, but I'm not inviting them. What did you hear?"

"My aunt says we're going to wake up and find them in the living room. We should put purple at the doorways; purple drives away."

"These people are pretty determined. And probably colorblind," Kate said.

Ned turned off the water in the kitchen. "Don't be surprised if some of them show up and want to talk to you, Mindy. They feel a connection."

"Tell me about it. All of a sudden I'm in some spotlight." Mindy leaned toward Kate. "A woman came into the store yesterday, bought three dollars' worth of polished cotton, and then asked me to sign her receipt. I didn't get it—I thought she wanted some kind of guarantee about the fabric. But she wanted my *autograph*. Like I was a movie star."

Kate shook her head. "People don't begin to understand."

"I picked up the pen, but my hand was shaking so bad I couldn't write my own name."

"Adrenaline," Ned said. "Did you feel sick later?"

"I went in back to work stock and get some water. After a while, the shaking stopped."

"She meant well," Kate said. "I guess."

"If there hadn't been a counter between us, I think she would have tried to pat my stomach," Mindy said.

"She meant well, but she was an idiot. The world is loaded with them," Kate said.

Mindy let a moment go by. "I heard that Dr. Gussey praised you in Sunday School."

"Word gets around."

"My aunt said he held you up as an example."

"I did," Ned said.

Mindy said, "That's nice. If people were going to show up out of the blue some morning, I'd want my husband to be there to praise me. If I had a husband."

Before the silence became embarrassing, Kate said, "I know you don't feel this way now, Mindy, but believe me—you'll meet people. Other men. You don't have any idea of everything that's ahead. What are you thinking?" she added, watching the girl's face go sour.

Mindy batted her eyes lavishly. "'Oh, sure, I'd love to go out with you. By the way, this is my kid. You don't mind a little company, do you?'"

"For lots of men, a child is a plus," Ned said.

Kate murmured, "Dr. Gussey loves children."

"So does Pastor Gussey," he murmured back.

Mindy chewed on her bottom lip. "Bill-o told me once that the only completely happy people were couples. 'It only works with two,' he said. 'A third person throws off the balance; there's always an audience. It's never clean again.'"

"Typical," Kate said.

"I thought he was talking about us. But now it looks like he was talking about you and Dr. Gussey."

"I wouldn't bet on that," Kate said.

"Anyway, he's got it wrong," Ned said. He stepped around the divider, using a fresh kitchen towel to dry between his fingers with a doctor's unthinking diligence. Kate braced herself. If he started quoting Scripture, she would spring across the room and plunge his head in the dishwater. "It's easiest for outsiders to see the happiness of couples. Newlyweds. Mother and baby. Once you get more than two, you lose that perfect reflection. But there isn't any less happiness. It's just a little more refracted."

"Do you think you could tell Bill-o this?" Mindy said.

"He already knows," Ned said.

"No, he doesn't," Kate said. "He doesn't know squat about happiness, and he knows less about love."

"He knows," Ned insisted. "He just doesn't want to know. He's like a horse being trained to bridle. He knows the pain in his mouth will stop if he'll just turn his head, but he hates having to turn his head."

Tears rushed to Kate's eyes, the last thing she wanted. "Quite an analogy," she said faintly.

"You gave it to me when you were in seminary. It was your teacher's example of how people respond to grace."

"I remember. But you know what I've learned since then? Some horses would rather have a mouthful of blood than go where you're trying to lead them."

"Doesn't mean we should stop trying."

Mindy said, "Is this how you talked to him? Blood and metal in his mouth? No wonder he's hiding out."

"We didn't have to say a word," Kate said. "Marriage is like fire to him—he can't resist putting his hand into it. He gets burned and jumps back, but he still loves the sparks."

"You're not making things better," Mindy said.

"We're telling you what we see," Kate said. Then Ned started telling Mindy that the baby was a commitment, and that commitment would carry her through the hard days.

"Things will get better," he said. His smile was directed at Kate, who said, "You'll get your feet on the ground."

"Better than that," Ned said. "You'll find a real closeness with someone. More happiness than you'd ever imagined."

"I can imagine a lot." Mindy yawned. "Bedtime. I'm sleeping for two."

"We won't be far behind you," Kate said with a little more heat than she'd intended. When Ned went into the kitchen to make popcorn, her treacherous brain replayed Bill-o's rough voice talking about her hungers. Her hand rattled as if it were a china cup.

Returning with the popcorn, Ned picked up her hand and squeezed it. "I read somewhere that when soldiers come back from active duty, they and their spouses have to start all over again," he said. "Their biggest mistake is thinking they can just pick up where they left off."

"You haven't been away."

"Psychologists say the couples who do best think of the return as a new courtship. Don't rush, they say. Find out what your partner is thinking."

"Okay. Tell me what you're thinking."

"I'm thinking that you've had a lot of decisions to make. You're becoming a whole new Kate."

"No different," she managed to say. "What decisions are you thinking of?"

"You've been in the news. Bill-o calls you the Lady Minister On The Move. Where are you going to go from here?"

Kate's lungs seemed to be filled with clotted, scummy air. "Ned, what has Bill-o told you?"

"What has he told me when? I haven't even seen the guy in three weeks. Although the last time I did he told me that you still make the same lasagna you made when you were twenty. He said it was like coming home again. He said it was great to have known you when."

As he spoke, Ned's body gently collapsed. Even his head, which he always thrust a little ahead of his shoulders, urging himself along, rocked back as if he were dazed. Not dazed, Kate corrected herself, vanquished. And she was vanquished with him. If he knew what she had done, her confession would rob him of the dignity he was trying to hold onto. If he didn't know, the information would strip away the dignity he believed he had a right to. She had made a commitment. She believed in commitment. If she didn't believe in commitment, what did she have left to believe?

"It's a different lasagna," she said. "Bill-o likes to pretend he has some special knowledge about me. But you know a Kate he's never dreamed of."

"He's been living here. He's seen you in action."

"He hasn't seen a thing; he might as well have kept sleeping on his office floor."

Still clasping her hand, Ned raised her fingers to his mouth. "So you're glad I'm here?"

"Yes," she said, a ferocious, foolhardy word. "Bill-o was my mistake. You are my husband. My *husband*. My life's nail. It's more than he could ever hope to be."

Ned dipped his head so that his lips grazed Kate's knuckle. A long time passed before he said, "Shall we go to bed?"

She turned out the light in the living room, and in the darkness Ned's arms slipped around her. It was easy to stand in his embrace, whose lines and angles she had long ago learned to fit.

"It's been a long day. I just need sleep," he said. "Do you mind?"

"I don't mind." She was grateful that the room's darkness disguised the relief and disappointment she could feel spread across her face.

Kate had forgotten to move the alarm clock back to the bedroom, so she and Ned slept deep into the next morning, hardly turning until after eight. Even then, only the sound of Mindy's methodical cursing was enough to drive them into the living room.

Hair uncombed, robe untied, her bare toes curled in the cold, Mindy stood in the front doorway holding the *Bugle*. "Fuck. Oh, fuck. Oh fuck, oh fuck, oh fuck."

"What?" Kate and Ned said together, Kate's tone a degree higher than her husband's. "We're up," he added, as she said, "Are you hurt?"

Mindy hardly glanced at them. Clutching the newspaper, she walked in a tiny circle and swore. Kate trailed a step behind the girl and read the headline over her shoulder.

GARDEN CENTER CLOSED; $4,000 MISSING. "I had a feeling," Kate said, pulling the paper out of Mindy's hand.

> Two days of investigation have revealed over $4,000 missing from the accounts at Elite's new NaturWise garden center. Following complaints from several disgruntled creditors, investigators began a review of the store's accounts and discovered unexplained gaps. The store's manager, William O'Grady, has not been seen for a week.

"Of course, it's too early to be making accusations," said investigator Darryl Binke. "But we certainly have grounds here to wonder about embezzlement. That's one of the charges we will be keeping in mind."

"Shit," Mindy said.

"Hush," Kate said.

"What was he thinking? There's got to be a mistake here. This is stupid, and he's never stupid." Mindy kept tracing her tight circle, her arms crossed over her breasts as if she could protect herself now. "All of a sudden I'm the last one to know. What does he expect me to do?"

"Nothing," Ned said. "He doesn't expect you to do anything."

"That's right," Kate said, not adding the rest: He isn't thinking about you. They all three knew it. "Anyway, you already have your work cut out for you."

"Do I? What's my work?"

"You have to have a baby." Kate meant for the words to sound gentle, but the tone slipped away from her and turned prim. She didn't blame Mindy for snarling, "Thank you for that bit of late-breaking news."

"This story doesn't change anything," Kate went on. "Are you thinking that if Bill-o had married you, he would have had clean payroll sheets? Take it from one who knows; absolutely nothing would be different."

"Jesus," the girl said, resting her face on the bookcase's hard edge.

"You're not the only one struggling with this," Ned said. "Last night I was thinking I'd go see him, take him out to lunch. There's one invitation I won't be making."

"Well, what do you know. Ned finally gives up," Kate said.

"We offered him a way to start a new life, and he took advantage of us. He might be in Bangkok now, living the high life off of our good wishes."

"He likes oriental women," Mindy said, her forehead still pressing against the bookcase. "He likes their small hands."

"Did he tell you that one day when you couldn't get a pair of gloves on?" Kate asked.

"A ring," Mindy said.

"Nothing has changed."

"Right. Nothing has changed a bit, except that my baby's father has become a felon. A wanted man—ha! Wanted by somebody other than me. I'm carrying a criminal's kid. And you're saying that doesn't make any difference?"

"Yes," Kate said. "Look. Bill-o was just waiting for his chance. So now's your chance. You've got his child; teach it all the things Bill-o never learned—truth telling, kindness. This is the baby who can make up for the sins of the father." She looked at Ned, her life's nail.

He said, "If you get away from him, you can make a whole new start."

Mindy shook her head. "You two. It must be nice to live in your world."

"I'm trying to tell you that you've got options," Kate said. "This doesn't have to be a tragedy."

"I appreciate your efforts," Mindy said, turning toward the hallway.

"Where are you going?" Ned asked in a tone so sharp and father-ish that Kate was startled, although Mindy's step didn't pause.

"To review my options," she said and closed the bedroom door.

"She doesn't really have many," Ned said.

"She's got more than she thinks," Kate said at the same time. "She does," she insisted in response to his questioning look and went into the kitchen to make coffee. She made it weakish, the way Mindy liked, although she and Ned were the ones who wound up drinking the whole pot.

For the next several days, Kate tended Mindy, and Ned tended Kate. She was content to let him keep up with the laundry and to field phone calls; later she would examine whatever exchange of power was going on between them.

Right now, Mindy stared for a half-hour at a time out the front window. After Mindy went to work, Kate looked out and saw blank sky, bleached grass, the last few sticks of a garden. Kate was prepared, if Mindy asked, to drive back up to the clinic, but she didn't think that Mindy would ask. Having walked out on that option once, she was unlikely to return. But watching Mindy's somber face, paler by the day, made Kate's heart flinch. She thought up new ways to please. She bought thick flannel sheets for the girl's bed and made an elaborate chocolate cake twice in one week.

"You can't afford this," Ned said, bringing her coffee while she frosted the sides.

"We have enough money."

"You can't afford three hours in the kitchen. Mindy isn't the only project in your life." The time had almost arrived, for instance, to write the church's quarterly budget, a chance to look directly at all of her diminished numbers and contemplate their meaning.

The time had also arrived to plan Advent services. Already Ellen had scheduled extra choir rehearsals, so on Tuesday and Wednesday nights Kate heard voices scraping through "O Come, O Come Emmanuel," and "What Child Is This," hymns that repeated mercilessly inside her skull while Ned slept beside her.

Gabe stopped in her office, and she assigned him the gift tree for Limestone Manor nursing home and Kris Kringle for the Boys' Club. She threw away The Sermon Sourcebook and labored through her own homilies, though they seemed too short and off the point. "It isn't easy to believe in new life now, when the world looks dead. But now is when we must believe." A ten-year-old could probably write better, but Kate couldn't. Strength was required, all she had, to sit with her Bible and dwell on passages that heralded the coming of a child.

And Mindy continued to grow more quiet, more considerate. Her radio played softly. She toweled down the shower walls every morning and helped Ned with the supper dishes. When Kate asked what she'd like to watch on TV, she had no preferences and went to bed at nine-thirty.

"I was wrong," Ned said. "I admit it. I thought she would be the world's worst houseguest, but she's become the world's best."

Kate held her tongue, although she found the girl's silent thoughtfulness unnerving. Like the Virgin Mary, Mindy was pondering things in her heart. Kate knew the insights that might lie there and wished she could protect the girl from them.

One night near Thanksgiving, when Ned was still at the hospital with seven-year-old twins who'd waded into an icy creek, Mindy thanked Kate for that evening's ham and scalloped potatoes, set down her glass of milk and said, "The baby just moved. An arm or something. It's been doing it for a week."

"A week! Mindy, for Pete's sake. Why didn't you say something?"

"I wasn't sure at first. The feeling isn't all that clear—it might have been indigestion."

"Aren't you blasé. We should have a party. You sound like you need somebody to remind you to be happy."

"That's probably right. I don't feel all that great."

Kate let her gaze sweep the table. The pink remains of the ham and the brilliant scraps of lettuce clinging to the salad bowl seemed luminous, infused with a light she couldn't possess. She could admire it, though. "How does it feel?" she asked.

"Real," Mindy said.

"Three months of throwing up didn't feel real?"

"It didn't feel different. That could've been the flu. This feels like I've swallowed a fish—a live one, whole. Anyway, it doesn't feel like feeling sick."

"What are you going to do?" Kate asked, meaning what did Mindy plan as a celebration. One of Kate's parishioners, a mother of five, bought a new hat as soon as the baby she was carrying started to wiggle.

"I thought—" Mindy began, "—give it to you."

Kate felt her jaw go loose. Undammed, Mindy's words poured forth, full of broken phrases, half-finished thoughts. Single mothers, she was stammering, a good home makes good opportunities—timing —security—stability… Letting Mindy's storm of words pass over, Kate seized on images. A crib wedged into the guest room, soft balls and blocks, Kate's own hands cradling a baby's head. The tiny shirts and shoes. And Ned, to whom happiness might be returned if they took in this salvation baby.

"—protection," Mindy was saying. "You have to start from where you are."

"Let me think," Kate said, holding up a shaky hand.

"Sure. You need to think. But what can you think, in the end? We're not in a normal situation. This baby should have been yours."

That was wrong, but Kate wasn't able to bring the words to her lips. In some ways—many!—Mindy was right.

After Mindy went to bed, Kate paced the narrow hallway, crazy for Ned to come home, but he was late, late. There must have been complications with the twins. She polished the words to show him this new window in their lives. The idea is full of problems. Don't answer right away. But when he pushed the door open his expression was already scoured; he kneeled beside her, cupped her chin and said, "How could we? This of all babies. You see that it's impossible, don't you?"

"She called you at the hospital?"

"She wanted to talk to me before you did; we stayed on the phone for a long time. After being mothered by you for all these weeks, she can't imagine anyone would be a better mother."

This stung; Kate pressed her eyes shut for a moment. "I can't believe Mindy told you I'd agreed."

"She didn't. She said you were thinking it over, but that she was hopeful. She wanted me to be hopeful, too. I didn't know she knew the word."

"She's been hanging around holy joes. She's picked up the lingo."

"Look at the situation, Kate." He pulled himself up to sit on the couch beside her. His hands, wrapped around hers, were stone cold. "Even if Mindy signs the baby to us, Bill-o won't. And how could we raise a child if we know that any minute he might come back to take it away?"

Kate licked her dry lips. "A baby, Ned. It needs a chance. This baby more than most. And Bill-o's wanted now; he's finally stepped over the line. If he comes back, we'll turn him in."

"Listen to yourself. This is Bill-o we're talking about. Nothing sticks to him; you've told me that often enough."

Kate's lungs ached. "Well, aren't we just an illustration of cosmic irony. Here's the thing I've wanted more than anything, the thing we've both wanted. Prayed for. And now you—you of all people—don't want to let it in."

"Ironic, all right," Ned said. She heard the tears in his voice. "You've begged me to stop bringing complications into our lives. You've reminded me over and over again that charity has a cost. Now all I can see attached to this baby is a lifetime of payments due. It's more than we can afford, Kate."

"I don't know what we can afford. Lately we've been getting into costs I can't calculate."

"It will ruin us," he said.

"I know," she said. "That doesn't change anything."

They didn't stumble to bed until past midnight, and though they lay still, crackling anxiety filled the space between them. Even Ned was rigid, his sighs betraying his raging wakefulness. After an hour, he crept from the room, and she turned her pillow and stretched her legs.

She couldn't dim her mind though, and kept thinking about the distilled dread on Ned's face. Kate didn't often have the opportunity to relieve him of a burden, and now the urge to do so pulled at her like a fierce current.

But the baby exerted a tide of its own. Her mind raced from bassinets and formula to soft, tiny shoes. A sleeping child, a curious child, a child to be nursed through colic and shadowy terrors. Desire racked her body like a cramp. She let herself imagine the new, vague hands, the soft baby jackets and sweet socks.

Going further, flogging herself, she envisioned an older child sitting in a high chair, joyfully banging its tray while she diced cooked chicken and carrots. The child's whoop when Kate placed the food on the tray; the child's wild laugh when it scooped up a piece of chicken and beaned Kate between the eyes. And then the second of calculation crossing the child's face, the flash of cunning. The day Bill-o would arrive with arms open and his smile slicked back. Kate groaned into her pillow and thrashed. From the living room she heard a page turn.

Five more times, or ten, she straightened the blankets and tried to think about how heating costs were going up or—hopeless—a possible homily for Sunday. Her breath was twined around the baby, its clucking murmur and birdlike shrieks. Bill-o, she reminded herself, but all she heard in response was the baby's chuckle as it kicked, happily naked on the changing table. By the time morning came, her arms shook as if she'd been pushing pianos.

Ned asked, "What are you thinking?" as soon as she entered the living room, and though she knew, she waited two more days before she gave him an answer. She wanted to say something admirable and clear, to make Ned know she wasn't choosing only for herself, or even for them, but also for him, him alone, who knew all about desire but was so late to learn about fear.

But two more sleepless nights only made her brain a murkier stew of conflicting longings. She began to lose track of what was admirable and of which gifts were meant for whom. Coming back into the parsonage and seeing Ned look up, his face a screen of trepidation, she blurted, "I've given up a child for both of my husbands," and let him comfort her while she wept.

Seventeen

Kate waited until well into the next morning before telling Mindy. She wanted to be steady on her feet when Mindy mounted the vivid portraits of a blighted childhood that Kate herself had painted. But Mindy only said, "I see," then moved toward the door with a dignity she seemed to have learned overnight.

"Do you understand?" Kate asked.

"How could I not understand? But I'm sorry."

"Please don't apologize."

"I'm not apologizing," Mindy said. "I'm sorry that the baby could have been lucky, but now it won't be." She closed the door behind her, and Kate rubbed her hot eyes, then got up and went to the church.

Work didn't block out the hoarse debate that muttered, day and night, at the base of her skull, but it drove the words back. Whenever she paused in making phone calls or taking notes in meetings, the words surged up again, and she heard her own voice drearily re-explaining every tired reason for not taking this baby. "I have made my decision," Kate reminded herself, but still she kept reasoning, defending, arriving again and again at the same hateful conclusion.

"I'm doing nothing. And this is still the hardest thing I've ever done," she told Barb.

"Nothing's firm yet," Barb said, lifting her hands from the keyboard. "You can change your mind."

"You don't need to remind me of that," Kate murmured, flinching from her friend's imploring eyes. "How are things on the home front?"

"Everybody's off the high horse. Dick says Mindy's learned a thing or two. Mindy says Dick's going to like knowing his own grandchild."

"What does he say then?" Kate asked.

"He still wants to know his grandchild's father."

Kate sighed and looked at her frayed cuticles. Barb said, "You know who he is, don't you?"

"Yes. Believe me, you don't want to pull him into things."

"It would be better to know. At least then we'd all have the same ground under our feet."

"It wouldn't make any difference," Kate said. "His feet haven't touched Elite ground in a while."

When Kate looked up, Barb was shaking her head, her face close to colorless. "I can't believe it. How stupid can one girl be?"

"He's a pro. You can't blame her for being taken in."

Barb's lips were parted and her eyes closed, her head moving slowly back and forth. Kate stroked her arm. "Listen," she said, "I wouldn't tell Mindy's folks. It's not going to help them to know this."

"No," Barb said.

"It's not as if he were a local boy, somebody we could talk to."

"I get it," Barb said, pulling away.

"There's really nothing we can do." Kate didn't try to check the pleading note in her voice, and neither, when she spoke, did Barb.

"There's one thing. But you won't do it."

"I can't. I can't. Don't you see that?"

"Yes," Barb said. "But it's still the only thing." She swiveled away and stared at the letter on the computer screen. Kate went back to her office. "I have made my decision," she murmured to the air and felt, as usual, unconvinced.

A knock on the door saved her from having to ponder any further; Kate looked up, then steeled herself as Barb ushered a pale, grim Judy Leiper into the office. Judy and her husband, Arden, had had their bad stretches—he'd slept around, and everybody in Elite knew about the morning Judy came downstairs to find her wedding picture in the middle of the floor, where Arden, drunk, had taken it from the wall and defecated on it. But in the last year they seemed to have come into the clear, attending church together, buying a new split-level.

Now Judy sat stiffly before Kate, her hands squeezed around the top of her handbag. "He acts like he's listening when I talk, but I can see he's miles away. He tells me exactly when he'll be home, and then he's home on the dot—not even five minutes late because he wanted to buy a magazine. All of a sudden he won't walk out the door without taking a shower."

"None of this has to mean anything," Kate said gently.

"I know that. Maybe Arden's just preoccupied. He gets that way. But maybe not." Judy loosened her grip on her purse long enough to fish out lip balm and apply it, then put the tube away and throttle the purse clasp again. "Last time it started when he quit eating dinners I fixed and sat for whole nights without saying a word. I can't pretend I don't remember."

"Have you asked him what's going on?"

"'Arden, why aren't you listening to me?' And he says, 'I was listening. You were talking about string beans.' And I was. I'll bet other gals can find more exciting things to talk to him about."

"So could you, Judy, if you wanted to."

"I'm his wife! We're not there to entertain each other."

You're not there to bore each other, either, Kate thought, but said, "You're afraid and you're angry. What do you want to do?"

"I want to believe him. But he won't let me."

She sniffled. Kate gauged whether she wanted a hug. No. "Judy, you can live like this, day after day, watching him and trying to figure out whether he's keeping a secret from you. Or you can ask him. It's a judgment call."

"Just like that. Don't you make it sound easy."

"I know it isn't easy—" Kate began.

"Could you stand living like this?" Judy demanded. "Not ever knowing, not ever being able to rest?"

Kate paused. No matter what people said, nobody really wanted to know the pastor's problems. But Judy was waiting for an answer, and her pastor owed her one. "Yes," Kate said.

After Judy left, Kate stared out her office window and contemplated the Bradford pear. Come spring, the tree would bloom, thrive, thicken and extend its branches, and if Kate had sense she'd go out and chop it down right now. Still, it was a beautiful specimen, and the church would never have been able to afford it on its own. "What's the moral?" Kate said aloud. Pulling herself to her feet, she went to the outer office to see if Barb wanted to go to the mall.

"What's the occasion?"

"Christmas is coming. Pretty soon I'll have to preach about how we shouldn't be focusing on material things. Let's go out and buy stuff."

Barb rummaged in a drawer for her purse. "I'll drive."

Kate smiled, taking in her friend's clenched, freshly permed hair and the lipstick that clung to the tiny creases in her lips. This primping had been silently taken on after Lucinda Akins complained about a lack of professional appearance in the church office. Kate said, "You're good to me. I was feeling the walls close in."

"You need to get more rest."

"I rest enough. I just don't know what to do with my hands."

"Now you know why expectant mothers knit," Barb said, and Kate laughed, even though the comment rankled.

On the drive over, Kate studied people's frozen gardens. Twice in the last week a drizzly, half-frozen rain had sniveled through town, deflated the cotoneaster berries, and heaved the lawns until the ground looked churned. Now everyone wished that snow would just come and cover the mess.

The mall was packed, naturally, and shimmered with noise. Store owners had adopted an old-fashioned Christmas theme. Carols bleated from speakers disguised as steeples, Salvation Army bell ringers stood in long gowns at the entrances to Sears and Penney's, and a giggly children's choir wearing velvet and lace wound through the food court singing "God Rest Ye Merry Gentlemen" over and over. "What do you need?" Kate yelled.

"I thought I'd go to Mother-To-Be and get Mindy a decent-looking pair of pants. She's not going to be able to button those pink ones much longer."

"She can't button them now; I had to give her a big safety pin last week. But you might as well save your money. She'll wear a barrel before she wears maternity clothes. Cotton knits probably attract bad hair."

"I'll look anyway. They must have something for the fashion-minded youngster in the family way." She paused. "I guess you don't want to come with me."

"I need to look for a present for Ned." Kate scuffed the neat toe of her shoe across the filthy floor. "Why don't I meet you back by the arcade in an hour?"

"I could use your advice. You know what she likes."

"You'll do fine. Right now I have to get into my annual holiday struggle with Mr. I-Reject-Crass-Materialism." Barb laughed and relented; Kate watched her shoulder her way through the crowds until she rounded a corner. Then Kate turned in the other direction.

She had picked a bad day. Irritable shoppers, oldsters walking for exercise, and packs of teenagers clogged the walkways. She nearly knocked down a high-wheeled, Victorian-style bicycle outside a cosmetics boutique. Striding past displays of athletic shoes, ovenware, purple geodes laid open like glittering mouths, she became irritable herself. Nothing here was remotely Neddish. She'd wind up combing the stores until a day or two before Christmas, when she would bring home an expensive sweater that he would wear twice, then put away. Envisioning the annual scenario, she rounded a corner without looking and took a teenager's elbow sharply in her waist. Snapping around to shout at him, she found herself face to face with a store called NEW!, and forgot what she'd been ready to yell.

In the window, suspended from invisible wires, pastel blankets floated like flying carpets, little rompers and overalls soared over a line of dancing socks, and an old-fashioned buggy hung upside down like a gravely silly bumbershoot. Someone must have spent days to set everything up. An electric train wound around a long track with pink and yellow velvet bears, small enough to fit a baby's hand, sitting in every car. High above the train, a toddler's cowboy suit of bright red chaps and bright green shirt tipped back and forth on a rickety ladder. The hat, its chinstrap tight, was jammed on the embroidered shoulders. A tape recording cried, "Yippee-yi!" or at least Kate thought it did —it was hard to be sure over the din.

She moved toward the window as a voice behind her chuckled, "Well, Reverend. Don't tell me you're on the nest too."

Blushing as if she'd been caught looking at crotchless panties, Kate found Jeff Rankin grinning at her chummily, a plaid felt cap covering his thin hair. "Come to the mall and see everyone you know," she said and gestured at the window. "I was just thinking about Mindy Leaf. Soon she'll be needing so many things."

"What that girl needs is a husband, pronto. Have you gotten her to tell you who the father is?"

"It doesn't really matter, Jeff."

"She'll need his salary if she ever wants to buy something in a place like this. She can't expect other people to underwrite her mistake."

Kate dampened her lips. Jeff had forbidden his teenage daughter from seeing her boyfriend since the boy's second DUI, though Kate had seen them twined together in movie lines and football games. If the girl wasn't sleeping with him Kate would eat her hat, and if the girl was using protection, Kate would eat her hat twice. "It's a good time of year to extend a little charity. Besides, you never know when you're going to want some help yourself."

"Asking for help is a bad way to get started in life," he said, rubbing his eyebrow as he did at Finance Committee meetings when he explained that the numbers didn't lie. "I wouldn't hire her. A girl like that —she's already proved that she doesn't follow rules."

"She's going to need a decent job. Who's going to give her another chance?"

"I represent clients," he said, his voice sharpening. "I'm responsible to them."

"I'm not asking you to do anything. I just wonder who's going to help her now." Kate herself had no employment to offer—even the cleaning and repairs at the church were done by volunteers.

Jeff nodded at the store window. "Tell her not to start buying just yet. Norma and I can go through our attic and send some things over."

"You're kind to offer," Kate said.

"I think we've got a high chair and a baby tub. No telling what all's up there. We'll send it over." She knew he would be as good as his word, and his high chair would help Mindy, even if it wasn't the help she needed most.

They spent another five minutes in front of the store, while Jeff detailed a glitch he'd found in the budget. She promised to go over it that afternoon and thanked him warmly before she slipped back into the crowd. There she veered around two Christmas trees and, twenty feet further down, skirted a bright red wooden sled stationed at the opening to the video arcade. From inside, a hoarse bark punctured the air, and Kate walked a few steps over the dark threshold to make sure no one was choking. The sound was just part of the cacophony rattling out of the machines—pings, screeches, an electronic car crash that happened over and over. Rings of yipping teenagers leaned into the screens as if they could warm themselves. They were couples, mostly —the girls standing with their hands wedged into their boyfriends' hip pockets, the boys slapping the machines and moaning.

If they followed the statistics of an article Kate had just read, two or three of the girls were pregnant already. One might come to her for counseling, sessions that mostly consisted of girls asking Kate what she thought of "Star" as a middle name. That the girl would have the baby went without saying. Any pregnant girl who would come to a minister was already borrowing blankets and changing tables and baby spoons and crib sheets, already talking daycare to friends and mother and sisters. Already her life was so filled with babybabybaby that she might miss the exact moment the baby's father drifted off to school or work or to get a pack of smokes, and didn't come back. "I just love all this *stuff*," a seventeen-year-old had confided to Kate the day after her boyfriend left her.

Now a girl whose brown hair sprang around her face like a mass of startled feathers sidled closer to her oblivious boyfriend, whispered something in his ear and fit the length of her leg against his. Kate turned away, but her imagination rampaged along. She envisioned all of these girls groaning with child, marching to Elite's maternity ward while the boys skittered across the countryside like dandelion seeds. But seeds could blow back again. Everyone knew stories about fathers who appeared at the front door, well dressed, nervous, mannerly, sur-prised at their need to hear their child's voice.

Kate could go further. Everyone knew stories about other fathers, fathers who surprised their ten-year-olds at the schoolyard and bought them ice cream, then sadly discussed the jealous vindictiveness of the children's mothers with a meanness like insanity. Twice a year a local story would surface—some felon father who, silent as a cat, broke into a house and promised to leave only if he was given money, or sex, or safe passage, and—always—a chance to glimpse his sleeping child. "She's my *kid*, man," one had said on the late news as he held up his handcuffed wrists so he could wipe his eyes. "My issue, you know? Time doesn't destroy a bond like that."

"So what?" Kate said aloud and was rewarded by seeing two kids standing near her glance up and frown. She muttered the words again, more fiercely: "So what?"

There at the mouth of the arcade, she started to pace, clenching and unclenching her hands and her jaw, blinking, and shaking her head. So Bill-o might come back. So he probably would. So the child might have his eyes, his hands, his smooth ways. She would still be the one to look in on that child every morning and every night. She would know the child's voice among a dozen others, would know the step to listen for. What had she been thinking of? She was going to do the prudent thing *now?* Her heart beat quick and high, as if it were climbing out of its cavity and rapping up in her throat.

At the corner of the arcade stood an old-fashioned wheel of fortune —a little bit of wit in front of a video arcade. She wrenched the big gilt wheel around, and it actually spun, ratcheting around loudly to rest on One Free Turn. The spin meant nothing—like all of the decorations, the wheel was only for show. Nevertheless, she closed her eyes. Her hand still resting on the painted plywood knob, she tried to filter out the mall noise, to concentrate, to listen. She strained until her ears throbbed as she tried to make out a sound she had never heard. And then, failing to hear even the lightest noise, she listened for the silence that had always attended her when she made decisions and that always left her so frighteningly free.

What she heard, and this with great clarity, were the cries of shoppers, the booms and squeals of video games, "Deck the Halls" tootling out of the mall speakers. No deep stillness underlying all, no silent exhalation. Not one thing in the world or in heaven to stop her from doing what she wanted to do.

A bench stood in the open area where three walkways came together, and she sat down. Her thighs trembled. In a moment, when she felt less strange, she would buy a cup of coffee and some gingerbread. It was time she got into the holiday spirit. She closed her eyes, then opened them when she heard someone calling her name.

"Kate, it's only me."

She reached up to touch his hand. "Oh, Ned."

"I didn't mean to scare you." He stepped around the bench and sat beside her. "I came by the church, and Gabe said you were here."

"What's wrong?"

"I just wanted to say hi. See your face."

She smiled. "Same old face."

"Same old." He smiled back. "How come you're over here? You're not getting enough teenage life at home?"

"I guess not. I stood looking in and thought about how every one of these kids has parents that they're driving crazy. And half of them are fixing to be parents now."

"I can tell you which ones."

"Don't bother. I can guess."

"Another generation that doesn't finish high school. More kids shutting doors that are hardly even open yet."

"They're right in the middle of their own lives. Making decisions, doing things. I can't tell you how tired I am of just standing and watching." Her voice cracked.

"This morning I called a couple of adoption agencies. Talked to some people. We'll be getting questionnaires."

Kate looked back into the arcade. A different boy was working the machine near the entrance, leaning over so far he might have been embracing it. Profanity streamed from his mouth. She said, "Do you know that many adoption agencies won't consider infants for couples who are over forty? Do you know that the wait is often years? That's after they check and double-check your background and finances and references."

"I know all that."

She kept her gaze fastened on the boy. "I don't want to wait years. I don't want—forgive me—a twelve-year-old. I want the first tooth, the first smile. I'm going to take Mindy's baby. I can't say no."

Calm slipped from Ned's face like a veil. Underneath raged the expression she had feared—the tight, despairing jaw, the red eyes that strained to see some better world. Kate felt her own eyes sting. He said, "So. Just like that. All by yourself."

"I can't refuse this baby, Ned. We can't. I know every reason in the world, everything that might go wrong. But even if I got pregnant tomorrow, the baby could be hydrocephalic. A child we adopted could get hit by a bus. Having a life means that things can go wrong."

"We're not talking about possible birth defects. We're talking about a life joined at the hip to Bill-o. You've shown him what a good life looks like, and he told you what he thought of it."

"Ned, I'm sorry." She tried to catch his eye and make him see that she was more than sorry. But he wouldn't look at her, even when she asked what, for God's sake, he was thinking.

"'For better, for worse.' I never thought worse would come just because you said so. Because you changed your mind."

"I didn't change my mind. But I have to take this baby. I really have to. Do you believe that?"

"You believe it. Apparently that's enough."

"We're low, the two of us," she said.

"Rock bottom."

"We won't get any lower than this."

"No."

"That's our hope." Catching his bleak look, she went on, "It's the one thing we know for sure. We won't sink lower. We've hit the foundation."

"You see a foundation. I see a hole in the ground."

"Ah, no, Ned. Not now."

"You're pulling us into a nightmare. You know it, and you won't stop."

A wave of sorrow swept through her, regret that he couldn't have married someone more deserving. She couldn't imagine loving anyone more. "No, I won't stop."

"I can't—," he began, but then, just at that moment, Barb called Kate's name, her tone turning apologetic when she saw Ned.

"Am I interrupting a date?"

"We were just talking," Ned said.

"You two are the only people in the world who could talk through this racket."

"It's not hard. We both know what the other one's going to say," Ned said.

"We'll just finish up a little business here," Kate said. "Ned can drive me back to church."

"Soon," he added.

They waited until Barb was out of sight before they stirred. Kate felt herself trembling as if she were a glass of water filled to the lip; the merest tap on the arm would make her overflow. But Ned didn't touch her and stood a silent pace away when she went to a food stand and ordered them each coffee and a cookie. Not until they sat back, the food spread untouched between them like a tiny picnic, did he say, "Starting now, and for the rest of our lives, we'll be paying for this."

She ran her dry tongue over her dry lips. "I'll pay. I don't mind. But will you?" She cleared her throat. "Will you?" Past shame or dignity, past fairness, she watched his sorrowing, loved face. "Will you? For me?"

The words hung in the air. His face held the look of a man who had broken free to dry land, or had pulled her to it. "I thought you knew. We've already started." He watched Kate until she held up a cup of coffee, which he took. Silence wrapped around them. Kate offered a cookie to her husband, and he absently broke off a piece. Satisfied, Kate took a sip of her own coffee, then began to eat.